HEALING DANGER

A Fortis Security Novel Book 1

MADDIE WADE

Healing Danger

Fortis Security Book One

Maddie Wade

Healing Danger
Maddie Wade

Published by Maddie Wade

Copyright © June 2016 Maddie Wade

Cover: Envy Designs

Editing: Black Opal Proofreading

Formatting: Black Opal Proofreading

Published by Maddie Wade June 2016

Copyright

Acknowledgements

This book has only been possible because of all the wonderful support I have received.

Thank you to two amazing authors, Tonya Brooks and Abbie Zanders, for all their incredible support and encouragement.

Thank you to Charlene @ Envy Designs at for the spectacular cover.

Thanks to the very lovely and talented Linda @ Black Opal Editing for my editing. You have been wonderful and didn't cry or shout at all my grammar bloopers!

Thanks to all my beta readers for steering me in the right direction and giving advice on plot line and flow.

Special thanks to Clementine Parsons, my wonderful friend, for allowing me to bounce my crazy ideas off her, and always being there for me.

Lastly, but definitely not least, thank you to my family for always having my back.

Dedication

This book is dedicated to my wonderful husband
and my children, who are my life.

Glossary

Banter: Playful and friendly exchange of teasing remarks.

Boot: Trunk of a car.

Boxing Day: The first day after Christmas when Christmas gifts or boxes are given to employees. A national holiday in the UK.

Butties: English slang for sandwich.

Carazon: Spanish term of endearment meaning *heart*.

Charlie: Cocaine.

Chosen Sisters: Three sisters who will be the mothers of the future leaders of the new world.

Cockney wide boy: Wide boy usually refers to a working-class male who lives in London and who lives by their wits and wheeler dealings.

Conifer: Evergreen tree.

Consultant: Consultant is a Doctor who has reached the senior level of doctor or surgeon. They are then normally referred to by the title of Mr, Mrs, Miss, or Ms. They are obviously still a doctor but not referred to that way.

Cwmbran: Cwmbran is a town in South Wales and is in the County borough of Monmouthshire.

Cwtched: Welsh for Cuddle.

Divine One: The One true leader of the Divine Watchers who will rule the new world.

Divine Watchers: A cult group who believe that the world can only be saved by gifted people. Beginning with the un-gifted being wiped from existence.

Dushka: Russian meaning 'Sweetheart'.

Fugly: Short for 'Fucking Ugly' (Slang).

GCHQ: The Government Communications Head Quarters.

Gi: Two-piece suit worn for martial arts.

Gifted Ones: People with abilities like healing predictive dreams, seeing the future, or communing with the dead.

Jogger: Someone who is obsessed with jogging.

Jumper: British for sweater.

Kitsch: Something of tawdry design or appearance created to appeal to popular undiscriminating taste.

Mardy: Sulky/Moody.

Mucka: Northern word for 'friend'.

Misogyny: Hatred dislike or distrust of women.

NHS: The National Health Service is the publicly funded healthcare system for England. It is the largest and the oldest single-payer healthcare system in the world.

Parachute Regiment: The Parachute Regiment colloquially known as the 'Paras' is an elite airborne infantry regiment of the British Army.

Plaster: Band-Aid.

Prime Fecund: The man who will sire the off-spring of the chosen sisters of the new world.

SAS: The Special Air Service (SAS) is a Special Forces unit of the British Army. The SAS was founded in 1941 as a regiment and later reconstituted as a corps in 1950. The unit undertakes a number of roles including covert reconnaissance counter-terrorism direct action and hostage rescue.

SIS: Another name for MI6 in Britain 'Secret Intelligence Service'.

Slag: A person who sleeps with many partners not caring beyond the sexual high.

The New World: The World after Armageddon has destroyed most of the population.

The Shard: The Shard also referred to as the Shard of Glass, Shard London Bridge, and formerly London Bridge Tower, is a 95-storey skyscraper in Southwark London that forms part of the London Bridge Quarter development. Standing 309.6 metres (1,016 ft.) high, the Shard is the tallest building in the United Kingdom.

Tidy: Slang for 'Okay good I agree'.

Toff: A rich or upper-class person.

Tosser: Literally someone who masturbates. More commonly refers to anyone who you have a low opinion of.

Trainers: The English term for sneakers or runners.

Vest: Singlet.

Newton's Cradle: Normally found on a person's desk, it is a device that has spheres hanging from an overhead bar. When you lift one sphere and release it, it hits the stationary spheres, transmitting a force through the stationary spheres that pushes the last sphere upward.

Re-sus: A room in an emergency department at the hospital where patients who are admitted by ambulance are taken for resuscitation.

Kip: A nap or short sleep

Stay Frosty: To keep cool and look after yourself

Cyka: Russian for 'bitch'.

Vicar: A minister in the Anglican Church.

Wellies: Shortened form of Wellington boots that are made of rubber and are worn in wet weather.

Treacle: a thick sticky dark syrup made from partly refined sugar; molasses. It can be spread on toast or used in desserts. It is very sweet.

Table of Contents

Healing Danger

Fortis Security

<u>Prologue</u>

Martha Cassidy lifted the sleeping child from her bed as quietly as she could and moved quickly, her face etched with fear. They had to get away before he came home. Her heart raced as she ran to the front window and listened to a car pull into the drive. A flash of the lights in the inky black night revealed it was her long-time friend, Larissa.

Adjusting the child's sleep-warmed weight and holding tightly to their meagre possessions, she looked around at the small sparse house that they had called home for the last three years. She fought tears as she remembered the hope and love she had put into making everything perfect.

She had loved Marcus with everything she'd had but he'd changed so much since Lauren had been born. He'd become increasingly obsessed about the beginning of the 'New World' and how people who had gifts—like she and her daughter—would be the ones to save it. However along with his obsession came violent outbursts and mood swings and, while she could take the abuse, she would not allow her daughter to become a victim.

Turning, she shook off her melancholy, stiffened her spine and closed the door on her old life.

Larissa met her at the front door and took her bag. "You settle Lauren with you in the back," she said kindly.

Martha eased into the back, careful not to wake her sweet child.

As Larissa drove them away, she explained that her friend had sorted out fake identities and new national insurance numbers for them, and there was money in a locker at the train station. Martha listened with only half an ear, deep in thought, trying to understand how it had come to this. She knew Marcus had loved her in his own way, but it had bordered on obsessive and he wasn't the man she'd loved any more.

They had met at a friend's party; he had been so handsome with blond hair and sky-blue eyes and had talked all night. He'd told her he was studying psychology and wanted to be a counsellor, and she'd told him of her desire to be a nurse when she finished college. They had married six months later, on her nineteenth birthday. Lauren had been born nine months after that.

She should have seen what was happening. He'd encouraged her to stay at home and look after Lauren instead of going back to college. She'd thought how lucky she was to have a man that wanted to take care of her and their daughter, but he'd soon become consumed with her gift of predictive visions and kept pushing Lauren to see if she was gifted too.

She had tried so hard to hide Lauren's gift from him, but she was such a loving child and he'd discovered it anyway. He had cut his finger one day and, when Lauren wrapped her pudgy little fingers around it to offer him comfort, it had healed. He'd become out of control then. His behaviour had become increasingly erratic and disturbing. She knew she had to get herself and Lauren away. Martha grieved for the man she had once loved but that man was gone. In his place was a violent stranger.

Chapter One

Present Day

Lauren looked at the bright green grass and beautiful vibrant flowers that surrounded her. The sun shone and the air was sweet with the smell of mown grass and freshly-turned soil. As she listened to the vicar talk about Claire—her wonderful, funny, and kind friend—she pondered how the universe didn't realise that it had lost someone so beautiful. That her best friend for the last twenty-six years was dead. It should be raining or thundering, but instead the world seemed happy, even peaceful.

Wiping away the tears that seemed ever-present these days, Lauren looked over to Claire's husband Daniel, who was clinging to their two-year-old daughter, Paige. He looked broken and she could see his pain and grief as if it were a living breathing thing. Paige looked so confused and overwhelmed by all the different emotions flowing around her. Children always noticed other people's pain, and she knew Paige was trying to soothe her father because she kept rubbing her little hand along his face.

Lauren felt a physical ache in her chest as her heart broke for them. How would they cope? How would Daniel work and take care of Paige? How would he show her what a wonderful, kind, and strong woman her mother had been?

Beside Daniel was his best friend Dane Bennett, along with the rest of the Fortis team. She knew two of them, Nate Jones—who had gone to school with her and Claire—and Dane's sister, Lucy. She wasn't sure exactly what it was they did, apart from some kind of security or protection thing. It was all a bit vague.

She studied Dane unobtrusively. He was a tall man probably six-foot-two with wide shoulders and the defined muscular build of a swimmer. His short dark brown hair was styled longer on top with shorter sides and his bright blue eyes always sparkled with something she couldn't quite define.

She'd been drawn to him since Claire had first introduced them. They had emailed for a while and became good friends. At least until Jeff—whom she'd started dating—had seen the emails and got jealous. He'd wiped all the emails between her and Dane and had forbidden her to have any contact with him.

She should have seen it then but had put it down to him liking her so much that he wanted her all to himself. What a fool she had been. If it hadn't been for Claire and Daniel, she didn't think she would have survived that period of her life. But she had, and Jeff and that horrible episode was over now.

She regretted that the contact had stopped between her and Dane so suddenly and knew he probably thought she was fickle, dropping his friendship like that. He had been nice and friendly and always easy to talk with. Maybe if she hadn't started dating Jeff things would have been different.

The emails between them had become something she'd looked forward to. It was only after things with Jeff had gone so wrong that she realised what a mistake she'd made. But she had and now she had to live with that choice.

They had talked since when they had seen each other at parties or gatherings that Daniel and Claire had hosted, but it had been a little awkward and she'd been embarrassed so Lauren tried maintaining some distance from him. When he was near, her heart beat a bit faster and the way he looked at her made her insides go all funny.

She knew that he felt her reticence and kept his distance as well. She just hadn't been ready to put herself out there yet and knew he would think she was a weak idiot for allowing Jeff to do what he had. She couldn't bear to watch him look at her with pity before running for the hills. She had seen that happen with her mother and didn't want history to repeat itself. No, it was easier to just stay away.

He must have sensed her gaze because he looked up and caught her studying him. She blushed and offered a small sad smile, but it felt forced. She glanced back to see Claire's coffin being lowered into the ground. Watching her closest confidant, the woman who was more of a sister than a friend being buried almost brought her to her knees. She tried to make sense of it. Claire must have known this might happen. Why hadn't she said anything to anyone?

Since the age of four, the girls had bonded over being different. Claire would often have precognitive dreams. Some were just little things, like running into a friend in the supermarket or that it would rain. Others were more important, like the day she met Daniel, but they were always right. That was why Lauren found it so shocking that this had happened.

Lauren felt tears prick the backs of her eyes. She and Claire had always laughed about their 'freaky' abilities as they called them. Now who would she talk to? Lauren never made friends easily; she got on with people well enough but the trust that true close friendships required was hard won. It wasn't that she'd had any awful experiences, except for Jeff, but her abilities made her different, and that made her wary trusting people with that knowledge. The last thing she needed was for the wrong people to get hold of that information.

Her mind drifted back to the first day they'd met. Lauren had been so nervous about starting a new school. Everyone already seemed to know each other, and she felt like an outsider. She had walked onto the playground, trying so hard not to cry in front of her mum. Her bottom lip had wobbled, and she'd turned around to see Tommy Wright and his little band of horrors looking at her and laughing.

She had wanted to cry so badly. Claire had seen the way she'd looked and had gone right up to Tommy and, with hands on her little hips, had said a few words to him that had sent him scurrying off with his friends behind him.

Claire came over to her then and, as if it was a foregone conclusion, said, *"I'm Claire and we're going to be the best friends ever."* And they had been. Claire had told her later she had threatened to tell everyone that Tommy wet the bed if he was mean to Lauren again. They had often laughed until they'd cried about it as they got older.

It wasn't until that Christmas when Claire had fallen off her bike breaking her arm that they had realised that they were special or 'freaky'. Lauren had healed Claire's arm without anyone knowing. Claire had confessed that some of her dreams would come true, but it wasn't until they were teenagers that she became aware how accurate they were. They'd kept each other's secret all their lives.

Claire had been shot ten days ago in her home at point blank range. It was still hard to come to terms with the fact that she wasn't coming back. That she wouldn't just turn up on a Friday with a bottle of wine and Chinese take-out. They had spent so many nights like that—putting the world to rights and laughing over silly things. Lauren already missed her terribly.

She followed the procession of people who walked past the graveside on shaky legs stopping to gently drop a small bunch of forget-me-nots on the coffin. They were Claire's favourite and it seemed fitting because she would certainly never forget her beautiful friend.

Slowly, and with her steps heavy with grief, she turned to look at Daniel and Paige. As a healer, she wished she could take his pain away but that was not how her ability worked. She could only heal physical injuries or pain, not the gut-wrenching emotional pain she could see on his face and in every step he took.

Chapter Two

He seethed inside as he watched them. Crying and snivelling at her graveside while he had to hide in the shadows. Nobody would understand the love they had shared. Where the fuck were they when she'd needed them? He was the one who had talked to her and watched over her. Even though she hadn't acknowledged his presence, he knew that she'd appreciated it but couldn't publicly tell him because of that useless husband of hers. His Claire had been so loyal. It was the thing he loved most about her.

The people who claimed to love her hadn't known about her illness and were too wrapped up in their own lives to notice the pain she was in. That bastard of a husband. It was Daniel's fault that *his* beautiful Claire was dead. Daniel should have known and protected her. What sort of a husband was he? He watched them and vowed he would avenge her death.

He would start with the bitch daughter of the man that had sentenced her to death. He had been shocked when he'd realised the connection between them, but it was fate telling him that he was doing the right thing. It was almost as if the universe was lining things up for him.

Now they would all see that he was a god among men when he tortured the daughter before mailing her body back to them, piece by piece. He wished that he could be there to see the pain and fear on their faces when they got each of his gifts. But no matter; his time for vengeance was coming. Excited to put his plans into action, he silently slipped away from the graveside unseen.

Chapter Three

Dane had never felt so helpless as he watched the man he'd known almost his whole life - the man who was like a brother to him - slowly fall apart with guilt and grief. Knowing he could do nothing to help ease Daniel's pain was crippling. He looked at his beautiful innocent goddaughter who would never really know her mother and it shredded him.

They had met at primary school and, after a little scrap over whose football team had been the best, had become best friends. Now all these years later he found himself watching his friend and wishing he could do something to ease Daniel's suffering. He knew the only thing he could do for them was to find the bastard that had killed Claire and make him pay for the pain he had caused. He had loved her like a sister from the minute Daniel had introduced them and couldn't imagine a better woman for his friend.

Walking into the house Daniel had shared with his wife, he felt anger filter through his blood with the need to avenge his friend's pain. He didn't know how Dan could stand it. Everywhere he turned were reminders of Claire and the life she had shared with her husband, and at the centre of everything was Paige—so innocent, so young. Daniel said it was a comfort to be around everything that she had touched, and it was better for Paige too, but he wasn't sure that he could do it. Hell, he couldn't do any of this.

Dane made his way through the living room towards his team, trying to get hold of his emotions, only briefly stopping to share pleasantries with old friends of his and Daniel's on the way.

He reached the team who stood slightly apart in their own little huddle, looked at the men and woman that made up Fortis Security and instantly felt more relaxed. He could feel his fists uncurl and his anger abate.

They were an eclectic group to say the least. His baby sister Lucy was the data analyst/tech geek. Today she was dressed in an elegant black dress and jacket and, even though it was a funeral, she still managed to wear a pair of her kick-ass high-heeled shoes that she was infamous for with the team. Nate Jones was an ex-parachute regiment guy and the team's best sniper and resident team joker. Then there was Zinoviy Maklavoi whom everyone called Zin. His history wasn't exactly clear, but Dane suspected it was intelligence related. He was a giant Russian that nobody really knew much about except their boss, Zack Cunningham. Zin was a solid operator and definitely highly trained. He liked and trusted him. He'd proven himself on several missions and Dane was happy for Zin to have his back.

The group was close, and each had felt the pain of Claire's loss. Daniel was a damn good team leader and Claire was always the one that remembered the team's birthdays and bought cakes and cards. She was like a sister to them all.

Lucy leaned in and hugged him. "How's he doing?"

"I don't know. He's so eaten up with grief, guilt and rage that nobody can get close to him except Paige. Honestly I think she's the only thing making him hold it together."

"Do we know anything about who did it?" Lucy asked.

"No not yet. They're still waiting on forensics and DNA." *And God only knows how long that will take.*

Dane would be glad when Zack was back from dealing with whatever crisis had taken him away from the team for the past three months. He didn't mind being in charge short term, but he wanted to get back to doing what he did best, which was being out in the field running ops from the ground. Not managing from the office and dealing with the politics of the job.

"Don't worry, man. We'll find the son of a bitch that did this," Nate told Dane resolutely.

At thirty-two, he was the next youngest in the group after Lucy. With his Hispanic colouring, huge muscles, and tendency to break out in his mother's native Spanish when he was around them, Nate drew a lot of attention from the ladies. But they were wasting their time. Nate didn't trust women; not after finding his fiancée in bed with his old high school nemesis twelve months prior. It was a shame. Dane hated to see any of his team get hurt, and Nate hadn't been the same since.

He didn't really know what it was like to have his heart broken because he hadn't ever been in romantic love. In fact, he hadn't had a serious relationship since he'd been nineteen and thought he could have the army and a life outside it. That hadn't lasted much past his first deployment. No, most women really couldn't handle the long separations and uncertainty that foreign deployments brought and honestly, he had been fine with that.

The army, and later the SAS, were all he'd ever wanted and there was never a shortage of single women willing to help him scratch any itch. The SAS even had their own set of groupies, and they could sniff out an operator better than any sniffer dog. He'd always made things clear beforehand that it was just for fun though, so nobody got overly involved. He wasn't cruel, he just didn't want anyone to get hurt by the brief hook-ups he preferred, and he prided himself on always being straight with people.

He nodded in agreement to Nate's statement. No, they wouldn't rest until Claire's killer was brought to justice.

"I'm sorry I won't be around," Zin said in that thick Russian accent that seemed to make women go all googly-eyed. He didn't get it himself but hey, he was a guy, what did he know about what made women tick? It surprised him that Zin's accent was still so strong after so many years living in the UK.

He inclined his head to Zin. "That job for Zack... it's a go then?" he asked in surprise.

"Yes, I got word about two hours ago. I will be, how you say, wheels up in two hours."

Dane nodded. "Stay safe man and keep in contact. Don't go dark for too long."

The big Russian managed to convey his answer with just a twitch of his eye and a slight tip of his head. He wasn't sure anyone else noticed it, but Zin had excess energy rolling off him in waves and, although he seemed relaxed, he was also hyper-alert. Dane needed more info on this mission Zack was running with Zin, but he needed to focus on Daniel as well. If anyone knew what he was doing, it was his boss, so he would just have to trust him for now.

Dane didn't trust easily but Zack, in fact everyone at Fortis, had his trust and his respect. Even his baby sister who was now a fully-grown woman. Lucy had surprised him when she'd gone to work for GCHQ—he had always thought that, with her flair for art, she would go into graphic design. This suited her though, and he was immensely proud of the woman she had become.

He glanced around the room and saw Daniel talking with Claire's parents. He watched Lauren go over and hug him and Paige, before kissing Sylvie and Malcolm. He didn't know what it was about Lauren Cassidy, but the petite pre-school teacher just set his blood on fire. He'd liked her since they'd met four years ago at Claire and Daniel's engagement party. They had hit it off straight away. She was easy to talk to and they had stayed in touch when he'd deployed.

The emails started as friendly exchanges with news from home but over the months they had become something more personal where he looked forward to every email she sent. They hadn't talked about the future except in general terms. Dane's feelings had grown for her over the course of those months, but he hadn't told her how he'd felt. Which was just as well because he hadn't really known then. He'd thought it was a deep friendship that maybe had the potential to be something more but hadn't been sure.

That changed when she'd had emailed him one day talking about a guy she had started dating—'Jeff-the-jerk' as he liked to call him. He'd felt sucker-punched by the feelings that seeing her with another man had evoked. From then, the emails had become less frequent and, after a highly classified mission where he'd had to go radio silent for an extended period, they had stopped altogether.

Dane had almost been relieved that she had stopped emailing. He found it too hard to talk about her life with Jeff when he wanted her for himself but perversely, he had missed her. Now here he was again, and he still felt pulled into her orbit whenever she was around. Of course, it didn't help that she was stunning, with ocean blue eyes and naturally golden hair that fell down her back in waves. At a little over five-foot-four she only came up to his chest but oh, she had those killer curves and a heart-shaped ass that made his body tighten painfully.

It wasn't just that though. She was kind and genuine and had lovely little dimples in her cheeks when she smiled. Lauren never put on airs and graces either. What you saw was what you got. Her sense of humour and her ability to put almost anyone she met at ease and make them feel relaxed was one of the things that had first drawn him to her. Yes, Lauren was fascinating, and he wanted to know more about what had happened with her and Jeff-the-jerk.

He knew they weren't together anymore and hadn't been for over two years, but nobody would talk about what had happened. Lauren was still the same on the surface, but something was different with her. She seemed unsure of herself and less confident. Not shy exactly but something he couldn't quite put his finger on. Wary perhaps?

For the first time in his life, he was fed up waking up alone. He didn't necessarily want happily ever after, but he wanted…something. And Lauren with her sweet gentle nature and intelligent mind—not to mention that drool-worthy body—was always top of the list when he thought about dating. Maybe he should just go for it and ask her out.

Dane cursed himself. What sort of bastard thought about his love life and pondered his own relationship woes at a wake for Christ's sake? Furious with himself, he marched outside to get some air and get his thoughts under control.

~~~

Lauren watched Dane slip outside and wondered why he looked so annoyed, but Claire's mum Sylvie was calling her name. Swivelling around, she shook off thoughts of Dane Bennett and concentrated on what Sylvie was saying.

"Would you mind taking Paige outside? I think she's feeling a little overwhelmed."

"Yes of course," she said, reaching for the little girl.

Smiling down at the precious child, Lauren crossed to the French doors that led out to the deck and garden. It was so peaceful; she had always loved it here. The decking blended out into a beautiful lawn bordered on all sides by flowers of different colours, their scents mingling to make a fragrant perfume. Claire had loved her garden and was always weeding or planting.

Spying Dane in the corner by her playhouse, Paige wriggled to get down. She clearly adored her Uncle Dane and toddled off towards him calling, "'ane 'ane!" Lauren watched as he crouched down so that he was at eye level with the child. The affection they had for each other was so touching that it made Lauren's throat constrict with tears. He twirled Paige around as she threw herself towards him for a big hug.

Lauren eyed Dane as he held tight until the child started to squirm.

"You want to play on the swing?" he asked, and she nodded eagerly. Straightening up, he noticed Lauren coming towards them.

"You're very good with her," she said.

He responded with a smile. "She's so easy to be around," he replied, starting to push the child gently on the swing. "I can see why Daniel can't bear to be away from her at the moment."

Lauren felt her throat go tight again at his words. "I still can't believe it's happened. It's like a nightmare nobody can wake up from," she choked out.

Lauren could feel the tears coming but was helpless to stop them, so she turned to hide her face from him. She felt a tug as Dane pulled her into his arms where all the emotions of the day overcame her.

~~~

He didn't know what prompted him to offer comfort. Crying women scared him to death. He never knew what to do but he'd acted when he saw the pain and anguish overcome her pretty face. He hated to see her so upset and felt helpless. He just held her and rubbed her back soothingly while she sobbed silently. She felt so small and vulnerable in his arms and he had the overwhelming urge to fix things for her, just to put a smile on her face again.

She moved against him slightly as she cried, and Dane was disconcerted to feel the familiar tightening of his body that seemed to happen whenever she was around. He adjusted his grip, easing his lower body away so that she wouldn't realise what a bastard he was for getting an erection while her heart was breaking.

Slowly her sobs ebbed, and he eased her away. She cast her watery eyes towards him, and he sucked in a breath. He wondered if the unchecked desire that had darkened her eyes mirrored his. Heat flooded her face and he felt her body go soft and lean into his. His hands flexed on her arms as he tried to control his reaction to her.

She wet her lower lip and it took everything in him not to kiss her. He wanted to kiss her almost more than his next breath.

They both stood transfixed as different emotions passed across their faces. He raised his hands slowly, and tenderly swiped the tears from her cheeks with his thumbs.

"Push push, Unc' 'ane!" Like a slap, Dane and Lauren jumped apart.

"Of course, sweetheart," he said moving away from Lauren.

Dane watched as Lauren rubbed her arms as if she were cold, which was unlikely because it was eighty degrees today. It was probably left-over emotion making her shiver. She seemed embarrassed by her meltdown and he was about to say something when she babbled her thanks and made a speedy retreat to the house.

Watching her go, Dane smiled inwardly. She had definitely felt the spark between them, and he decided that he was going to pursue that attraction. He just wished the timing was better.

Whether on purpose or not, and to his great frustration, Lauren kept herself busy and was unavailable the rest of the afternoon. *Maybe it's for the best* he thought, as he and the Fortis team departed. Now was neither the time nor the place and he needed to keep focused on finding Claire's killer. Lauren was a distraction he didn't need right now and yet she was one he couldn't stop thinking about. Zack had vowed to Daniel that Fortis would find out who'd killed Claire and none of them, especially Dane, wanted to let Daniel down on this.

Chapter Four

Sitting behind a large oak desk in his grand office a hundred miles away, Marcus Preedy looked at his son with barely-contained disdain. At twenty-one, his son was a big muscular lad with a talent for martial arts. Which was just as well as he had no *special* gifts.

The only reason Marcus kept him around was his size—and his freaky technical skills. Nevertheless, the boy was soft. His heart bled too easily and lately he'd been able to tell how discontented the boy was feeling. It wasn't anything he could put his finger on. Maybe he was just a paranoid bastard, but he didn't think so.

He sighed. His life would have been so much simpler if he had been the one with gifts instead of his snot-nosed little sister Joanne. Just thinking about her made his stomach twist in anger. She had run away when she was thirteen, making his teenaged life a misery. Marcus couldn't understand what made someone run away from the power that their special abilities gave them. However, she had, and his parents had blamed him for it ever since because he was the one looking after her when she had left.

He, for one, had been glad when she had run away since they had always hated each other. There had never been a moment she hadn't plagued his life. He'd thought having a younger sibling to mould into what he wanted would be amazing.

From the minute she'd been born though, she'd shied away from him and acted as if she was afraid of him. It made his parents think it was his fault and that he was to blame. He had tried. Really, he had, but when he'd realised she didn't like him, he'd stopped trying and just treated her with the hatred and disdain he felt she'd deserved.

It wasn't until she was thirteen and he read her diary that he realised she was an Empath. At the time he hadn't known what an Empath was—he was only sixteen himself. But her diary had said she could feel the feelings of others as if they were her own. After that, he had made sure to let his hatred towards her show when she was around and revelled in the pain and fear it had caused her.

His life had gone to hell when she'd run away because everyone blamed him. They hadn't come right out and said so, but it was there in the disappointed looks his parents gave him, when they could be bothered to acknowledge him at all. It just made him hate Joanne even more.

He'd left home at eighteen and gone to college. Marcus had wanted to study psychology so he could understand how other people's minds worked. He was reasonably clever, but it was his drive and determination that had gotten him through. He hadn't seen his parents since the day he'd left home and hadn't grieved for them when they'd died. They hadn't deserved to have him as a son.

Now Marcus had power if not special abilities. People feared him and that gave him power like no other. He loved the feeling and thrill it gave him to see someone cower in fear of him. Perhaps that made him sick in the eyes of others, but he'd never cared what others thought. Nobody had ever heard from his sister again, despite a large police investigation. It was as if she had just vanished. He for one hoped that he never saw her again and, with a bit of luck, the stupid bitch had gotten herself killed. Standing from his desk he brushed aside his thoughts of his family and focused on the present.

Turning to the other man, Marcus eyed him quizzically. "What do you mean you think you've found her?" he asked his head of security.

Michaels looked at him with a smug smile. "When I took care of Claire Thompson, there were pictures of her with this woman." He handed Marcus a picture. "She looks just like your ex, so I thought..."

Marcus tensed and grabbed the picture—and there she was, his little Lauren. All grown up and she did indeed look just like her betraying bitch of a mother. The shock of seeing the picture made him sit down heavily in his chair. She had the same shaped face and her eyes were the same shade. She also had the same full mouth as her mother.

His hands clenched on the picture in anger as he remembered her betrayal. He had offered her everything and how had she repaid him? By disappearing and stealing his daughter from him. Marcus felt the anger towards Martha mix with the longing he still felt for her, and it made him feel weak and angry. This, in turn, made him want to strike out at her and make her hurt for all she had done to him. He'd had to make do with taking that pathetic bitch Larissa to his bed. She had always fawned over him when she'd thought Martha was not around. It had been fun for a while having her on the side, but she was not wife material and had proved that when she had given him the useless boy as his only male heir.

Nevertheless, and against his will, he still loved Martha and if she walked back in now and begged him to take her back, he would. Obviously, he wouldn't allow her the freedom or privileges that she'd had before but she still had his love and what more could she ask for after everything she had done?

He turned again to Michaels. "Find her and bring her to me. Do it quietly and see that she is not hurt in any way."

"No, Father. Let me," his son Drew implored. "Please I can do this. I'll bring my sister to you."

Marcus looked at him for a long while considering his request. This might work better, and she might be more compliant if she met her long-lost brother. Drew obviously wanted this badly. The way he leaned forward like an eager puppy and practically begged made Marcus realise that he could use this. *Yes, this could work.*

"Very well, do it. Go now and make sure you check in with Michaels every twelve hours."

~~~

Drew turned and strode quickly from the room. This was it! His chance to find his sister. He wanted to find her badly, but he didn't intend to let his father get near her after what they had done to that Thompson woman. His father was losing it, and this was his chance to get away from him and keep his sister safe.

Drew had always wanted a brother or sister growing up. His existence had been a lonely one. He'd known about Lauren since he was a small boy—it had been the only time he'd heard pride in his father's voice. Marcus had shown him pictures of Lauren as a child and told him all about his wonderful half-sister. He should have been jealous of her but all he'd felt when he had seen the pictures was longing for someone to share everything with. He'd wondered what it would be like not to be alone.

He had been home-schooled by private tutors at the direction of his father. Marcus hadn't wanted him to make outside connections. Marcus hadn't really bothered with him though, except to come around occasionally when he was younger to check him for *abilities*. He'd never felt loved by his father—he hadn't felt anything from his father except indifference. Drew was more like a possession that he owned, and it was Marcus' duty to take care of him financially rather than treat him like a son.

Drew loved his mother but watching her simper and beg for the scraps of affection that Marcus threw her—normally in the form of them disappearing upstairs for hours—made him eventually resent her weakness. He still loved her but didn't particularly like her. She had never stood up for Drew or defended him when Marcus had criticised or bullied him. He knew that she loved him in her own way, but it wasn't enough to love your child. You were meant to protect them too. He hated that he felt that way about his mother and felt disloyal for it.

He took the stairs to his room two at a time and rushed to pack a bag, dismissing his self-indulgent thoughts. He needed to concentrate on the task of finding his sister and maybe finally having the loving family he'd always dreamt of. Maybe then some of the guilt he'd felt for not speaking up sooner would leave.

Marcus watched his son leave and turned to Michaels. "Follow him and make sure he gets this done properly. And I want regular updates."

~~~

Michaels would do anything for Marcus Preedy, even if that meant watching the pathetic son who kept trying to wheedle his way into his father's affections.

Chapter Five

Lauren prowled around her flat feeling restless. She'd put a call into her therapist and booked an appointment for the next week. She had regained a lot of the confidence that Jeff had stolen from her, but losing Claire had thrown her for a loop and she wanted to touch base and talk things through with the therapist.

It had been a week since they had buried Claire and she just couldn't settle. She felt edgy and full of energy but at the same time couldn't concentrate on anything. Thank goodness her boss had agreed to let her take some time off because there was no way she would be able to concentrate on her kids.

Lauren loved being a teacher, especially in Reception class. Loved watching their little faces fill with awe over the simplest things like learning to read and write their names. Not that there weren't days when she wanted to scream. Like the day little Scotty James had poured glue into Jenny Sampson's hair. It had taken some explaining when Mrs Sampson had picked her up. She could smile at that now. Mostly she loved it though.

She couldn't wait to have kids of her own one day. She wanted a large family of four or five and her biological clock had certainly been letting her know that, if she wanted that, she needed to get started. Stupid body didn't realise it wasn't that simple though. To have a baby you needed a partner.

Putting herself out there and trusting people was a risk, and being rejected for things she couldn't help was hard. And honestly, after Jeff she didn't trust her own judgement anymore.

Her mind involuntarily skipped to Dane and she wondered what it would be like having little brown-haired, blue-eyed Danes running around. She sighed at the direction her thoughts had taken. Yeah, like that was ever going to happen with her fears paralysing her.

She could not believe she had cried all over him like that. And then to get turned on? *Oh God*, she was still mortified. What would he think of her behaving like that at her best friend's wake? God, she was a horrible person.

She tried reading a book on her tiny balcony but gave up after reading the same page four times. Walking to the fridge, she opened it enjoying the cool air. Even at seven at night it was still hot. *Great. No wine.* Her luck just kept getting better. Slamming the fridge shut with more force than necessary, Lauren sank dejectedly onto the couch.

Lauren loved her home with its pale cream walls and accents of gold and turquoise. It was calming and classy. But not tonight. Tonight, she felt unsettled and couldn't put her finger on why.

A run! That's it, she'd go for a run. Rushing to change into a sports bra and running shorts, she threw her hair into a ponytail and grabbed her iPod.

Stepping from her flat, she set off at a fast pace towards the park. She waved to Mr Aden who lived below her and was watering his garden. He liked to wait until the sun wasn't so strong or so he told her. Personally, she thought he just liked to talk with Mrs Fielding—the widow from two doors down.

Lauren loved living in this part of the country with its historical buildings, including the Cathedral and the old Tudor house. The town was a real mix with old historic-listed buildings right next to new architecture. It was generally quiet, except in May when the fair came to town for three days and the whole of High Town was closed off for fairground rides and food stalls of every description.

She also loved how the change of seasons made the town look picturesque. Loved that everyone knew everyone else and was friendly. It was reassuring. She knew that was one of the reasons her mother had settled here.

She'd always felt safe here—it was a good-sized town but nothing extraordinary ever happened. That was why it was such a shock when Claire was murdered. It just didn't happen. But West Mercia police did have a good track record so she hoped they could figure it out soon. Daniel had told her Fortis was looking into it as well.

Running into the park, Lauren stopped by a bench to do some stretches and get her muscles warmed up. She loved to run. It always gave her time to let her thoughts go free. No phones ringing, no school work to prepare, just her and her thoughts.

Bending to adjust her trainers, she started to get the creeps. It felt like someone was watching her. A prickly feeling at the back of her neck had her slowly straightening. She surveyed the area around her, but nobody was there apart from a few students enjoying the early evening sun and a couple of parents with kids on the swings. Shaking it off, she plugged in her earbuds and put on her jogging playlist.

Lauren started a lap around the park and enjoyed the feeling of freedom. As she passed the benches, she noticed a well-built young man watching her from the bench in the kid's park. He looked familiar but she couldn't place him. He didn't look like a nutter, so she dismissed him and carried on.

On her second lap, she noticed that he had moved closer to the trees by the river but was still watching her. She felt slightly nervous now though, and her heart began to pound. He was definitely watching her. She sped up a bit deciding it was time to go home.

Turning to leave the park she ran straight into a rock-hard chest. Big hands grabbed her arms and she opened her mouth to scream.

"Lauren."

She stopped with her mouth open.

"It's me, Dane. I'm sorry, I didn't mean to scare you."

She yanked the earbuds out making him release her arms and take a step back. She took a breath to calm her galloping heart before she spoke. "Jesus Christ, you scared me to death," she replied a little shakily. "What are you doing here? Is everything okay with Paige?"

"Yes, they're all fine. I was just walking through the park and spotted you. Are you okay? You seem nervous."

"I'm fine. I was just being silly. I thought some guy was watching me, but he's gone now," she said casting her eyes around the park for the young man. She turned back to Dane and saw that he too was looking around the park. She felt his posture ease and realised that he hadn't seen anything suspicious. "I was probably being silly. What happened to Claire has me spooked."

"No, you're right not to ignore your gut instincts. Not ignoring them is what will keep you safe."

Lauren noticed him take one more look around the park before turning to her with a smile. "Come on, I'll walk you home," Dane said placing his hand on the small of her back as he steered her in the direction of her home.

Lauren let him take control. She was relieved he was there. She was very independent and as a teacher always had to be in charge. If she wasn't, the kids would walk all over her. It felt oddly empowering to have someone take the lead for a change. To let someone look out for her.

They fell into a comfortable silence as they walked, enjoying the balmy evening. She noticed he kept a vigilant eye on his surroundings. She found it reassuring that he wasn't just discounting her feelings.

"Have you eaten?" Lauren asked him, not hungry but not wanting to be on her own just yet.

"No."

"Good. I have homemade vegetable pasta sauce in the fridge if you want to join me." She hoped he would say yes. She felt a bit pathetic wanting him to say yes but right now she didn't care. She just didn't want to be on her own.

"That sounds great," Dane replied with a smile. "I can't remember the last time I had a home-cooked meal. My culinary skills are fairly basic and mostly restricted to breakfast."

He smiled again and she could see that his lack of prowess in the kitchen certainly didn't bother him. He'd probably been too busy being a badass in the army to learn how to cook. He had a certain take-charge alpha personality and she wondered how she hadn't realised it before.

In hindsight it had always been there, and she *had* noticed it, she guessed—although mainly with his interactions with Daniel and his friends. They were always innately competitive whether it was cooking on the BBQ or playing football, and yet they never fought aggressively. Maybe there was a bond that men got from fighting together that allowed there to be more than one alpha in a group. Nate was another member of Fortis and he was about as testosterone-filled as it got.

She snapped her thoughts back to the now. *Where the hell did that thought process come from?* She was clearly in need of some food.

~~~

Climbing the stairs behind her, Dane wondered who'd been watching her in the park. He'd have to keep an eye out. He didn't like the idea of anyone scaring her or watching her. He followed Lauren up the steps and couldn't help but admire the view. *That outfit should be illegal!* The material clung to her like a second skin showing off her breasts and ass to perfection and *God*, he was only human.

Snapping his eyes upward, he was pleasantly surprised when he stepped into her home. It wasn't what he'd expected. It had clean lines with comfortable fabric couches facing the big bay windows and a small TV in the corner. The floors were polished oak with big, cream throw rugs covering the main living areas and filmy curtains at the windows.

It was an open floor plan with a small kitchen and a dining area at the back. It had a lovely homey, airy feel with none of the frills and froufrou he expected from someone who was a healer. It wasn't really what he had expected from Lauren. She was so girl-next-door and he had expected… he didn't even know what he'd expected but this wasn't it. Which was silly because as he looked around, he realised it suited her perfectly.

He hadn't ever thought of himself as narrow-minded but God, he couldn't think straight around her and he was having a hard time not thinking about her constantly. He was royally screwed.

She didn't know that Daniel had told him about Lauren and Claire's special abilities and, although he'd been initially surprised, it did explain how insightful Claire had always seemed. He'd come across people with special abilities in the forces and found them to be very normal people who just had extraordinary abilities.

Daniel had felt bad for breaking her confidence, but after losing Claire he'd felt that every avenue should be explored in the hunt for her killer. Dane wasn't sure it had anything to do with Lauren's abilities, but the excuse to keep an eye on Lauren was okay with him. Which was how he'd found himself in the park that evening on the pretence of taking a walk.

He wasn't so unaware of himself that he didn't realise he was using this as an excuse to be around Lauren more. But he liked her and missed the friendship they had developed a few years back, even though it had all been via email. Lately he had felt the need for something more permanent in his life. He wasn't sure if that was Lauren, but he did know that the feeling went away when she was around.

He knew what he was—a trained killer and he was good at it— but he hadn't enjoyed taking lives, it was just part of the job. He loved the camaraderie that being in an elite Special Forces unit like the Special Air Service gave a person, but the constant barrage of extremists that just wanted to kill unrepentantly in the name of religion—and in the most heinous ways—had worn him down until he felt like any difference they were making wasn't enough. In a job like that you had to believe in what you were doing and love it, or you lost your edge. And after that last FUBAR mission, he was done with all the political red-tape bullshit.

With Fortis he could do the job he loved without all the strict rules. He'd been surprised when Zack had contacted him out of the blue just before his discharge. Zack offered him everything he wanted as far as the job was concerned and he liked and respected him.

After serving with Zack on several tours of Iraq and Afghanistan, Dane could attest to the fact that his reputation as a coldly clinical yet loyal operator, who never failed a mission no matter the cost, was well earned. He had certainly set fear in the hearts of his enemies.

Everyone had been shocked when Zack retired two years ago and set up Fortis Security. If anyone had "career forces" written all over them, it was Zack. There was a lot of speculation over his last black ops mission. The rumour was that his team had been ambushed while meeting with an elder and held captive, but nothing was ever confirmed of course, and he'd never asked.

Fortis did do off-the-books black ops jobs for the government although that wasn't common knowledge, but Zack chose those with meticulous care.

No, his life was almost perfect, but it was missing something. He thought maybe that something could be Lauren. The bond they had started to develop still pulled at him. What would have happened if he'd fought for her and told her how he felt? He'd wondered about that on more than one occasion.

He knew his job would put some women off taking a chance on him and questioned if that was the case with Lauren. Oh, she wanted him, the incident in Daniel's garden proved that, but she seemed more reticent over the last few years. Dane wondered if it was his job or if Jeff-the-jerk had anything to do with that.

His fists clenched at his sides as he thought about that bastard hurting her in any way. He was going to ask her about it but knew from previous discussions that she avoided all talk of her ex. He would need to tread carefully so as not to scare her off. He would ask her on a date and see what happened.

~~~

Lauren was very conscious of the man prowling around her home and was suddenly a bit nervous about what he might think, which was silly. They had known each other for ages, why should she care?

"I love your home," Dane said.

He didn't elaborate but smiled that panty-melting smile of his. She was ridiculously pleased by his compliment. *Oh boy.* She was in trouble if that was all it took to make her melt. *How the hell am I supposed to ignore that?* And why had all these strange feelings for Dane appeared since Claire's funeral?

Oh, who was she kidding? She'd always liked him and found him completely drop-dead gorgeous. But that wasn't all that drew her to him, it was his kind and patient nature and his obvious love for his family. She'd seen him with Lucy, and the bond they shared was tangible. He also had confidence and an ingrained sense of honour, which she loved.

But like a wimp she'd chosen Jeff who she thought was the safe option with his job as an estate agent. Well hadn't she been wrong? No, she should have gone with her gut instinct and let things happen with Dane the way she thought it might have. Her gut had never been wrong, and she would do well to remember that in the future.

Smiling and blushing at the compliment he had given about her home, Lauren excused herself. "I'm gonna take a quick shower if that's okay?"

"Yes, of course that's fine. I'm just going to admire the view." Then realising what he had said and seeing her blush, he quickly added, "From the window."

~~~

Watching Lauren race off to the bathroom he could have kicked himself. *God damn it what is wrong with me?* Every time she said anything he put his foot in it like some awkward teenage boy.

Wandering to the aforementioned window, he did indeed admire the view of the street below. With the Cathedral and grounds, which dated from 1079, at one end and the beautiful 12th-century castle house hotel on the other corner it was beautiful—almost like this part of town had been left in the past. Dane knew that all the period properties along this street had been renovated and some turned into flats, but all had listed building status stopping any developer from ruining the feel and beauty of the street.

Watching the quiet road for a while, he was about to turn away when he noticed a young man who was tall and built like a Rugby prop at the corner of the street. The kid clearly wasn't trained as he'd been so easy to spot but he was definitely watching the flat. Stepping forward he tried to get a better look, but the kid must have realised he'd been made because he ducked back and disappeared. Better let him think Lauren had company. He would ask Lucy to pull the CCTV from the camera on the corner and see if they could identify the kid.

"Would you like a drink?" Lauren said from close behind him.

Dane had heard her coming, he seemed to intuitively know when she was close. He sucked in a breath and ran his hand through his hair and in the process inhaled the lovely citrus scents of her shampoo and body spray and the lingering scent of jasmine that was all Lauren.

It made him think of her in the shower which was not a good thing. He ignored his body's response to those thoughts and was careful not to let on that he was now sporting an erection with which he could hammer nails. Lauren deserved more than that. He wanted to get to know her again as they had before over their emails. She had a wicked sense of humour and was easy to talk to. He missed that.

He looked up, realising that she wanted an answer. "Yes, whatever you're having is fine." God, he had to get his shit together and not behave like a teenage boy. Thank God his soft denim jeans concealed his current condition.

Lauren looked at him quizzically before crossing to the fridge to grab two bottles of water and handed one to him. "Dinner won't be long. The pasta's just boiling, and I have a salad ready in the fridge," she said smiling.

Crossing to stand in front of her, he watched her put plates and cutlery on the breakfast bar "Is it okay to eat here? I'm not much on formality."

"Yes, of course."

He smiled as he remembered how it had annoyed his dad when he and his sisters tried to eat in front of the TV instead of at a table. Those were good times. Good until everything with his sister and mum, and then family life had gone to hell. Things had settled down eventually after his mum's death, but it had never been the same. Much as his dad tried.

Dane was distracted from the depressing direction his thoughts had taken by Lauren who was bending over to retrieve the salad from the fridge. He knew he should stay away and keep his distance, but his brain wasn't obeying him tonight. He felt the battle he was waging with his body was about to end.

His eyes swept her from her toes to her head. She turned and saw him watching her and her eyes went dark and sultry with desire as she looked at him. The look in her eyes caused his dick to strain against his zipper painfully. She seemed frozen on the spot—the want and vulnerability he saw cautioned him to go slow.

He watched as her body responded to his slow perusal. The lace edge of her white bra made him want to sweep his finger along the curve of her soft-looking skin as it dipped and disappeared into the valley of her breasts. Her nipples beaded against the white tank top, just begging him to take them into his mouth.

He could see from the pulse in her neck that she was as affected as he was. Her breathing became choppy and shallow as he watched her eyes glide from his face to travel slowly down his body. The desire in her eyes made his body hum with suppressed need. His eyes once again travelled over her then met hers. He watched them dilate in response to what she saw.

He stepped forward so their bodies were almost touching, and he could feel her heat. His body tightened even more. His gaze lingered on her face and the curve of her neck. *God she is beautiful.*

Dane moved in even closer and heard the hiss of her breath as she felt his erection brush against her lower belly. He bent his head towards her slowly giving her every chance to pull back but all he felt was the first soft brush of her lips against his. He felt her body go slack as she slowly and completely surrendered to him.

He grasped her neck in a commanding yet gentle grip and tilted her head so he could deepen the kiss. She rose on tiptoes as he pulled her body flush against his. Her arms went around his neck bringing her body closer, and he felt his control slip.

He felt like a man possessed. He wanted to consume her, to worship her glorious body but tried to keep things light and gentle as he instinctively knew she needed to be the one to move things to the next level.

He was trying hard to restrain the power pulsing through his body as she leaned into him even more and wrapped her leg around his hip. Dane teased her mouth with his tongue; he couldn't get enough of her. He could feel the heat of her core against his hard length and revelled in feeling her need.

His hand moved up her rib cage and cupped the perfect mound of her breast. Pulling his mouth from her lips, he trailed kisses down her neck. Tilting her head with the hand that was now buried in the silken curls of her hair gave him better access, while her hands danced all over his back and shoulders, sending electrical pulses to his throbbing cock. Dipping his head, he trailed hot kisses down her neck before he caught one plump peaked nipple in his mouth and began to suckle it through the material of her top.

~~~

Lauren arched towards him, wanting more and burning with the fire that was starting to flow through her veins. She slowly became aware of a loud hissing noise behind her and spun back to see that the pasta had boiled over.

Turning the knob for the stove off, she turned around and faced Dane. He still caged her with his arms around her waist. He rested his head against the top of hers as they both tried to regain their equilibrium and regulate their breathing. She'd never reacted like that before—so wanton and uncontrolled. Suddenly she felt shy.

"I'm not sorry, Lauren. This will happen, this thing between us. It's been simmering for a long time." Looking down he was incredulous to see she was laughing. "What's so funny?" he asked indignantly.

"Seriously? The pot boils over and you start talking about simmering!" she said smothering a laugh. "I couldn't help it, sorry."

Smiling, Dane dropped a light kiss to the top of her head and said, "Come on. Let me help you clean this up and we can order pizza. That soggy pasta looks past saving."

~~~

Other than her near monumental mistake of trying to tear his clothes off in the kitchen earlier, Lauren found herself thoroughly enjoying her evening with Dane. Laughing and talking the way they used to it felt almost like Jeff never happened. They slipped back into the relaxed friendship they had before. None of the awkwardness that she might've expected after that steamy make-out session in the kitchen was there. They kept to safe subjects though, like sports, movies, and their jobs.

She could feel the undercurrent of attraction between them, but it was nice and exciting and didn't make her feel pressured or embarrassed. She also liked that he kept wanting to touch her. It wasn't overtly sexual, just light touches as his shoulder brushed hers and the way he kept playing with her fingers as they talked. It was nice and it made her feel special. She was sad that it had taken losing Claire for her to realise that life was not a dress rehearsal and she needed to grab onto it with both hands.

~~~

As Dane got up to leave, he was surprised it was so late. He couldn't remember a time when he'd had so much fun with a woman who wasn't naked, except that he did. It had been at a BBQ Claire and Daniel threw before his last deployment. He'd spent most of the night talking to Lauren. Just remembering how beautiful and relaxed she looked that night and looking at her now, all soft and comfortable, made him think that maybe he wanted something more with her, something real.

She made him smile and he liked being with her. She was intelligent and he loved that she had her own opinion on things. She made his body burn with the need to touch her. He knew that he needed to go slow with Lauren despite his earlier stupidity in the kitchen. He didn't regret kissing her, but he regretted moving too fast. She was so responsive, and his body had taken over, but he couldn't allow that to happen again. He needed to stay in control, or he would mess this up. He wanted to make her laugh. Lauren had been so serious the last few years. He'd seen the old Lauren again tonight. The one who laughed freely. Losing Claire seemed to have changed something in her. She looked so carefree when she laughed and after the pain of the last few weeks, he was glad he was the one to put a smile on her face.

~~~

"I want to check that all your windows and doors are locked before I leave," Dane said seriously.

Lauren nodded. She'd feel better if he did. She remembered the feeling from the park and although she thought it had been nothing, she would rather be sure everything was secure before she went to bed. Dane walked from room to room checking that everything was locked down tight.

"You need a security system," he stated firmly as he stood with her by the door. He pulled her closer to him by her hips so that their bodies were close but not touching. He could feel the heat of her body but ignored his own response. He looked down at her intently. "Call if anything seems off or you get any funny feelings. I'm only five minutes away."

"I'm sure earlier was nothing, I was just feeling spooked. I feel kinda silly now."

Dane gave her a stern look that brooked no argument and nodded. "No matter. Call if you need anything. Okay, Lauren? It doesn't matter what time."

"Okay. I will. Goodnight, Dane." She leaned up and put a chaste kiss on his cheek. "I had fun tonight. Thanks for keeping me company."

"It was my pleasure. I'd forgotten how much we have in common." Moving his hand from her hip, he took her hand. "Would you have dinner with me next Friday night?"

Lauren looked a little shocked and he wondered if he'd said the wrong thing. Maybe it was too soon after Claire's murder. "I'd love to have dinner with you," she said, her smile beaming.

"Great. I'll pick you up at eight o'clock," he said, trying not to grin.

"I'll be ready."

He waited until she closed and locked the door before he left, and once on the street noticed that she'd crossed to the window to watch him walk towards town.

Dane walked down the road and kept a close eye on his surroundings. He'd had fun tonight and, despite the awfulness of the last few weeks, he felt excited about the future. He couldn't believe even a peck on the cheek made him feel like a fourteen-year-old boy where Lauren was concerned. He needed to get a grip and behave like the gentleman his father had raised him to be.

Chapter Six

Lauren sat up in bed with a start her heart racing. She didn't know what had woken her but something had. Staying stock-still and listening intently, she tried to figure out what she'd heard. A scratchy, bumpy noise. Getting out of bed and tiptoeing to the wardrobe, she grabbed her hockey stick and crept to the door.

Cracking open the door she stopped and listened. It was coming from the window in the bathroom. *Oh shit. Someone is trying to open the bathroom window*! Heart hammering and feeling panicked, Lauren looked around. What should she do? She spied her phone as she locked herself in her bedroom and quickly dialled Dane's number. She didn't want to think about why she was calling him first. "Dane!" she whispered when he answered. "It's Lauren. Someone's trying to get into my flat through the bathroom window."

"Okay, sit tight. I'm on my way, and Lauren? Lock yourself in the bedroom and don't come out until you hear me or the police."

"Okay," she said to the dial tone.

~~~

Dane checked that his Browning Hi-Power was loaded and slipped it into his shoulder holster before slipping a Ghoststrike fixed blade into an ankle sheath. It always paid to be prepared in these situations and knives drew less attention than a firearm. He grabbed his phone and keys from the side table and ran for the door.

He ran out of his house at breakneck speed nearly barrelling into Nate.

"Wow. Man, where you off to in such a hurry at this time of night?" asked Nate.

"Lauren just called, someone's trying to get into her flat."

"And she called you?" Nate said with a raised eyebrow.

"No time to explain, man. Jump in the car and I'll fill you in on the way."

"Sure, I could do with some action."

"Cool, you carrying?"

"Seriously, Dane, do bears shit in the woods? Of course, I'm carrying. Don't go anywhere without my baby," he said, referring to his Sig P226 handgun.

"Okay, let's move," Dane said as he reversed out of his drive at full speed.

Although it was illegal to carry a weapon in the UK, all of Fortis team had a PPW licence, which allowed them to carry for personal protection and, at times like this, he was glad he did. He felt naked without his firearm.

"So, what's up? What are you doing at my place at one-thirty in the morning?" Dane asked as he drove.

"Couldn't sleep so was out getting some air, saw your light and I wanted to talk to you about something." Nate shrugged, making Dane think it wasn't as casual a visit as he said.

"Is it something that can wait until tomorrow?"

"Yeah, sure. No problem."

~~~

Arriving at Lauren's house less than five minutes later he could see it was completely silent and in total darkness except for the streetlights. The back of his neck was itching like hell and he definitely felt eyes on him. But who and why? He turned to Nate who was surveying his surroundings carefully. "You too?"

"Yeah, man, my neck's crawling," Nate responded.

He had learnt very early in his career that when a person got that itchy neck feeling they should watch their ass. It had saved his hide more than once. Parking his Ford Explorer down the road a bit, they stalked silently towards the old Victorian style house that made up the apartments of Mr Aden and Lauren.

Falling into a natural routine from working together for a long time, they split up, weapons drawn with Dane going up towards Lauren's door and Nate going around the back. Dane silently ascended the steps, listening for any noise that indicated that someone was there.

Reaching the door, he could see that someone had unsuccessfully taken a screwdriver to the lock. He was about to knock when he heard a crash followed by swearing in Nate's deep rumbling voice. Running down the black wrought iron steps he saw a large figure run off down the street with a very pissed-off Nate behind them.

Deciding that Nate had things under control and not wanting to leave Lauren unprotected, he went back to check on her. He was very conscious of further threats and could still feel the prickles on his neck. Stopping at the door, he quietly listened for any movement to indicate what the situation was inside the flat. He quietly took out his phone and pressed Lauren's number. He couldn't hear anything except the phone at his ear.

"Hello," she whispered

"Lauren, it's me," he said. "Are you okay?"

"I'm fine. Where are you?"

"I'm outside. Open the door."

He could hear shuffling and locks being undone. He waited impatiently to see she was okay. Opening the door and peeking out, Lauren seemed so relieved to see Dane she threw herself into his arms.

"It's okay, honey," he said gently stroking her hair and cradling her close. "You're safe now."

"I was so scared," she said the sound muffled by his shirt. "I just kept picturing what happened to Claire."

Walking with her into her flat and kicking the door shut behind him, he sat her down on the couch gently. He pulled the blanket from the back of it and wrapped it around her shaking body.

Dane crouched in front of her and tipped her head up so that she could see his eyes. "I'm just going to take a look around and make sure everything is clear and secure, okay?" he said gently. Lauren just nodded.

Walking from room to room with his weapon drawn, he was fairly certain that they were clear but, as he'd seen in the past, rookie mistakes like only being *fairly certain* got people killed. Once he was sure that the flat was secure, he went back to Lauren who was shaking with shock.

He sat down beside her and lifted her onto his lap. He rocked her and stroked her hair until her racing heart slowly calmed and she stopped shivering.

She sat up. "I'm okay now," she said slowly moving off him.

"Will you listen for Nate?" he asked. "I'm going to go secure the bathroom window better."

Lauren nodded again and seemed a little surprised to hear Nate was there.

Dane checked all the windows and could see that the bathroom was the only one that had been tampered with. Someone had been trying to jimmy it open with a screwdriver. It was lucky they'd gotten there when they did, or God only knew what they would have found, although he felt they weren't dealing with a professional. This guy was strictly amateur but that could make him more prone to mistakes and erratic behaviour, so he wasn't going to take this lightly.

Walking back into the living room, he saw that Lauren had moved to the window and was peeking out. In her hand she had a wooden hockey stick with the local high school's name on it.

Turning she noticed that he was staring at the stick. "This was the first thing I could grab to protect myself and I have a pretty mean swing," she said with a self-deprecating smile. She was getting some of her grit back.

He smiled then. "Well done, honey. You protect yourself however you can. I can teach you some basic self-defence moves if you want so you'll feel less vulnerable in the future."

Crossing to the front door, he opened it to Nate who he'd heard coming up the steps. "Hey man did you catch him?"

"No, the bastard was fast, and I lost him."

"Did you get a look at him?" Dane asked.

"Not really but I would say he's a young white male and is built like a brick shit house." Which considering Nate's size must mean he was huge.

"Shit!" Dane swore softly.

"What's the matter?" Lauren inquired. "Do you know him?"

"No, but I saw him earlier. That's why I said to make sure your place was locked. I should have stayed and protected you." He moved closer to Lauren and slipped his hand around her waist from behind pulling her back to his front.

~~~

"Oh God, it's the man from the park. He was young and built like a tank. Why is this happening? What does he want from me? Do you think it has something to do with Claire?" Lauren's mind was going a mile a minute trying to make sense of things. She leaned back into Dane, enjoying the warmth and strength he provided.

Nate stepped forward. "Hey, Lauren. I didn't get a chance to say so at the funeral but I'm so sorry about Claire. I know you were close."

Lauren looked up at the tall handsome man with his tan Spanish colouring and dark chocolate eyes as if only just realising he was there. "Um thanks, Nate." Manners and etiquette seemed to kick in, forcing her brain to calm down. "How's Josefina?" Lauren asked politely.

She, Claire, and Nate's younger sister Josefina had been good friends in school. Nate had always been kind and sweet to his sister's friends. She'd always wished she'd had a brother like him when she was younger. Nate had a beautiful calmness about him usually. Tonight though? Tonight, she could see some tightness around his eyes and in his stance indicating he had pain in his life. As a healer she had learnt over the years to spot the little signs that indicated someone was hurting.

"She's good. She and her husband just moved to Aberdeen with his job and they are expecting their first baby in December."

Lauren was happy for her friend, but she couldn't help the pang of pain that flitted through her that her friend was having a baby and she wasn't. God! What sort of selfish cow was she envying her friends' happiness? She shook her horrible thoughts away. "That's wonderful," she said, and she did mean it, she just wanted the same for herself. "Thank you for tonight."

"You're welcome, Chiquita."

~~~

 Good old Nate. He could always be counted on to diffuse a situation. And by getting Lauren to talk about Josefina, Nate had totally stopped her impending meltdown. Dane watched the exchange with interest. There seemed to be a lot of tension coming off Lauren when she had talked about Josefina but of course, that could be the stress of the evening. She sure was a complicated one. He ground his back teeth. Absurd though it was, he wanted all her attention on him not Nate. He wanted to be the one to calm her. *Shit.* He was in trouble.

Dane leaned forward and dropped a kiss to her temple staking his claim like a dog pissing on his territory. God, he had never been like this. He knew he was behaving like a prize prick but couldn't seem to help it. Nate knew it too because he gave him a stupid grin as if to say, 'Ah, like that is it?'

~~~

Calmer now, she realised nobody had answered her question from earlier. Lauren asked again, "Who do you think was trying to break into my flat and what do you think they want with me?" She directed her question at Dane who shared a look with Nate.

"Honestly, we don't know, honey, but I promise you we will find out. I won't let anything happen to you."

"So, what was that look for between you two?" she asked waving her finger between the two of them. "And don't play dumb. I really want to know."

The fright was wearing off now, leaving anger in its wake. Anger that some low-life had tried to break into her flat and nearly frightened her to death in the process. How dare they do this to her. She wasn't just gonna sit back and let the big badass men handle it. This was her life and she wanted to know what was going on. Although she really liked having Dane's arms around her and though it was an unfamiliar gesture, it felt right.

~~~

Pulling Lauren in closer to reassure himself she was okay Dane decided honesty was best. "It was just a look to say we need to watch our backs more and that yes, something is going on. I'm sorry we don't know more than that, Lauren, but we will."

~~~

"Wow, all that with a look," she said dubiously, not quite believing him, which caused Dane and Nate to chuckle. Lauren accepted his embrace and turned slightly into him. She also accepted his explanation for now—she was just too tired to argue anymore tonight.

"I'll stay here tonight with Lauren," Dane declared. "Nate, you can take my car and bring it back in the morning."

"Are you sure you don't mind?" Lauren asked.

"I'm sure, and tomorrow I'll get some added security on this place."

"I can make a start on that tomorrow if you like," Nate said.

"Great. Thanks, Nate."

"Well, I'll get going. Call if you need anything," Nate said.

~~~

As Nate was about to leave, Dane remembered that he had come around to his house earlier. "Did you want to talk to me about something earlier?"

"Nah, don't worry. It can wait."

"Are you sure?" he queried as he walked him to the door. He had been worried about Nate lately. He was quiet and that was not the normal Nate Jones. He was usually ribbing everyone about everything.

"Yeah, I'm good," Nate replied. "So, you and Lauren, hey?" he queried, trying to deflect Dane's attention. "She's a nice girl, man. I like her for you."

Dane looked at him thoughtfully. "Yes, me too and uh sorry for being a prick back there."

Nate laughed. "No worries, man."

Dane watched Nate walk to his car. Yes, he and Nate were going to have a man-to-man soon so he could find out what was going on with him. Maybe they should go for a beer or maybe a sparring session. Yes, that was more his style. Have a hard-sparring session. See if that helped him work out his problems without them having to do any touchy-feely talking.

When Nate had driven off, Dane locked up behind him making sure everything was secured. He would rather be paranoid than dead. Lauren was still standing in the living room when he came back. She looked a little lost, so he walked over and tugged her into his arms.

~~~

Lauren wasn't really sure what to do. She couldn't really offer him her bed without seeming like a forward hussy…even though at this moment she couldn't think of anything she would like more. And not just because she wanted to tear his clothes off. No, she just wanted to feel the safety of his arms around her.

Feeling him pull her into his arms she instead said, "Um, I haven't got a spare room." Lauren wanted to smack herself upside the head. *Well duh, he knows that, stupid. He just checked your flat for bad guys.*

"Don't worry. I'll just stretch out on the sofa."

She hesitated. "Are you sure?" Half of her wanted him to drag her to bed while the other half knew she wasn't ready for that yet.

He nodded. "Yes, it's fine like this. Believe me, I've slept in worse."

"Well, okay. I'll just go to bed then. If you want to grab a shower or food or drink, help yourself. I'm not much of a morning person, so don't wait for me."

She pulled herself free from his arms and stepped back. Dane let her go but stepped forward and put a gentle kiss on her temple just next to her brow. "Goodnight, Lauren. Sweet dreams."

"Goodnight, Dane, and thanks for coming to my rescue."

"My pleasure, honey," he said settling down on the couch.

Wow, what a night. First the scare in the park then the hot make-out session in the kitchen and now this. Her life had become a bad TV show. And now she was lying there, feeling completely frustrated due to the hot and sexy man in her living room. She so wanted to talk to Claire right then. Just thinking about her friend made her feel heartsick. *God, I miss her.*

~~~

In the living room Dane was faring no better. He was cramped and too hot. He could smell her scent everywhere and imagining her in bed one door away wasn't helping his body relax. Dane knew she wasn't ready for anything more just yet and seeing her discomfort earlier had come to her rescue.

He was sure he was going to be dead from blue balls by morning though. *This is gonna be a long night!*

Chapter Seven

He watched from the street below as all the lights went out in Lauren Cassidy's home and he fumed. Who the hell was after Lauren? Who the fuck did they think they were, targeting his prey? And now that bastard staying with her was going to make it even harder for him to get to her.

He wondered if it was Marcus Preedy or his head of security, Michaels, but didn't think so. Michaels was shorter and stockier. Maybe it was that son of his. Preedy thought he was the one in control all the time. They would all soon see that he was the one running this show, and nobody was gonna fuck it up for him or get in the way.

Pulling out the dog-eared picture of himself and Claire, he ran his finger along her face "Don't worry, my precious love," he muttered to himself. "I will make sure they pay for not noticing your suffering." Putting the picture back in his inside coat pocket, he mused to himself *Was it Preedy or someone else?* And if it was Preedy, how had he found out?

He needed to speak to that arrogant consultant, Mr Hale, from the hospital. He hated the self-opinionated prick, but he needed to find out if he knew about his interest in Lauren and, as one of Marcus Preedy's minions, he might know.

Hale was one of the leading oncology consultants in the country and if he'd managed to control his little gambling problem, he would've been one of the best in the world. However, by allowing his habit to get out of hand he'd become Marcus Preedy's little bitch—and all for money and status. He hated men like Hale who had it all handed to them on a plate while men like him had to struggle to find their place in society.

Focusing his mind back on the here and now and away from his hatred of Hale, he knew this development would mean he had to be more careful and creative, but he was the master of creation. A genius among men at blending in and going unnoticed but soon they would all see his masterpiece.

Chapter Eight

Opening one eye, Lauren looked at the clock which showed 08:47 in bright numbers. What a night. She had finally drifted off around five after much tossing and turning. Between sexual frustration and holding her breath at every noise, it had been impossible to relax. Dragging her tired body upright, she headed for the shower.

She was halfway out her bedroom door before realising she could smell coffee. It took her foggy brain another moment to realise that she was midway across the living room in nothing but sleep shorts and a vest while Dane stood watching her from the kitchen.

"Good morning," he said as he stood there with his arms crossed over his impressive chest, emphasising his huge biceps with a mug of coffee in one hand.

Looking all perfect and chipper he had obviously showered and looked as fresh as a daisy while she knew she must look like a scarecrow. He was dressed in soft denim jeans and a black t-shirt that clung to his impressively muscled chest and arms. Realising that she was staring and hadn't answered him she mumbled a quick "Morning," and hurried towards the sanctuary of the shower.

Rushing through her shower and morning ablutions, Lauren pinned her wet hair up off her neck with a clip and applied a light layer of tinted moisturiser to help conceal the dark circles that lack of sleep had given her. Giving her eyes a quick swipe of mascara, she realised that she now had to make a dash back to her bedroom for clothes in only a towel. *Come on, Lauren,* she coached herself in the mirror. *It's a towel—you're covered to your knees and it's not like he's gonna throw you to the ground and ravage you as soon as you walk out the door.*

Now why did that thought have her hoping that he might? She was a hot mess. One minute hoping he jumped her and ravaged her on the living room floor and the next hoping she could slip into her room unnoticed. *Come on, pull yourself together!*

Opening the door, she saw Dane standing by the window watching the Saturday morning comings and goings in the street below. She ran to her room and was annoyed with herself because she was disappointed that he hadn't jumped her.

She quickly dressed in navy knee-length shorts and a white, vest top. It was gonna be another hot one today and she wanted to be comfortable. Slipping her feet into flip-flops, she cast one last glance in the mirror. Yes, she looked almost human now.

Walking out into the living room she was met by Dane who was holding out a coffee mug.

"I wasn't sure how you liked it, so I left it black," he said.

Taking the fragrant coffee, she smiled and inhaled the scent of the rich brew. "Thank you, it's perfect," she replied taking a sip of the steaming coffee. Feeling slightly better after her caffeine hit, she asked, "So, what's the plan for today?"

"Well, Nate's going to come over this morning and fit one of our state-of-the-art alarms for you and then I'm going to have a look around and see if I can spot any signs of our friend from last night."

"Okay, what should I do?"

"Whatever you normally do on Saturday but stay in crowded places."

"Right then. Well, I have a few errands to run this morning and then I normally go into the hospital and visit with the kids in the paediatric ward. How long will Nate be here?" she asked.

"He'll probably be here until early afternoon."

"Okay, I'll bring him back some lunch. Will you be around?" she asked and then blushed and ducked her head.

"Yes, I'll be around all day, so I'll see you later."

"Oh, okay. Great," she said smiling and feeling inordinately pleased that he was staying. "I'll get you something for lunch as well." She needed to stop being so ditzy around him and start behaving like the competent woman she was.

~~~

Following at a discreet distance so that nobody would notice him including Lauren, Dane watched her go into the dry cleaners. She then headed for the food market.

After abandoning sleep at around seven that morning, he had grabbed a quick, torturous shower. He'd been surrounded by all her shower gels, body lotions, and that little shower puff women liked to use. The smell of her was everywhere. He had quickly washed and then turned the setting to cold hoping to freeze his erection into submission, which had worked until she'd stumbled out of her bedroom looking all soft and sleep-rumpled. Her hair had been tangled as if she had been making love all night. Then his cold shower had counted for nothing.

Listening to the shower come on had nearly killed him—he had imagined her in the shower running that little puff with shower gel all over her wet, naked body. It had nearly had him running in there to join her. Luckily his restraint had kicked in and he had managed to control his thoughts if not his body.

He had been pleased to see her a little rattled at seeing him and had watched enraptured as her gaze had wandered all over him. He'd stayed perfectly still while she'd feasted her eyes over his body, her desire unchecked. It had taken an iron will to not act on that look and luckily for them both, she had come to her senses and run for the bathroom. He wasn't pleased however to see the dark smudges under her eyes that she had tried to conceal. She'd obviously not gotten much sleep either and it made him angry that someone had dared to frighten her in her own home. Well, it wouldn't happen again. Not on his watch.

Lauren was special, he mused as he watched her. He was starting to recognise that, but she was also vulnerable. It was up to him to make sure she was taken care of both physically and emotionally. Somehow in the last twenty-four hours she had become his. He didn't know how or why, just that it was. But he also knew he needed to keep a clear head to do his job and it was his job to catch a killer and protect her.

He and Nate had spoken that morning and had decided that she should go about her business as normal and he would tail her to keep her safe. Nate was going to watch his six so that the guy couldn't get the jump on them. The hope was that the idiot from last night would try again and Dane could grab him. He wasn't entirely happy with the scenario. But if he looked at it objectively, he knew it was the best plan to catch the guy quickly. While he was determined, he hadn't seemed trained.

He tried to stay close enough that he could protect her. He had his weapon tucked into his jeans with his shirt covering it but didn't want to use it in this crowd. Luckily the SAS had taught him some very special hand-to-hand moves. He inched closer, watching everyone around her, hoping the guy from last night would make a move so that he could grab him.

Part of him didn't want to believe that it was linked to Claire. However, Dane didn't believe in coincidences and for Lauren to suddenly have someone watching her and trying to break into her house a month after her best friend was murdered in a professional hit, just didn't sit well with him.

He had put a call into Zack earlier, who was always up early, and brought him up to speed on what had happened. After promising to keep his boss apprised of the situation, he had called Lucy and told her to put the whole team on notice.

~~~

 Lauren stopped at the dry cleaners to drop off the suit she had worn to Claire's funeral. It was a lovely black silk dress and jacket. She had loved it when she'd bought it and didn't think she'd ever wear it again but she didn't have the heart to throw it away.

The early morning sun warmed her body as she carried on to the outdoor food market that was held every Saturday. Wandering around, she picked up fresh salad stuff and some fragrant giant peaches. At the bread stall, she bought some freshly baked rolls and, at the meat counter, chose a selection of meats. She was about to go to the cheese shop when she turned and looked up into the face of the man from the park.

Stepping back quickly and nearly tripping, she panicked but his hand came out to steady her.

"Please I'm not going to hurt you. I just need to talk to you, Lauren."

"H... h...h... how do you know my name?"

"Please, we have to be quick before he sees us," the man said, grabbing for her arm.

Yanking her arm back, she turned and fled, running through the crowded market towards home. She could hear him behind her, calling her name.

"Lauren, please!"

Running blindly, she screamed and kicked as large hands grabbed her. Fighting for her life, she got in a good elbow to the ribs, which resulted in, "Shit, Lauren, stop it!"

Recognising Dane's voice and suddenly catching the scent of him as he wrapped his arms around her to stop her hitting him again, the fight left her.

She looked up at him then, with blind fear showing in her eyes. "Someone's after me," she said in a shaky voice, holding on to him for dear life.

"Shhh, it's okay. Let's get you home. I had a feeling that guy was still around. Nate and I have been following you to make sure you were protected. Nate's gone after him." He was ushering her out of the market and back towards her house, having picked up her shopping before she comprehended what he had said.

Pulling herself away from him, Lauren felt the fear turn to anger and, in a deadly calm voice, said, "So you decided without consulting me, and knowing that this could happen, that I could be bait?"

Dane looked contrite. "Well, yes. We're trained for this sort of thing and you were never in any danger," he said calmly.

"But that wasn't your decision to make," she said. "He was close enough to touch me! I could have been dead before you got to me," she continued, her voice rising with each word. Lauren could tell by the dark look on his face that he didn't like being questioned but she didn't care; she was furious. How dare he take her choices from her!

"I am only going to say this once. We would never ever let anything happen to you. I was right behind you and you never saw me. I promise you were safe."

Lauren fought to control her anger. She knew his intentions had been honourable, but she was having a hard time letting this go. He didn't seem to understand what he had done wrong and she didn't know how to explain it when she was feeling so emotional. She walked off but kept close to him as he followed her. She wasn't a dumb blonde!

~~~

Dane put a hand to the small of her back as he guided her towards her home. She was pissed with him and he felt bad about how he'd handled things. He never would have treated Lucy like this, so he shouldn't have treated Lauren like it either. He didn't know what made him act so out of character around her, he just had the overwhelming need to protect her. He would have to go about things better or he would ruin this before it got started.

He could tell by her reaction that she needed to be treated as an equal and that's what he would try to do, but she also needed to stop being stubborn and realise that he was in charge when it came to her protection. Dane sighed. He had a feeling this might be a bit of a sticking point. Oh well, good things were never easy, and he had a feeling this thing between him and Lauren could be a very good thing.

~~~

"Listen. I know you know what you're doing and you're good at it. However, I'm used to making my own choices, not having them made without my knowledge. I understand you're the expert in security and the like and if you're willing to help me, then I'm grateful. But please talk to me first. Tell me what's going on. I'm a big girl. I can handle it." Lauren was calming down as they walked towards home and she let her anger go. It was wrong to be angry with him. He didn't know that he'd hit a trigger for her insecurities and he was just doing what he thought best. Although he could have behaved a bit less like a douchebag in her opinion. She didn't intend to tell him that though.

"No, you're right and I promise to try and make sure you're involved from now on."

They both turned when they heard her name called. Nate stood beside the Fortis truck that was parked outside Lauren's place. He had a man on his knees with his arms zip-tied behind his back in front of him.

"Lauren, I don't want to hurt you. Please listen to me."

She watched as Nate pulled the man to his feet and frog-marched him towards her. Stopping ten feet in front of them, Nate shook the lad. "Shut up before I gag you.

Is this the guy from last night?" Dane asked.

Nate nodded. "Yes."

"I don't want to hurt you, Lauren," the lad implored and strangely she believed him. "I don't want you hurt like the Thompson woman was."

Her blood ran cold at his statement and for the first time in her life she knew what the saying 'seeing red' meant. Without any thought for herself, she launched herself at him. Grabbing his t-shirt, she shrieked, "What do you know about Claire?"

For the second time that day, she was seized around the arms as Dane hauled her backwards. "What the fuck, Lauren? Stay back, he could be a killer and you put yourself right in front of him."

She wriggled until he let her go and then whirled on him. "I thought you said you could protect me," she snarled, feeling more than slightly feral.

She could see him grind his teeth and clench his fists trying to stay calm. "I can, but not if you're going to throw yourself at danger," he barked angrily.

"Oh, so it's okay for me to be in danger as long as you've made the decision? Is that right?"

She didn't know why she was baiting him; it wasn't like her. He ignored the taunt and put his arm around her waist, pulling her back into his front, then turned to Nate.

Well, two could play that game.

She ignored the arm around her and stubbornly concentrated on the man in front of her.

~~~

"Get him to Fortis, we'll follow you."

Dane could feel the animosity coming off Nate in waves. Nate had known Claire nearly his whole life and was pissed to be standing next to the man that may have killed her.

Lauren was studying the man from the protection of his arms. He could feel her trying to control her fear and anger in front of this man. She had one heck of a temper and for some reason that made him smile. He was proud of her for not wanting to show weakness to anyone. She was strong and he realised it was a complete turn on. He was even happy when he realised that she'd stood up to him. Not many people did that, and he liked that she did. Even if it did tick him off to have his abilities questioned by this tiny woman. She was a little firecracker.

"What's your name?" she asked, her voice strong and steady despite the fear she was feeling.

"Drew. My name is Drew Preedy and I'm your brother."

Lauren staggered in Dane's arms. "What…how? I don't have a brother!" she exclaimed.

"We have the same father. Marcus Preedy," he said, looking defeated.

Dane watched as the blood drained from Lauren's face. She looked terrified. It was too much for her to take in. He needed to get some answers and get her somewhere safe.

"Come on," he said. "Let's take this to the Fortis office. I don't want to stand on the street with targets on our backs and we're starting to draw attention," Dane finished looking at the interested faces of people passing by.

~~~

Dane drove Lauren while Nate took Drew with him in the van. Despite the lad's size, he knew Nate could handle the kid.

"Are you okay?" he asked her gently.

She nodded. "Yes, I'm just trying to get my head around everything that's happened. I had no idea I had a brother. I mean, I've thought about it over the years but never thought it would happen and never in these circumstances." She went quiet suddenly. "Sorry, I'm babbling and I'm sorry for being such a crazy bitch back there. I'm just…I'm all over the place."

He laughed then. "No problem. I kinda like your crazy. It's hot." He winked and reached over to give her hand a squeeze of reassurance.

It also served to relieve the tension and bring a small smile to her face.

~~~

Her heart picked up speed at that small gesture. *God my poor heart isn't going to survive.* She turned to look out at the scenery going past her. It was a beautiful day. "He didn't seem like he wanted to hurt me," she said quietly, almost to herself. "But my mum was terrified of my father right up until the day she died. She was always scared he would find us one day."

"I didn't know that you had lost your mum," he replied, steering the conversation away from her father and her alleged half-brother.

"It was five years ago. She had very aggressive ovarian cancer. She was diagnosed and, three weeks later, she was gone. I still miss her every day. We were so close. It was only the two of us," she paused. "How about you?" she asked as she turned to look at him. "Are you close to the rest of your family? Obviously, I've seen that you're close to Lucy."

Dane smiled then and she could see the love he felt for them in his eyes.

"Yes, I am. My older sister Lizzie lives in York with her husband and they have a son Mateo, who's four. You're right about Lucy and me, we are close. Although of course we still bicker like kids. It drives my dad mad. But there's nothing I wouldn't do for any of them. My dad still lives in the family home in a little village called Weobley. We're very close. I couldn't ask for a better father. He broke his back raising my sisters and me. He was both mum and dad to us, especially Lucy. I try and see him as much as possible."

"And your mum?" she queried, noticing he didn't mention her. She watched his face as pain crossed it fleetingly.

"She died when I was ten. She was an alcoholic and decided to get in her car one night after one brandy too many and drove herself into a tree. Luckily nobody else was hurt but she was killed instantly," he said it so bluntly, as if talking about someone else's mum and yet she could see it hurt him.

"I'm sorry," she said. "I didn't mean to drag up painful memories."

"It's okay, it was a long time ago," he said shrugging. "It tore my dad up pretty badly. She was the love of his life and he blamed himself for a long time. We were a normal middle-class family and she was a wonderful mum until the day my baby sister was taken from us." He looked over at Lauren, who was looking at him with sympathy in her expressive blue eyes.

She saw his fingers tighten on the steering wheel as he relived that horrible time; it obviously still had the power to hurt him.

He deliberately relaxed his hands and continued. "She was stolen from the Maternity Ward when she was only a day old. My mum had been showering and she had been put in the nursery. When she went to get her, she was gone. There was a massive police hunt, but they never found her. She just never got over it and I guess the drink helped."

She rested her hand on his arm in comfort. She could see this brought him a lot of pain even after all these years. Her heart ached for him. She couldn't imagine the pain that they had suffered. Some wounds were just too deep to ever heal properly. His eyes looked so bitter and the set of his jaw was slightly stiff as if trying to contain his emotions.

"That must have been awful for you all. God, I'm so sorry." Lauren had forgotten her earlier anger with him now.

"Don't be, it wasn't your fault." Dane turned back to the road then. It was obvious he hated talking about any of this and she wondered what had made him spill his guts like that. They drove the rest of the way in silence, each lost in their own thoughts.

Chapter Nine

Reaching the renovated concrete and metal warehouse on the edge of town, Dane pulled into the parking lot at the front. There were a few vehicles already there including Lucy's flashy, yellow Mazda convertible. Zack was constantly on her about the car. He said it screamed hairdresser not badass security firm but she loved her car and refused to get rid of it. As her brother, Dane was silently proud of her for standing her ground with their boss who could intimidate most grown men. But he could also see Zack's point. It didn't give the right company image.

Zack had been very careful to maintain the public presence of Fortis as a corporate and private security specialist. But the private government work was the main focus for them, and they had earned a very good reputation for both in the two years they had been operating. Maybe he would talk to Lucy about parking her car around the back from now on.

Lauren stepped out of the Ford Explorer as he opened the door for her. She followed him, Nate, and a sombre and scared-looking Drew into the building.

"Take him into the conference room, Nate," Dane instructed.

~~~

Walking into the interior, Lauren took in her surroundings absent-mindedly. She was expecting a large, cold space but the small reception room she stepped into, with an oak desk and muted sage green walls with pot plants on the table, was lovely.

There was a little sectional couch and a coffee table with magazines and leaflets in the middle and a coffee station in the corner. The beautiful paintings in the background added a splash of brightness to the room, giving it a nice vibe. She was impressed.

Lauren noticed all the details with half a mind as her focus was on Drew. She couldn't get the revelation that he was her brother out of her mind. If that wasn't bad enough, he knew about Claire's death, which made her feel nauseous just thinking about it.

Following through a secure door to the back, she noted what looked like four offices on the left and a big glass conference room at the back. Seeing another door on the right with a retina scan ID. she asked, "What's through there?" She felt interested in what Fortis did for the first time.

"Our weapons and training facility and the tech room," Dane explained.

"Oh," she replied because really—what could she say to that? She didn't really understand the whole set up. Lauren knew they were a private security company, but she still wasn't sure of the exact details, and she wondered to herself if there was more to it than that. Daniel had often disappeared on work trips that were hush-hush. She had never thought to ask Claire before and now she would never get the chance.

Swallowing back tears and stiffening her spine, she was determined to get some answers out of Drew Preedy. She wasn't ready to think about him as her brother yet. She would ask about Fortis later perhaps.

Pushing open the door to the conference room, they stepped in. Dane took the seat at the head of the long polished oak table and indicated Lauren take the seat beside him. Nate was leaning against the wall behind him, his arms crossed over his muscled chest.

"Right, start talking and don't leave anything out," Dane directed Drew.

Lauren sat watching them. She felt a little sorry for Drew. He looked dejected but he didn't look guilty. Not that she would know—her record for reading people and situations was appalling.

No. She had made one mistake in judgement with Jeff, that was all, and that was because she hadn't trusted her instincts. She had to keep reminding herself that she wasn't a failure just because of one bad call. Yes, it had been a doozy of a mistake, but everyone made mistakes. They didn't have to define a person. She repeated the mantra over in her head.

Lauren knew that she was only having a confidence wobble because of everything that had happened in the last few weeks but was determined not to let it derail the progress she had made. She felt better after her inner pep talk.

Recognising that she would need to keep some distance from Drew until he proved himself, she hardened her heart towards him. He knew what had happened to Claire and she wanted answers. It didn't come naturally for her to be hard, but she was determined.

She tried to look at him with objective eyes. He was handsome with the same honey blonde hair as hers, but his eyes were green and hers were blue.

"Does he have to be cuffed?" she inquired, indicating the zip-ties.

Drew offered her a small smile of thanks and she faithfully did not respond to it.

"Yes, he does," Dane stated patiently. "He's been stalking you for days and either he killed Claire or knows who did. So yes, he will remain cuffed until I decide he's not a threat to any of us."

"You're right. Sorry. This isn't exactly my comfort zone."

Dane's face softened momentarily as his eyes met hers. "I know, honey, that's why we're here," he said motioning to himself and Nate. He turned back to Drew and all trace of gentleness was gone, in its place was a cold hard operator. "Start talking," he said in a deadly calm voice that caused her to shiver.

She tried hard to concentrate on Drew but was also dealing with the way her heart had flipped when Dane had called her 'honey'.

"Okay. So, as I said I'm Drew and I'm Lauren's half-brother. I've lived with our father, Marcus Preedy, since my mum died in a car accident when I was fourteen. My mum's name was Larissa. She knew your mum, Martha," he added, looking at Lauren.

"Yes, I remember my mother talking about her. She helped my mother escape. How did she end up with my father?"

Drew shook his head. "I don't know, we weren't exactly a close family. I'm sorry," he said, looking contrite before he turned back to Dane and continued. "I'm twenty-one now and I always knew about your existence," he said again turning to her. "Father talks about you all the time. He's been looking for you for the last twenty-six years."

Lauren shuddered *God, all this time he has been looking?* It was amazing he had never caught up with them. She leaned her body towards Dane, automatically seeking his comfort.

"Our father is not a nice man. He's cruel and twisted and thinks everything and everyone is expendable. I didn't realise quite how far he would go to get what he believes is his divine right until he had one of his henchmen kill Claire Thompson.

"I don't know if you know, but Claire Thompson had special abilities. He was trying to get one of his associates at the hospital to manipulate her into using them and join the Divine Watchers. He believed that her abilities would give the Watchers an advantage over other mere mortals. But she flat-out refused to have anything to do with them and threatened to report them."

Nate looked quizzically at Dane, who shook his head indicating now was not the time.

"You have them too don't you, Lauren?" Drew stated. "Father always knew you were special. What is it? Your ability?" he asked softly, looking at her.

She couldn't detect any malice or jealousy from him—only interest. Everyone seemed to turn towards her. *Shit! Now what am I supposed to do?* It seemed that she was going to have to trust Fortis to keep her secret. Stopping to take a calming breath, she decided she had to tell them so she could help get justice for Claire. "I can heal physical wounds," she said and turned to see Dane's reaction but there wasn't one—he just nodded. That was strange. Usually people reacted in some way. It made her wonder if he had already known, which would certainly make things easier for her.

"Wow. Very cool," Nate said with a massive smile. "But I can see why you keep it quiet; you would be inundated with people wanting you to heal them if you didn't."

Lauren nodded her agreement. "I volunteer at the hospital once a week in the paediatrics department as a play specialist. If I can help some of the children heal faster with my gift, then I do, but obviously nobody knows this. I can't tell people about it or I might attract the wrong kind of attention. But when you have an ability, you must use it. It's part of who you are, and it would be wrong somehow not to. So that's how I do it without putting myself in danger of people finding out."

Nate slowly nodded and she could see him processing this revelation.

"Doesn't the staff find it funny that every time you come in the kids improve?" Dane asked.

"No, because I don't heal them completely. I just speed up the process and the medical profession puts a lot of it down to the children's resilience."

He nodded as if agreeing with her then turned back to Drew. "Continue," Dane stated coldly.

"You have to understand. I didn't know about any of this. I overheard a conversation between my father and his head of security, Michaels. They were talking about Claire. Father said that Michaels would have to deal with her. I know you're going to think I'm lying or just stupid, but I honestly didn't realise he meant to kill her. But anyway, after hearing this I decided I wanted to know more about what was going on. I sneaked into his office when he was out and found a book of names. They were all listed as Watchers and believe me, they are everywhere and, from what I can determine, they are ruthless.

"Inside the drawer with the book, was a picture of a man who had been hung, drawn, and quartered. It was then that I realised what they intended to do with Mrs Thompson, but it was too late. It was a warning for those who didn't follow the path correctly. I put the book back. I was going to come back and copy it but when I went back, it was gone. Anyway, our father was sending Michaels to retrieve you, but I persuaded him to send me instead. I wanted out and I wanted to find you."

"How did you know it was too late for Claire?" Lauren asked.

"I hacked the police records and found out she had been murdered."

She felt Dane tense beside her.

"It's okay, he isn't going to hurt me," she said more confidently than she felt.

"No, I'm not. I had no intention of letting him know where you are, but I wanted to warn you and meet you. Ever since I was a little boy, I wanted to find you. I've wanted to meet you. You all might think I'm stupid for not realising earlier or getting away sooner, but I really didn't know." Drew hung his head in defeat. She could be wrong, but she had a feeling he meant every word. "I promise you, Lauren, I had no idea he would kill her. I never would have stood back and let that happen." He said it so quietly that she hardly heard him.

Standing, Lauren walked around the table to Drew. She saw Dane stand as if ready to defend her. She bent down and hugged him. Drew tensed, not used to physical demonstrations of affection and then hugged her back as best he could with his arms zip-tied.

She could feel the shudders rack his body as he gave into long-suppressed emotions. She squeezed him to let him know she heard and believed him. This man had obviously never been shown love or affection and it hurt her to know that he had been hurting.

~~~

Lauren turned to Dane. "Now what?"

He looked at Drew. "If your father doesn't trust you, why did he let you come on your own?"

"He doesn't trust me," Drew emphasised every word. "And you're right. I have to check in every twelve hours with Michaels."

Nate and Dane shared a look and then Dane turned to Lauren. "Well first we'll check out his story by doing some background checks on him and asking around. If that checks out, we will see."

Before anyone had any chance to say anything else, Lucy came rushing into the room like a whirlwind. As usual she was dressed in her black skinny jeans, a black tank top, and 3-inch black leather knee-high boots that made men want to worship at her feet.

"We have a problem, bro. I need a word please."

Following Lucy out into the hall Dane tried to tamp down his frustration at the interruption. He knew Lucy would only interrupt if it were important. "What's going on?" he asked impatiently.

"It's Daniel. He was on the phone looking for you and going on about Claire having an affair. He sounded drunk."

"Shit!" he exclaimed looking at his phone. "When is Zack gonna get over his obsession with having this room as some sort of 'cone of silence'?" He brushed a hand down his face tiredly. He was anxious to get the interrogation with Drew over so that they could get some leads to follow but knew he couldn't leave Daniel alone. *Shit.* "I'll go over there now. Can you find out where Paige is please, Luce?"

"Already done. Claire's parents have her for the day."

"Okay. Call and see if they can have her for the night. I don't want her seeing her daddy like that."

"No problem. So, who's this guy?" Lucy asked, indicating the conference room.

"He's the guy who's been trying to get into Lauren's flat. Now he's saying he's her brother."

"Well, I can definitely see the family resemblance," she said, peering over his shoulder.

"Yes? Well maybe, but until I'm satisfied he is who he says he is, and isn't a threat to her or anyone else, he'll be treated as hostile."

Lucy rolled her eyes at him. "You're not in the SAS now, big brother, but you are the boss," she said holding up her hands as she saw him frown.

"Ha! You only humour me, and I know it." Dane smiled feeling some of the tension go. He knew he tended to take things a little too seriously. Lucky for him, Lucy was always there to pull him back and kick his butt to keep him grounded.

Marching back into the room with a frown he swore again. He still didn't have the full story from this Drew Preedy character and though Lauren seemed to trust him, he didn't. He wasn't sure he trusted the ignorant and innocent act but for now they would bring him into the fold and get Nate to shadow him as a 'friend'. Nate was good with people and he was great at 'good cop'. God, he wished Zack would get his ass back here soon.

Returning to his place beside her, Dane spoke to Nate. "Nate, can you show our guest to the den. He looks like he could do with a meal and some sleep. Make sure he checks in with Michaels as per their routine. I don't want to tip our hand just yet."

Seeing the unspoken 'keep your eye on him', Nate nodded and herded Drew out the door towards the back of the warehouse.

Dane stopped Drew as he was about to leave. "Drew, do not let on to Michaels that you are here or what has been discussed. If I find out you're lying about any of this, I'm gonna make you wish you had never set eyes on Lauren. Do I make myself clear?"

Drew nodded. "Perfectly."

He couldn't see any attitude in his response, but time would tell. Catching Lauren's eye, he could see she was worried. "Don't worry, he'll be fine," Dane reassured her.

"Don't you think you were a little hard on him?" she asked.

"No, I don't. Look, I know you want to believe him and so do I, but we don't know anything about this lad, and we have to be careful." She nodded. "Listen, we have a situation. I'm not ready to let him out of my sight just yet and he did look like he could use the rest. It will also give Nate time to feel him out and see if he is who and what he says he is."

Kneeling so that he was eye level with her, he took her hands in his and gave her a strange look. "Was Claire having an affair?" he asked bluntly.

~~~

Lauren was speechless for a second. She snatched her hands back from Dane. *How could he ask that?* Claire had adored Daniel and would have never jeopardised what they had. How could anyone even think it?

"What the fuck? Of course, she wasn't! She loved Daniel and would never have cheated on him." Dane was so shocked to hear her curse that he couldn't suppress the small smile that tugged at his mouth. "What's so funny?" she demanded, looking at him angrily. "How can you ask that and then smile?"

"I'm sorry," he said, all serious now, "but Daniel's been on the phone talking about Claire having an affair and he was drunk, which isn't like him."

The anger left Lauren and was replaced by worry for Daniel. "Well, let's go see him then," she said, striding to the door.

~~~

Dane followed, shaking his head. This woman was a complete contradiction. She made his head spin. He liked to compartmentalise things and she just didn't seem to fit any particular box. The thought both unsettled and excited him.

Chapter Ten

Arriving at Daniel's house, they were shocked to find him slumped in a lounger on the back deck with a bottle of whisky in one hand and a piece of paper in the other. Daniel hadn't even heard them approach. The way he just looked up at him with such desolation in his eyes made Dane wince. He looked so grief-stricken and dejected. Dane crouched down to eye level with him. He noticed that Lauren hung back while he talked to his oldest friend.

"What's this all about, Dan?" he asked softly using his nickname for his friend.

Daniel didn't say anything, just thrust the piece of paper at him and took another swig of the whisky. Taking the paper, Dane was surprised to see it was a picture of Claire with a man he didn't know. It was recent by the looks of it and seemed innocent enough. Claire was sitting in a canteen of sorts and the man, who looked to be around forty and was average height with thinning blonde hair and a pasty complexion, stood behind her with his hand on her shoulder. It was almost like a 1920s family portrait.

"Where did you get this, Dan?"

"It came in the mail with a note."

"What note?" he said more urgently now.

"This one." He picked it up off the floor and thrust it at Dane.

Reading the note, Dane felt a coldness seep over him. He had a bad feeling about this.

> *She was mine and you let them murder her! None of you loved her like I did and now you will all pay the price for neglecting her!*

"Do you still have the envelope?"

"Yeah, it's over there somewhere," Daniel said waving towards the kitchen.

"Okay. I need to take this and get it checked for prints," he said gently, realising how fragile his friend was right now.

"Fine, take it," Daniel said belligerently.

~~~

Just then Lauren stepped forward from the shadows and hesitantly approached them. "Daniel?" she said softly.

Daniel looked up at her angrily. She felt her heart start to race. She'd never seen him like this, and she didn't like it one bit.

"Did you know?" he asked with an angry sneer. "Of course, you did. She told you everything," he said, answering his own question.

Before she had time to process that, Daniel had pushed by Dane and was storming towards her.

She froze and at that moment all she could see was Jeff rushing at her with his fists raised. Dropping her head, she raised her hands in a defensive pose trying to ward off the blows she knew were coming.

"Lauren," she heard Dane call her name urgently and looked up into his worried face. "Are you okay, sweetheart?" he asked cupping her shoulder gently.

She turned to see Daniel looking pale and shaken a few feet away. Daniel looked at her then. "God, Lauren. I'm so sorry I scared you. I would never, ever hurt you. You're like a sister to me," he said as small sob slipped out. "I was just so angry and upset and I reacted badly." Daniel ran his hands through his hair agitatedly. "I was only going to speak to you. Please say you forgive me?"

Standing up straight and angry at her reaction but still slightly wobbly, she strengthened her resolve. Dane let her go but stayed close to her so that his arm was touching her shoulder. She pushed down her feelings. This was about Daniel, not her and she didn't want Daniel to feel worse than he already did. She took a deep breath and shook it off for now. She would deal with this later.

She could feel Dane looking at her and avoided his eyes and the questions she knew would be there. She walked over to Daniel and hugged him tightly. "I know you wouldn't. I overreacted. I haven't reacted like that in over a year. It must be the stress and tiredness of the day getting to me."

Dane joined them then and she felt his hand at her back. "I don't know what that was about but don't ever blame yourself for your reaction to others," Dane said addressing Lauren.

~~~

He pulled her into his arms—he couldn't resist holding her after seeing that reaction. He didn't know what had caused it but he vowed to find out.

He turned to Daniel then. "What the hell, man? Why would you speak to her like that? She doesn't know anything more than you do and if you sobered up maybe you would see that." Dane's words were harsh, but his tone was gentle. He knew his friend was in a very bad place right now. He would never have gotten through losing his mum if it hadn't been for Daniel's friendship and he wasn't gonna let him down now. But he also wasn't gonna allow anyone to speak to Lauren that way—not even Daniel. Daniel sat down on the lawn and sobbed as if his heart was broken.

"I'm so sorry, Lauren. I didn't mean it. I know you don't know anything. I'm just so confused."

~~~

Lauren crouched down beside him and rubbed his back as she would a child. This was hitting him hard. She had a feeling that Daniel hadn't let himself grieve for Claire yet. He had been so focused on the funeral and looking after Paige that he hadn't given himself time. Letting his grief out was a good thing and would help start the long healing process.

"Listen, Daniel, I'm fine. Just a little tired that's all. I understand, please don't worry about me. Come on, let's get you cleaned up. You could do with some food and then sleep."

"Just sleep. I just want to sleep forever until this nightmare ends. Oh, God, Paige. My baby can't see me like this."

"Paige is fine—Sylvie and Malcolm are keeping her tonight. You just get some sleep and we'll talk later," Dane told him.

Daniel nodded like a zombie and let them guide him into the house.

Between the two of them they managed to get Daniel into bed where he promptly passed out.

Shutting the door gently, they headed for the kitchen.

"Can I see the picture please and the note?" Lauren asked to fill the silence.

Lauren could see Dane didn't want her to see the note and, as he hesitated, her spine stiffened ready to argue and she could see him give in. "Yes, fine. But don't touch it. I'm going to see if I can get some prints off it."

~~~

Dane went to retrieve the note and the picture from the lawn where he had dropped them when Daniel had flown at Lauren. He still couldn't get her reaction out of his head. He had seen men who had been involved in horrific things in combat react like that. It made his stomach twist to think that she had been involved in something that would cause the same kind of reaction.

He made a mental note to talk to her about it when things had calmed down. It went against everything he believed in to harm a woman and to think someone had harmed Lauren made his blood boil. She was getting under his skin in a big way. The feelings she evoked in him were things he hadn't felt before—the need to protect her was overwhelming.

Thinking back to this morning when he'd let Drew get close enough to touch her made him shake his head. He couldn't believe he'd done that. What had he been thinking? What if he had stabbed her? His belief in his abilities was fine on a mental level and it had been a solid plan but suddenly, the thought of her broken and bleeding froze him in his tracks.

How had things changed so much in a few short hours? He was going to have to sort this out in his head as soon as he had a spare minute. Second guessing himself was not Dane's style.

Concentrating on the job at hand, he carefully picked up the note with tweezers he'd found in a drawer and turned to carry it inside. He quickly found a clear bag and dropped the note and the picture into it to try to preserve any evidence that might be on it, although he wouldn't hold his breath.

Inside he found Lauren waiting for him on a stool by the breakfast bar.

"I need to get this back to Fortis and see if we can get any prints off it. How about we all look at it together there?" She looked at him and he could tell she was trying to decide if he was just trying to put her off. "Look, honey, I'm not trying to put you off. I just think it would be good to get everyone's thoughts on this."

She smiled at his use of 'honey' and seemed to accept his reasons when she nodded. "Okay you're right. Let's go."

~~~

The drive to Fortis was quiet and Lauren knew he was probably wondering about her reaction to Daniel that afternoon. She really wanted to see if things could work between them and to do that she knew she would have to tell him everything that had happened with Jeff. It was just so humiliating and she felt so stupid for allowing it to happen.

Her feelings for Dane were already stronger than those she had felt for Jeff and that scared her. Allowing someone to have so much control over how she felt was terrifying, but it wasn't like she could stop anyway. And really, she knew he wouldn't hurt her or treat her like Jeff had.

He was honourable and kind. She kicked herself for not seeing it before and wished she could turn back time. She recognised now that her feelings for him had already been strong then and instead of being brave she had gone for boring and average Jeff and look where that got her. No, she was going to be brave from now on and take a few risks. She would let this thing, whatever it was with her and Dane, play out and see what happened. She just wanted her life back; this was another step on the road to recovery.

Sitting back and looking at the surroundings as they drove, she was happy and felt like a weight had been lifted off her shoulders. There was a certain freedom that came with being brave.

She turned and offered a small smile to Dane as they came to a stop outside Fortis. As they walked in, she slipped her hand into his large calloused one and he rewarded her with a heart-stopping smile. It was the first contact she had initiated, and it felt good.

Dane punched in the security code to get to the tech room and, as he pushed through the doors, Lucy and Nate turned to see who it was.

"Hey, I thought you were gone for the day," Lucy said. Her gaze dropped to their linked hands, pointedly causing Lauren to blush. Dane just ignored it. He was obviously used to his sister teasing him.

"Yes, well something came up at Daniel's and I need everyone to look at something before I send it to be checked for prints."

Everyone had turned serious now as if sensing that something bad had happened.

Dane placed the clear bag on the computer desk next to Lucy and stood back so everyone could get a look at it.

Lauren studied the picture intently. It did seem innocent, but she was dismayed to realise she didn't know the man who was so obviously fond of her friend. Studying it more she noticed the sign on the wall behind them was slightly out of focus, but she recognised it as the Gloucester Royal Hospital. *What was Claire doing there?*

She pointed to the sign. "Look." Dane peered over her shoulder. "What was Claire doing at the hospital and why Gloucester?" she mused aloud.

"I'm not sure. We could ask Daniel but I'm not sure if that's a good idea after his outburst earlier," he said. Lauren could see he was still angry with his friend for shouting at her.

"What outburst?" asked Nate.

Dane then explained what had happened and how Daniel had been drunk. He thankfully left out the bit about Lauren's reaction.

"Shit, that's not like him. I've never seen him raise his voice in anger to a woman. It's just not him," Nate said looking at her sympathetically.

Lucy reached out and squeezed her hand. "Are you okay, sweetie?" she asked.

"Yes, I'm fine. I know he wouldn't hurt me."

"Like hell you are," Dane said. "He scared the crap out of you, honey, and if he wasn't my friend and grieving, I would've kicked his ass."

"Please leave it. I'm fine, I promise."

He didn't look convinced but nodded. "Okay. So, what do we all make of this?" he said, directing everyone's attention back to the picture and note.

"Lauren's right," Nate said. "It is the Royal Gloucester Hospital. Someone should go and check it out. We should also show Drew, he might know who the guy is and how he is connected to all this."

Dane didn't like it, but he knew Nate was right. "How did his background check go?" he said, turning to Lucy.

"So far it's clean. No arrests or convictions. He was a good student and got excellent grades in his exams. He studied computer coding and I.T. security at college. He's also passed the licensed hacker course. He looks genuine, bro," Lucy said with a smile.

God, it looked like this boy had the entire female contingent of the building in his corner. Dane ran his fingers through his hair in frustration. "Okay, get him in here."

Nate left to get Drew, who was sleeping in the room set aside for guests or overnight work—which was mainly Zack and Dane as neither had lives outside of work.

Maybe Drew was everything he said he was, and he was just being overly cautious, but he'd been fooled once by someone he perceived an ally and it had cost him two men. He was never gonna lose someone he cared about again by being too trusting or losing his concentration.

Drew walked in looking sleepy and, in that minute, looked just like the kid he really was with his hair sticking up everywhere and rubbing his eyes. Nate followed behind him.

"Someone doesn't like being woken up suddenly. Boy wonder here tried to put me on my ass," he said laughingly, causing Drew to mutter something under his breath.

"Sorry, what was that?" Nate asked putting his hand to his ear.

"I said I'm sorry. I just don't like being woken up suddenly. It makes me nervous."

~~~

Nate nodded. The kid had reacted like a seasoned soldier and Nate had a feeling that Drew had trouble letting his guard down for some reason. It made Nate sad for the kid; something had made him that way.

"Are you okay?" Dane asked Nate.

"Yes, he let go as soon as he realised it was me and, to be honest, I'm insulted that you would think I wouldn't be," Nate said with a pissed-off look at Dane.

~~~

He had a tendency to be overprotective. He knew Nate could handle himself. God, he hadn't met anyone yet who could rival Nate's hand-to-hand combat skills and yet his instinct was always to make sure everyone was okay.

"Yes, well, if it happens again, I'll put you in cuffs," he said to Drew.

"I've said I'm sorry and it won't happen again. Just shout to me first next time. It's gonna take a while to adjust."

"Fair enough," he said giving him the benefit of the doubt.

Dane walked up to him and Drew stood up slightly taller. He was wary of him and rightly so.

"Drew, I want you to look at this picture and tell me if you know the people in it," he said pointing towards the desk.

Drew looked at the picture carefully while Dane and Nate studied Drew watching for any little tells that would let them know if he was lying. "The lady is Claire Thompson, but I don't know who the creepy-looking guy is."

Dane looked at Nate and Nate nodded. Nate thought Drew was telling the truth and so did he. *Shit, nothing about this was going to be easy, was it?* "Nate, can you get this to your friend in forensics and get it tested for prints please?"

"No-can-do boss, she's on maternity leave."

"Fucking hell, can't we catch a break on this? Okay, what about Sly? Is he home? He has contacts in forensics through his cousin. See if he can do it, please."

"Sure, right on it," Nate replied, slipping from the room.

"Lucy—keep digging on that other thing," he said. "I want to make sure nothing is missed. Talk to as many people as possible. Drew, you can go back to your room now, but I want you at the briefing tomorrow at," he looked at his watch; it was now nineteen hundred hours, "oh nine hundred, okay?"

Drew nodded that he would be there. "I want to do anything I can to help."

Dane tipped his head, looking at the kid for any signs of dishonesty and not finding any. "Fine, see you then."

The back part of the Fortis building was secure so only people with the access codes could leave or gain entry. Dane followed Drew's progress on the monitor. The kid didn't seem like he wanted to harm them, but he wanted to be sure. He'd thought the doors all having access codes, including the kitchen, was overkill when Zack had done it, but now he was glad he had. It allowed Drew to think he was free but in effect allowed him no freedom at all. Moreover, it kept him safe from Preedy and his lot.

He looked down at Lucy who was giving him a funny look. "What?"

"Don't you think you're being a bit tough on him, Dane? He looks clean and I believe him. He even offered to do a DNA test earlier while you were out because he can see you don't believe him."

"No, Lucy, I don't. Trust is earned and a DNA test is a good idea."

"No!" Lauren, who had otherwise been very quiet the whole time, stated emphatically. "I believe him about that. He doesn't need a test."

"Lauren, honey..."

But she stopped him with her outstretched hand. "No. I won't be swayed on this. Trust goes both ways, Dane, and if we don't show him any he won't show us any."

He looked down at her beautiful stubborn face and knew she wouldn't be changing her mind any time soon. "Fine. No test but finish the detailed background check."

Lucy smiled a big smile at her. "Score one for the girls!" she said holding her hand out for a high-five which Lauren laughingly obliged. "He needs someone to stand up to him." She looked over at Dane then who was shaking his head and chuckling good-naturedly.

"Come on. You look dead on your feet, let me take you home," he said gently, holding out his other hand to her.

~~~

Lauren took it and followed Dane back out to his car and climbed in while he held the door. He was ever vigilant as he walked around the front and scanned the car park and surrounding buildings for any threats. She loved how he hadn't let her go once the entire time they were at Fortis and smiled, unable to contain the happiness that being around him made her feel.

She watched him as he rounded the front of the car after making sure she was secure and realised how wrong she'd been. This man wouldn't hurt her; she would bet her life on it. He was a protector. How had she not seen that before?

Laying her head back on the headrest, she let her mind drift over the day's events. A brother, her incident with Daniel, the note and picture, her fear in the market when she thought someone was trying to hurt her, her anger at Dane, her lust for him. Her mind was a jumble and kept zipping from one thing to another and she was just too tired to process it all properly. But one thing she could process was that she liked being with him. He made her feel special and safe. Maybe after some food and sleep she would be better equipped to deal with it all.

However, the thought of sleep brought a new wave of drama for her to think about. Where would Dane sleep? Was she ready to sleep with him yet? Oh, she wanted him in a bad way but was she ready for that final hurdle? To give herself to him in her most vulnerable state? She wasn't sure.

She looked across at him; his face was in profile as he drove. He had such a strong face with a square jaw that was covered in a fine dark stubble making him look even more rugged and handsome, if that were possible. His face was all hard angles and planes but the laugh lines at the corner of his eyes and the slight dimple he got when he smiled softened it.

She let her gaze travel over him. His biceps bulged and flexed as he drove, but it was his forearms that caught her attention—they were strong with corded muscle and a dusting of dark hair over tanned skin.

She remembered how those arms had come around her as he had kissed her in her kitchen just last night and the mere thought of that kiss almost made her moan aloud. God, she was getting hot and bothered over his forearms. How would she survive seeing him naked if the rest of him was as perfect as she had seen or felt so far? She'd probably pass out from desire and make herself look like a total idiot.

She had never been particularly hung up about her body. She ran and tried to stay in shape but there were still bits she didn't like, like her overly round bum and her two large breasts. How was she going to measure up to this hunk of sex beside her?

Taking a deep breath, she calmed herself. She was worrying over things she couldn't control again. She used the techniques her counsellor had taught her. She visualised putting the problem in her imaginary box and putting it in the imaginary cupboard. She let out a breath; there, she felt better already.

Lauren allowed Dane to lead her up the steps to her flat. He took her keys and opened the door, ushering her in ahead of him. He deftly switched off the alarm that Nate had installed earlier. He always seemed to be aware of her safety but never in an overt or overbearing way. It just seemed like it was second nature to him. She guessed that was down to years of training and being in highly dangerous environments, or maybe he was just a true gentleman.

She threw her bag on the side table in the entryway and went into the kitchen to get a bottle of cola.

"Do you want anything to eat or drink?" she asked, holding up the bottle.

"Yes, please," he said coming up beside her. "Can I help?"

Lauren looked in her fridge and realised someone had put away the food she had brought from the market. Who had done that and when? "Who put this away?" she asked, turning to Dane and pointing to the meats and cheeses.

"I had Lucy bring it over earlier. It's been in the fridge at Fortis so it's all still fresh. Nate gave her the key that we were using while we sorted the alarm. I hope that was okay."

"Yes, of course. Thank you," she said, touched by his thoughtfulness. She bumped her shoulder with his in a show of affection. She was getting more confident around him all the time and she loved how natural it felt to touch him. Just being around him felt so right.

Dane gave her a heart-stopping smile. "So, sandwiches it is then," he said, leaning down and taking out things from the fridge.

They worked side by side with Dane making the sandwiches while she cut up the large, juicy peaches. They carried them through to the living room and sat on the couch side by side, shoulders touching while they ate.

Both were quiet for a while until she asked him to tell her more about what Fortis did. "I have a feeling it's not just your average security company?"

"We do offer close protection to different clients, mainly VIPs and the like, but our primary role is more, shall we say, covert." He looked uncomfortable like he was waiting for her to freak out or judge him somehow. "We do black ops missions for different allied governments mainly, the UK and the US."

"Black Ops? What does that mean? I've heard it said before but don't really understand."

"Well, if a government has a job that needs doing that isn't strictly authorised or can't be acknowledged by the government, that's classed as 'black ops'. For instance, governments might send us in if there's a hostage situation that needs resolving and they can't acknowledge it. Or to help another country they wouldn't like to be seen helping, or to rid them of certain cell leaders that they can't openly come out and say they need taking care of because it would affect the fine balance that is politics."

"So, by taking care of, you mean kill?"

"Yes, Lauren, sometimes we have to kill to keep this country safe," he said defensively.

She reached out her hand to touch his forearm and he immediately took her hand and linked his fingers with hers. "No, don't misunderstand. I'm not judging you—I was just clarifying it."

~~~

She looked thoughtful and Dane worried that he had pushed her away and scared her. But she left her hand in his so that was a good sign and reassured him slightly.

So many people didn't understand this kind of work. They just thought of them as mercenaries, and there were those in the business that were cold ruthless bastards that just went with the money. But at Fortis, they were the good guys. Zack only ever took the jobs that he thought were for the greater good of the country and never knowingly took excessive risks with his team.

Dane was holding his intellectual breath as he waited to see what she would say.

"So, you're like the knights of the round table then," she said. "You keep us all safe and we don't even know you do it."

He laughed then, he'd been called many things, but he had never been called a knight before. "A knight. I like that. I rather see myself as Sir Lancelot," he said, striking a silly pose and smiling. She laughed then too, and it was a wonderful sound to hear. They settled into a companionable silence then.

Lauren yawned and Dane realised that she must be exhausted after the day she'd had. He was used to high adrenaline situations, but she wasn't, and it must be hitting her hard.

"I'm sorry," she mumbled, holding her hand over her mouth.

Dane stood and pulled her up. "Come on, let's get you into bed." Even though he knew she was exhausted, he was sure he saw the flare of desire shoot through her eyes before another yawn hit her.

He slipped his arm around her back and walked with her to the bedroom. "I'm gonna check all the doors and windows and set the alarm and then I'll sleep on the couch," he said as he stopped at the door.

"No, that's not necessary. We're both adults and I'm sure we can share a bed without things being awkward."

He looked at her then and she looked vulnerable. "Okay, honey, you go on. I'll be in soon."

He walked around her flat, checking that all the doors and windows were secure and wondered if he would get any sleep tonight lying next to her. She had looked so beautiful and fragile when she asked him to share her bed that he hadn't been able to say no. Didn't want to say no. He could see it had taken courage for her to offer. A person was so vulnerable when they were asleep, and he loved that she trusted him to sleep next to her. Ah well, he probably wouldn't get much sleep, but it would be worth being tired if he got to hold her.

Dane walked into the bedroom and, in the light from the moon, he could see her. She had changed into shorts and a vest top and was asleep on top of the covers. She was lying on her side with her hands tucked under her cheek, making her look so innocent and perfect that it made him catch his breath.

He had the overwhelming need to protect this woman. She made him territorial and possessive as if he wanted to mark her as his, which was stupid because he wasn't that kind of man, but that was the effect she had on him. Stripping to his boxers, he lay down next to her and was surprised when she rolled over towards him and tucked herself against his shoulder. Dane put his arm around her and pulled her close, settling her against him and thinking he'd get no sleep at all.

~~~

After Dane and Lauren had left, Lucy got back to work on the background checks for Drew. She'd already searched the electoral roll, the DVLA, the HMRC, and everything she could think of including colleges, schools, hospital records, and police databases. As far as she could tell he was clean. She'd even hacked his college reports and it seemed he was a good kid.

His medical history seemed good, just the normal childhood stuff. She felt satisfied with what she found. However, she knew Dane wanted more so she went deeper into everything looking for inconsistencies.

Satisfied that there was nothing odd or shifty about Drew, Lucy wrote her report and saved a copy to the hard drive.

She decided to see if she could enhance the picture that she'd scanned in earlier that had been sent to Daniel. She switched machines and opened the FRS programme. Will had tweaked the programme so it was much more sophisticated now.

She grabbed some coffee while she used the other monitor to start looking into Marcus Preedy and any of his known associates.

It was twenty-two hundred hours when Nate stumbled into the tech room. "What you still doing here, Luce?"

"Hey! Oh, I'm just running some software to see if I can get a hit on the picture. Nothing yet though. What about you?"

"I just took the letter over to Sly to check for prints. Thought I would crash here to keep an eye on Drew."

"What's your take on him?" Lucy asked.

"I think he is what he says. He seems a little immature in some ways but in others I think he's old beyond his years. I also think he's had a lot of shit to deal with that he will need to get his head around, but I think he's genuine. That's just my initial opinion though. I would have to be around him more to say for sure."

"Yeah, that's what I thought too. I feel sorry for him, he seems a little lost. He's very bright though, if his exam and college results are any indication. I think maybe he's never been allowed to be a kid and maybe that's why he comes across as not so much immature but naïve. He doesn't seem to know how to react to us and it's making him seem shifty."

"Well, if what he's said is true then he's had it pretty tough, and facing us couldn't have been easy for him. I guess time will tell. We just need to keep a close eye on him. Want some help?" Nate asked, indicating the monitors and Lucy agreed, glad of the company.

"Yeah, you can help me start cross-referencing these companies that have known ties to the Divine Watchers."

They worked together in a comfortable silence.

Chapter Eleven

Dane woke at six o'clock the next morning as he always did. The first thing he noticed was that he had a leg thrown over him and a hand on his chest. He was surprised he'd slept so well and felt strangely content waking up with Lauren in his arms. She felt like she belonged there.

Lauren let out a breathy little sigh in her sleep that had his body waking up and taking note. He lay perfectly still and hoped his morning wood would disappear but no such luck. He extricated himself from under her so that she wouldn't be embarrassed when she woke.

Dane knew that this had been a big step for her. Yes, she wanted him, but he knew to gain her absolute trust would take time. Something had happened to her and he needed to find out what had put the uncertainty in her eyes. He now realised that's what it was—uncertainty.

She seemed uncertain of people and situations as if she didn't quite trust her own judgement. She tried to hide it and did most of the time, which was why it had taken him so long to figure out.

Quietly he slipped from the bed and made his way to the bathroom. He freshened up as best he could. He had no clean clothes, but he had spare ones at Fortis so he could grab a shower there later. Coffee—he needed coffee. Dane set about making it and then settled in to wait for Lauren to wake.

~~~

Lauren had been having the most wonderful dream. She had dreamt that she had been lying in Dane's arms, their bodies pressed together. She stretched her body and couldn't believe how good she felt; she hadn't slept that well since before Claire had died.

She loved to sleep—it was one of her favourite things—and she was not usually so good-tempered when she woke. But this morning she felt okay.

She sat up and noticed that the other side of the bed was rumpled. She remembered telling him he could sleep in her bed, but she couldn't remember him coming in. Oh, please don't tell her that one of her favourite dreams had come true and Dane had been in her bed and she had slept through it. *Bloody typical!* For once she was pissed that she was so good at sleeping.

She sat up and stretched again as she looked at the clock. *God it was only seven in the morning.* She never woke up this early on the weekend.

Lauren grabbed some clothes and dashed for the bathroom. She spotted Dane in the living room doing something on his phone. He looked up and she mumbled a quick "Hi" before diving into the bathroom. She knew it was silly, but she felt shy around him sometimes.

She had a quick shower, threw on some clothes and tidied her hair so it hung down her back.

When she walked into the kitchen, the smell of coffee hit her senses and made her mouth water for that wonderful first fix of the day. She noticed Dane sitting on the couch—he was watching her intently.

"Good morning. Did you sleep well?" he asked.

"Good morning. Yes, I slept wonderfully, which I didn't think I would after the day I had yesterday."

"Your bed is incredibly comfortable," he commented and looked back down at his phone.

So, he had slept beside her and she had missed it. *Shit shit shit.* The image of him in her bed made her blush and her tummy flipped in excitement. Hopefully next time, if there was a next time, she would be awake for it. The time for fear and uncertainty ruling her life was over; it was time to be brave. With that thought and trying not to show any of her turmoil in her expression, she asked, "So what's the plan for today?"

"Well, Nate texted me and, as far as we can tell, everything Drew said checks out. It seems like he really is trying to help and escape his father at the same time."

Lauren poured herself some coffee and came and sat next to him on the couch. She tucked her legs up underneath her and relaxed against the cushions, her shoulder pressed to his.

"I'm glad and relieved," she said "I kinda thought that he was. But it's nice to have it confirmed. My instincts haven't always served me correctly."

"What does that mean?" he asked, looking at her patiently and with no expectation on his face. She couldn't believe she had been so foolish as to say that. She knew she needed to tell Dane about what had happened with Jeff if they were to have any hope of having a relationship. It was just so hard, and she was so ashamed.

Her logical brain knew it wasn't her fault but her emotional side still struggled to catch up. Lauren got up and started pacing around the room. She loved that it was all open but now she realised she had nowhere to hide. She held her hand up in front of her and took a deep breath.

"Do you remember me telling you about Jeff in our emails?" She saw Dane tense and then visibly force himself to relax.

"Yes, I do," he said through gritted teeth.

"Well I met Jeff when I bought this flat. He seemed nice enough and friendly, good looking in a forgettable way. Well about four months after you deployed, Jeff started asking me out. I didn't like him that way, but he was persistent and sweet, and he made me laugh. You and I had been emailing and things had gotten more intense between us but neither one of us had come out and said anything."

Lauren kept pacing, knowing that this had to be said and not wanting to look at him when she did it. "I had started to develop strong feelings for you, Dane, but your job was so dangerous, and it scared me. I was still getting over the loss of my mum and couldn't handle it, so the next time Jeff asked me out, I said yes. We went out a few times and he was nice. There was no spark, but it was safe, and I needed safe. God, what a fool I was."

She seemed lost in thought and Dane sat still, knowing that if he went to her as he wanted that she would clam up. He just waited quietly, hardly moving a muscle for her to continue.

"After a few months," she continued "Jeff started to change. He was staying here mostly, and he started to get obsessive about the tiniest things like the jars in the fridge facing the same way and the towels hanging the same length. Then he started to criticise what I wore what I ate—everything.

"I didn't realise how much it was changing me, but Claire did, and she begged me to end things with him. I knew deep down that she was right, but I didn't want to hurt him. I don't enjoy conflict and I guess I just put it off.

"One day I came home to find him deleting all the emails you had sent me. He went nuts, shouting and screaming that I was a slut and I was cheating and that I was to never contact you again. He said he had friends in the forces, and it would be a shame if you were to get injured by friendly fire."

Dane snorted at that but didn't say anything.

"That was the first time he hit me." Lauren looked down, so ashamed that she had been so weak. She forced herself to look up at Dane and all she saw was compassion and understanding. "I didn't tell anyone, I was so embarrassed. It continued for six more months. I wanted to leave but I just didn't see a way out without angering him and I was afraid. I'm not proud of that but it's the truth.

"One day, I'd met with Claire and she'd convinced me that he was going to kill me if I didn't get out. She was right and I knew it. I told her that I was going to do it as soon as I got home. Claire wanted Daniel and her to be with me, but I knew I had to do this on my own. I came home to end it with him and tell him to leave.

"He wouldn't go. He said I was his ticket to easy street, and he wasn't giving it up. I own this house outright after my mum left me money from her life insurance," she explained. "He wasn't even making any pretence of caring for me by then. Jeff said that he had been swapping my pill out for dummies and that I could be carrying his child. I told him I didn't care and that I would raise it alone.

"For the first time in months, the old me was back and I was seeing clearly for the first time in ages. Jeff said that no whore like me deserved his child and then he beat me. I won't go into details but when I came around in the hospital, Claire was there. She and Daniel had found me. I had a concussion, a ruptured spleen and four broken ribs and luckily, I hadn't been pregnant.

"Daniel had Jeff arrested and I'm not sure what happened, but he was murdered by another inmate while on remand in prison." Lauren stopped then and took a breath. Her hands were shaking slightly, so she put them behind her back. She watched from underneath her lashes feeling uncertain as Dane stood and came towards her. She dropped her eyes, not wanting to see the disgust in his.

He gently tilted her chin so that she had to look in his eyes.

"You are one of the bravest, most courageous people I have ever had the privilege to know. You didn't let that scumbag beat you, you picked up your life and carried on. If that isn't a sign of strength, I don't know what is. You could easily have given in and retreated into yourself but look at what you have achieved.

"You have a great job that you love, your own home and friends that love you, and make no mistake they do love you, Lauren, and I think you're pretty special too." He slowly leaned down and kissed her gently while fitting her body to his. It was not a kiss of passion but of promise. He leaned back and he could see the relief in her eyes. "Thank you for telling me, honey."

"Thank you for not judging me," she replied quietly.

"How could anyone judge you? You're a survivor and a warrior and I'm proud of you for it."

She put her arms around him and leaned into his warmth. She felt strong around him—not weak or scared. Oh, she was a lot better these days.

Dane's phone buzzed a text alert breaking the spell. He pulled back to look at his phone.

Lauren stood and walked over to look at the picture of her mother on the wall behind the table. She'd had the picture put on canvas shortly after her mother had died. She would have loved Dane. Her mum had been a sucker for a white knight and he certainly fit the bill. She thought she would feel sad after telling her sordid story to Dane, but she didn't; she felt empowered by his reaction to her afterwards. Somehow, she felt free and ready to move on and hopefully it would be with him.

He was everything she wanted in a partner. Sexy, kind, strong, brave, loyal, and funny. He made her feel all those things too.

~~~

Dane looked at the text from Lucy without really seeing it. His emotions were all over the place. He felt so much anger and hatred for Jeff the jerk that he wished he were still alive so he could kill the bastard.

Seeing Lauren opening herself to him and making herself vulnerable to him had humbled him in a way nothing else ever had. She was so brave and strong and if he hadn't been falling for her before he certainly was now.

He hated that he hadn't been here to stop her from getting hurt and thanked God that she'd had Claire and Daniel. He was angry that Daniel hadn't told him but at the same time respected that he had kept her confidence. He would be talking to him about it though.

He tried to give himself a minute to calm the rage that was trying to break free. Him losing his cool was the last thing she needed right now. He had meant every word he had said to her. She was a warrior and he was going to make sure she believed it.

He tried again to read the text. Lucy was running late and wanted to push the meeting back thirty minutes. That was fine; he could do with the extra time to get his head straight.

Dane looked over at Lauren, who was lost in thought looking at a picture on the wall. He wanted to hold her so badly but, after she bared her soul, he didn't want to spook her. He walked up behind her, making enough noise that she knew he was coming. She hadn't seemed jumpy in the past, but he was worried talking about it had opened old wounds for her and he was going to do everything he could not to cause her any more pain.

"Is that your Mum?"

"Yes, it is," she sounded proud.

"She was beautiful just like you," Dane said into her ear, causing goose bumps to spread out all over her skin. "And just as brave, it must be a family thing." He could feel the pulse in her neck quicken as he kissed her there. He looped his arms around her waist and pulled her back towards his body.

The air in the room suddenly seemed charged. His body started to react instantly, and he heard Lauren suck in a breath as she felt his hard length against her bottom. He could see a pulse start to flicker even faster in her neck and knew it wasn't from fear but from desire. He couldn't stop himself. Slowly, he bent his head and, sweeping her hair aside, brushed tender open-mouthed kisses along her neck to her collarbone. She sighed in response and let her head fall to the side.

Running his hands from her shoulders down the soft toned skin of her bare arms, he clasped her hands in his and raised them to the table in front of her. "Keep your hands there," he said in a gruff tone. She complied without hesitation and he felt his heart swell with pride for the trust she had in him.

Grinding his now painfully hard erection into the softness of her ass, he drew his hands up her rib cage and slowly cupped her heavy breasts, gently caressing them. She jumped when he pinched and rolled her nipples between his fingers and she pushed back against his hardness. "Do you like that?" He whispered so close to her ear that she felt his warm breath.

"Yes," she said on a breathless exhale.

"Turn around, Lauren," he said in a commandingly erotic voice. She turned to face him and slowly raised her eyes to meet his. The desire and trust he saw there nearly un-manned him. She was so beautiful to him and, in that moment, he knew that he would never get tired of seeing that look on her face and he would never give her a reason to ever feel differently.

"Keep your eyes open. I want to see everything you're feeling, you're so beautiful."

She looked up at him and her face was flushed with desire, her eyes dark and cloudy like a stormy sky. She raised herself up onto her tiptoes and pressed her lips to his. It started out as a gentle meeting then she ran her tongue over his lips. Suddenly, it became an all-out war as his control snapped. Lips met and tongues battled for dominance. Hands were everywhere.

Dane cupped her ass and lifted her onto the table as he stepped between her open thighs and ground his erection into her core. Lauren was grabbing at his shirt, popping buttons as she fought to touch his heated skin. She ran her hands over the hard ridges of his abs.

He was fighting to stay in control as she was so responsive. Running his tongue down her neck, he pushed her body back so that she was lying on the table and he was pinning her with his body. He kissed the deep vee between her bra-clad breasts, but it wasn't nearly enough—he needed more.

He needed to taste her. Pulling the front of her t-shirt up, he pulled the cups of her bra down, exposing the beautiful mounds of her breasts with their perfect pink nipples just waiting for his touch.

"Please, Dane," she said.

He bent his head, swirling his tongue around her nipple before sucking it deep into his mouth and suckling hard.

"Oh my God, that is so good," she said, clutching his head to her. He gave the other breast the same treatment before trailing hot kisses down her belly. Reaching into her shorts, he could smell her arousal. Unbuttoning them, he eased them down her long toned legs. He couldn't wait to have them wrapped around him but that would have to wait.

Using his index finger, he pushed the material of her hot pink underwear aside and slipped his middle finger into her hot soaking tight channel. God she was perfect.

Lauren arched off the counter and pushed back towards him.

"God you're so wet I need to taste you." Removing his finger, which caused her to whimper, he used his hot tongue to stroke along her labia and then he licked up all the gorgeous essence of her. Moving up, he swiped his tongue around her clit making her buck against his mouth.

"Oh God, Dane, I'm so close, please!"

Sucking her clit into his mouth, he suckled hard while thrusting two fingers up into her tight wet channel and curling them forward to hit her sweet spot, while bringing his hand up and pinching her nipple.

She thrashed and bucked as her orgasm hit and her body clenched around his fingers. She rocked and undulated until finally her body went limp in his arms. Withdrawing his fingers, he kissed his way back up her body and looked down at her. His heart jumped—he had never seen anything more beautiful in his life.

"I never knew it could be like that," she said softly.

~~~

She became aware of where they were and that he still had a rock-hard erection pressed against her core. As far as she had come, her inexperience with men wouldn't allow her to be so forward as to initiate the next step. She desperately wanted to feel him inside her but just couldn't say it.

Lauren was saved from making the decision by Dane's ringing phone. Dropping his head to her chest, he groaned.

"We could maybe finish this later," she said shyly, deciding to be brave.

"You can count on it, honey," he said, sounding slightly strained. Lowering her shaky legs to the floor, Dane bent and pulled her shorts up while she rearranged her top. Standing up, he kissed her gently. Lauren could taste herself on his lips and it made her body heat with renewed desire. He left his arms around her and buried his head in her neck, gently kissing it. He lifted his head.

"I like you, honey. I really do. I'd like to see where this goes. We've wasted enough time so let's give this a chance."

He looked so adorably unsure of himself at that moment. Most of the time he was Mr In Control take charge. Somehow spilling all the horrible details of her time with Jeff had helped to free her from her past and made her feel brave enough to try for a future.

Lauren was scared to hope that he meant it, but she really liked him, and she trusted him and that meant more to her than anything. As she had seen lately, life was short and maybe this risk would be worth it.

She smiled and said "I'd like that too. You're very cute when you act shy, Dane."

Burying his head in her hair. he groaned.

"Not cute, please not cute. That's like the kiss of death. Kittens are cute. I'm manly and tough," he said jokingly, and she laughed.

"Not in this case. I think it's kinda hot." He looked at her with a shit-eating grin then.

"Well then in that case 'cute' is my middle name," he said as he released her from his hold.

Walking around the table she grabbed her bag, just as her phone rang. she managed to answer it before it rang off.

"Hello," she answered happily.

"Lauren, it's Nate, you need to come quickly. Drew's been shot in the leg and is refusing to let me call an ambulance until he sees you."

"Oh my God, okay, I'm on my way," she answered quickly. The shock of the situation hadn't caught up to her yet.

"Oh, and Lauren, tell Dane to answer his goddamned phone next time."

Seeing the stricken look in her eye, Dane exclaimed. "What's wrong?"

"It's Drew. He's been shot and wants me."

"Where is he?"

"Oh no, I didn't even ask."

"Come on. I'll call Nate from the car and find out." Relieved that someone else was in control of the situation, she jumped into the car. Dane hit speed dial as he hooked his phone to the Bluetooth, finding out from Nate that Drew had been shot outside the Fortis office. He sped through the early morning traffic towards the outskirts of town. Wondering who the hell had found out about Drew and how they knew where he was.

Chapter Twelve

Arriving at the Fortis offices, Lauren was surprised to see no emergency services there. Rushing inside, they ran straight into Lucy. "Hey, he's through here," she gestured to one of the rooms at the back "and let me tell you that he is one stubborn man."

Following Lucy through the door with the retina scan, Lauren tried to calm her mind. Twenty-four hours ago she didn't even know she had a brother and now she was feeling sick at the thought of something happening to him.

Looking past Lucy, she saw Drew sitting on the edge of a single bed with his leg up and a bandage wrapped tightly around it. Blood was already seeping through, turning the white bandage a dark red. As if feeling her watching, Drew tried to stand up and come towards her, only to wobble.

"Hey, sit your ass down!" Lucy exclaimed with more than a little exasperation as she gently but forcefully pushed him back down onto the bed. Being bossed around was obviously annoying Drew because he frowned at Lucy. Although she didn't really know him, Lauren felt it was out of character for him to look so gnarly but that was probably the pain.

Approaching her brother, she knelt to look at his leg.

"What happened?" she asked while peeling back the soaked bandage.

"Looks like daddy dearest didn't trust me," he said with a grimace. "He must have had Michaels—his trusted little pet—follow me. When Nate and I stepped outside to get some breakfast, the bastard shot me. Luckily, I had just spotted him and was about to run at him when he took the shot. The movement must have thrown the shot off and he got my leg instead of somewhere more serious. Hurts like a bitch though."

"Okay let's take a look." Lauren had seen a gunshot wound once before when she was in the accident and emergency wards doing voluntary work. A police officer had come in with a gunshot wound to the shoulder and she had wanted to test her ability, so she'd snuck in on the pretence of talking to him and had healed him. Luckily, he had been unconscious and was completely unaware of what happened. It had been a close thing, but she managed to slip away unseen.

Drew's wound was a through and through, so there was no bullet to deal with, thank goodness. She wasn't sure how well she would fare if she had to dig around in his leg to get a bullet out. It might be that the healing process would push the bullet out, but she was glad not to have to test the theory.

"This only just missed your femoral artery, Drew. You're either very lucky or Michaels is a crap shot." Lauren said as she looked at the wound closely. "Stay here. I'm gonna go wash up and then I will sort this out for you."

"Are you sure? You don't really know me and you don't have to do this. I've had worse pain from beatings meted out by father."

Her heart broke. This poor young man had had so much to deal with on his own; *well not anymore.* "I'm sure, Drew. It's fine."

Walking through the door to the small kitchen, she moved to the sink and began washing her hands thoroughly.

"Are you out of your goddamned mind?" Dane demanded behind her. "You can't. I won't let you do it. You hardly know him. Let me call in a friend of mine to look at him."

Lauren's spine stiffened. She hated being told what to do and would never tolerate it again. If he wanted a relationship, he was going to have to learn right now that she didn't take orders from anyone unless it pleased her to do so. Straightening to her full height, she spun around and poked a finger in his chest.

"Listen up, Mister. Just because you gave me an earth-shattering orgasm does not give you the right to tell me what to do. Never again will a man dictate to me—do you understand me?" She enunciated every word with a poke to his chest. Lauren was so engrossed with her tirade she missed the shocked look of bemusement on Dane's face and the way he stepped back and crossed his arms over his chest. "Now either back off and give me some space or find me some pain medication for after," she continued.

~~~

Dane felt like a total bastard but at the same time found her temper very cute and very sexy. Jeff had controlled, manipulated and abused Lauren and, not an hour after she had bared herself to him, here he was telling her what to do. Granted his reasons were completely honourable but that didn't give him the right. He was going to have to curb his bossy nature a bit but seeing her stand up for herself and getting all feisty turned him on. So maybe him being a bit bossy was a good thing if it got her all worked up. As long as she knew it came from a good place, not a bad one. Damn she was something else.

"I'm sorry," he said pulling her to him by her belt loops and slipping his arms around her. "I just can't stand the thought of you putting yourself in danger."

"Oh my God! Are you turned on?" she asked, rocking her hips against the erection he was now sporting.

"Well you're kinda hot when you're angry," he said completely unrepentant for that part. "And 'earth-shattering'. I like that."

"Reall? That's the bit that got your attention?"

"Hell, yeah. I am a guy." He laughed. "But seriously I have become quite attached to this body and don't want to see it hurt."

~~~

Well hell, now she felt bad for ripping into him. Here he was being all caring albeit in an overbearing badass way and she had gone all 'taming of the shrew' on him. Bossiness was just a trigger for her. Resting her head on his chest she listened to his heartbeat, inhaled the heady scent of him and used it to calm herself.

"I really need to do this. I've never had a sibling and now I do. I want to be there for him, and I don't want you to treat me like a victim because of what I told you. I may over-react to things sometimes so just be patient with me, okay?" she said rubbing his chest where she had poked him. "This is the first relationship I've had since, well, you know."

"Lauren honey, that's not what this is. I would never treat you like a victim and that isn't what I was doing. I just care about you and can't stand the thought of anything happening to you. I'm sorry too for coming across the wrong way but I will never be sorry for trying to protect you. I'll try to handle things better in the future and I will be as patient as you need me to be. Come on, let's do this," he said, stepping away from her so she could wash up.

Quickly washing her hands with soap and then using alcohol hand gel, she walked back over to her brother. He looked a bit pale and pinched around the eyes and she could tell he was in pain. Crossing, she knelt in front of him, absently noting that Lucy had not left his side. Lauren gently placed her hands on the wound. She closed her eyes and concentrated all the energy in her body on the wound.

~~~

Drew felt his leg begin to get hot, the heat spreading outward from the wound and beginning to travel all around his body. His thigh started to feel tight and even hotter on the wound—almost too hot. He could see sweat break out on her brow as she concentrated, then all of a sudden the pain was gone and a lingering warmth just seeped into him.

~~~

Lauren released his leg and sagged back. All the energy left her body and she collapsed into Dane's arms.

"Shit, Lauren, you are amazing!" Lucy shrieked causing everyone to look at Drew's leg. It was completely fine, no wound, no scar, nothing. Just old dried blood from where the wound had been.

"Good," she said weakly.

"Are you okay?" Drew asked her.

"Yeah. just a little weak. I just need to lie down for a while." Going to help her up, Dane caught her as she stumbled and winced.

"What's the matter? Are you hurt?" he asked sharply, scanning her body as if he could see it. She shrugged.

"When I heal someone, I take on their pain. It should only last for a few hours or so and then I'll be fine." Dane swore savagely and swept her up into his arms. He carried her through the hall into another room with a big double bed. Setting her down gently, he sat next to her.

"Do you need anything?" he queried.

"No, just need sleep." He nodded and went to leave. "Can you stay for a bit?" she asked quietly, holding out her hand. Lying down next to her, he pulled her into his arms and fitted his body to hers. Lauren's last thought before she drifted off to sleep was how proud she was of the way she had handled their little confrontation in the kitchen and how not at any point had she been scared or intimated by him despite his size and obvious ability. He'd shown her respect and had talked to her. It made her smile and think maybe this could work for them.

~~~

He stayed like that with her in his arms for hours until there was a soft knock on the door.

"Dane?"

"Hey, Luce, what's up?"

"Can I have a minute please?" Gently extracting himself from Lauren, he went out into the hallway to meet Lucy, Nate and Drew.

"What's going on?" he said looking at them all.

"These were delivered here for Lauren." Lucy said holding out a bouquet of lilies. "Read the note."

Dane tilted the flowers so that he could read the note without touching it. A sinking feeling settled in his stomach.

"Sorry for the loss of your friend but you didn't deserve her anyway. None of you did. I will make you all pay for neglecting my Claire. We will meet very soon."

What the fuck! "Is this Marcus?" He aimed his question at Drew. He was feeling rage at the thought of someone threatening his woman.

"No. No way. Not his style. He would just straight out hurt someone; he thinks he's above games."

"Then who the fuck knows she's here? She has no ties to the place. Did you do a sweep of the area after Drew was shot?" he asked, sounding more frustrated by the minute.

"Yes," Nate said, sounding a little pissed that Dane would have thought differently. "I did, and the only sign of someone being here was over by the corner warehouse where the farming machinery company was but whoever it was, and we are assuming it was Michaels when he shot Drew, is long gone."

"So how did he find her last night and again today? Because I'm telling you we weren't followed," he said adamantly.

"Could she be bugged?" Lucy asked.

Dane looked at her as if coming to the same conclusion.

"Get her bag!" he demanded of Lucy who was about to call him on his rude behaviour but thought better of it. It was obvious he cared about Lauren and that was making him act out.

Lucy came back in carrying Lauren's handbag and the bug detector. She laid the bag down and carefully ran the wand across it, which then emitted a loud beeping sound. Everyone looked at the bag accusingly.

"Fucking hell, how did I miss this? The first thing I should have done was check for bugs. God damn it!" Dane stood with his hands on his hips, fists clenched in anger watching as Lucy cut the bug out of the bottom of the bag lining.

"It's not a particularly sophisticated device but whoever planted it had obviously been watching the crime network 'cause they did an okay job of hiding it," Lucy said as she removed the bug. She then dropped the bug to the floor and crushed it under her heel. "This must be the same guy that sent Daniel the note and the picture," she finished.

"Right, conference room now. We need to work this shit out."

Dane was furious with himself. He never made mistakes like that and now, when the stakes were so much higher with Lauren involved, he started. Well, no more. He had to take a step back and start doing his job properly.

He couldn't deny the feelings that he had for her, but he would have to keep them locked down until this was over. The thought of losing her to some psychopath made him feel light-headed. His father had never gotten over losing his mother and he couldn't face that being him, but ending things didn't feel like an option either.

Heading to the conference room, Dane noticed how friendly Lucy seemed towards Drew. Hell, no, that was not happening. He would have to have a word with her later about keeping her distance, although watching them now he could see that it wasn't worrying about. She was just trying to mother him as she did everyone else. However, for now he needed all the help he could get, and Drew could be invaluable with his inside knowledge.

Grabbing cold bottles of water from the fridge, Nate threw one to each of them and sat down next to Dane.

"Firstly, I don't want Lauren knowing about this. She has enough to worry about and this will only worry her more." Dane could see Lucy wanted to say something "Yes, Lucy, spit it out."

"You're making a mistake not telling her. She won't appreciate things being kept from her. I know you're trying to protect her, but this is wrong." He thought for a minute back to the promise he'd made her about telling her everything. But he didn't want her upset by this and if he could shield her from it, he would. "Maybe so, but it's my operation and that's what I want."

Lucy looked ready to spit nails. "Of course, boss," she said giving him the evil eye and letting him know that she really thought he was being an arsehole.

Dane was in complete work mode now, issuing orders and making demands. "Drew!" he addressed him. "I need all the details I can on your dad and don't leave anything out."

Drew seemed to pause as if suddenly unsure of himself.

"It's okay, Drew," Lucy said gently. "I know it's hard to feel like you're betraying your only living parent, but you have Lauren now and we need you to help us protect her." Drew straightened as if Lucy's words had hit home. Dane stood with his arms crossed waiting for Drew's answer and then started to pace.

"Sorry. You're right and as of now Lauren is my family—no one else. Okay, we live in a place called Bridport in Dorset. He has about four men who are very loyal to him, but Michaels is his right-hand man and head of security.

"The house is a massive old farmhouse that has been completely modernised. The security is very tight with armed patrols, alarms and guard dogs that stay in the house with him. He's one paranoid bastard."

"Okay, what does he do that warrants all this security?" Nate asked.

"Mainly imports and exports of high end luxury items like cars, paintings, jewels, etc. I'm not sure how much of it is legal, to be honest. He has many business meetings with clients at the house though. He wasn't the kind of father you had a conversation with, and he didn't trust me, so I don't know the details."

Drew couldn't hide the bitterness that telling them that evoked. Dane could see the hatred Drew felt for his father. It must be awful to want love and acceptance from your parent and never receive it. Sad really. It must be a bitter pill to swallow to never be good enough and to compete with a ghost.

Drew continued "He believes that people with abilities are superior beings sent from God to rid the world of evil." Everyone gasped.

"Is he for real?" Nate asked. Drew nodded solemnly.

"He's always believed that, but for the last two years he has been having secret meetings with a group called the Divine Watchers. I don't know a lot about them except they have the same beliefs and they make him look almost sane."

"I heard a bit about this when I was working for the Government Communications Headquarters," Lucy commented, looking at Drew. "They were rumoured to be a radical bunch who believed that the earth needed to go back to the start of creation to fix all the wrongs of man. There were even rumours that they wanted to create an Armageddon to do this. It was also rumoured that they had some very powerful allies although that was never confirmed. If they're still active, then we need to find out how high this goes. I have a contact at GCHQ that I'll call discreetly."

"Okay so why does Marcus want Lauren back? Is it because she's his daughter or because of her abilities?" Dane asked Drew.

"He's always wanted her back and never stopped looking. It was a pure coincidence that he found her. I think it's because he thinks she belongs to him."

"How did he find her and how does him killing Claire fit in?" Dane asked.

"Marcus has a team that monitors the emergency services and hospitals. They report anything or anyone that seems different somehow. Claire came to his attention after her brain tumour was diagnosed. Something in the electrical impulses in the brain is different in people with abilities. Most doctors wouldn't spot it necessarily, but the Divine Watchers have been studying people like this for decades and have found a way to single them out."

"Claire had a tumour?" Everyone turned to the door where Lauren stood, looking ghostly pale. Dane hurried around the table to her.

"Come and sit down, sweetheart," he said, urging her into a chair next to him. When she was seated, Drew continued.

"Yes. She had a stage three brain tumour and was having treatment. Margo, one of the scientists that work for the Divine Watchers, approached her. They wanted to get her into a trial at one of their private clinics. But Claire refused and when she kept eluding them or refusing to meet with them Marcus had her murdered."

"But why Claire? Why was she so special? There must be others out there with her abilities!" Lauren asked.

"I'm not sure, but from what I can tell it was a numbers thing. They wanted as many people with special abilities as possible and people with serious illness are more likely to try something like a trial. I'm so sorry, Lauren. I had no idea until after that he would kill someone.

"He's always been heartless but as I was explaining before you came in, he's gotten increasingly more unstable of late. When he sent Michaels to her home to kill her, there were pictures of you two together and Michaels must have recognised you.

"You're the very image of your mother and Marcus has pictures of her everywhere at home. It used to drive my mum mad. It was one of the reasons that Marcus got us our own place. I was too young to remember what it had been like but apparently he never let my mother forget that she was just a fill-in for his beloved Martha."

Lauren shuddered. That was creepy. She was almost glad her mother wasn't here to see this day.

"I still don't understand the trials though. Who is running them and how do they help the Divine Watchers with their plans for cleansing the earth?" Lucy asked thoughtfully.

"I honestly don't know. I'm sorry." Drew looked genuinely upset that he didn't have all the answers.

"So how do you know about the electrical brain impulses and the trials? That doesn't seem like something Marcus would tell you." Dane asked Drew sceptically

Drew shrugged. "I'm a hacker. I hacked his computer and found a file. Most of it was in some sort of ancient script but that part wasn't."

"Could've been a trap," offered Lucy.

"Maybe the info was but the hack wasn't," Drew said with the arrogance of youth.

Dane looked at Lauren.

"Don't worry, we'll figure this out," he said, taking her cold hand. "This still doesn't explain the man in the photo Daniel had or…" Everyone suddenly went silent and looked at her.

"Or?" she asked, looking around the room quizzically. Dane hunkered down by her chair rubbing her cold hands in his.

"You had some flowers delivered here earlier with a note from the same person who sent the note to Daniel."

"Where? Let me see." He pushed the note towards her which was now in a clear pouch to protect any evidence.

Lauren scanned it. "He's right, you know. There is so much I didn't know that she was dealing with. What sort of friend was I? I didn't even know she had a brain tumour, for God's sake."

"Hey stop that. She loved you and for whatever reason she kept it from everyone even her husband." Dane kept rubbing her knuckles with his thumb, knowing she needed the connection. "What we need to do now is find out as much as we can about the Divine Watchers and how Marcus fits into that. Then see if we can find any connection between our suspects and Claire.

"Lucy, I want you to speak to all your contacts at GCHQ and get as much info as you can on this. Nate, can you talk to your friend on the force and see if he can give us access to any CCTV in the area? I want to know if any of these pricks are close. Also see about getting some cameras put up on all the surrounding buildings. They're all unoccupied so nobody will care. I want to know if anyone gets within a hundred metres of this place.

"I'm gonna run this note through the handwriting database and see if I can get a hit anywhere. It seems strange to me that, in this age of computers, this perp is still handwriting his notes. I'm also going to talk to Zack and see if he can help with this. Drew, can you write down everything you know about your father's operation, including names, dates, times, and anything else that you feel might be important. Also is there any chance of you hacking his computer from here?"

Drew looked slightly smug. "Of course, no problem."

"Lauren, I want you to go back over the last few months in your mind and see if you can pick up on any change in behaviour with Claire. Sometimes hindsight is a wonderful thing." Dane crouched back down to eye level with her. "We will fix this, honey. I promise." He kissed her gently, not caring that everyone was watching, and then stood. "Come on, you can sit in my office." He turned to Drew. "Lucy will show you everything you need."

"Great but can we get some food? I'm starving. I never got breakfast"

Dane nodded and smiled to himself "Sure, I'll get some food ordered in for everyone." Drew grinned then and it made him look so young that Dane felt sorry for the kid. He surely hadn't had an easy life. Great, now he was going soft on the kid. "Let's all meet back here at eighteen hundred to go over what we have."

~~~

Lauren sat at Dane's desk and thought about everything that had happened since she had gotten up that morning. Her hand unconsciously played with the Newtons Cradle there. She felt heartbroken that Claire hadn't shared something as important as a brain tumour with her. Why hadn't she seen the signs or had she and she just hadn't realised it? Surely if Claire was having chemo or radiation therapy, they would have noticed the symptoms. She had seen lots of patients that had gone through chemotherapy and the side-effects were awful.

She cast her mind back over the last few months for any clue that her friend had given and there were none. Except for her will! Lauren got up and started pacing the windowless room, playing with the pendant at her neck. Claire and Daniel had asked her if she would raise Paige if anything happened to them both. She had agreed and been flattered that they would trust her to do something like that for them. At the time, they had said it was just a routine precaution as you never knew what the future held, and she had never questioned it. Did Daniel know about the tumour—had he seen the signs?

Lauren went over and over it in her head. Claire hadn't complained about headaches or blackouts or anything that would have raised a red flag, so what had made her go to the doctor in the first place?

The more she thought about it the more she was sure that Claire had deliberately hidden the signs from them. But why? Lauren would have tried to help heal her. Just because she hadn't been successful with that type of thing before didn't mean she wouldn't have tried. She knew it might have killed her to fail but she would have done it. Claire had everything to live for and while she enjoyed her life, she didn't have anyone depending on her like Claire had. The only explanation she could think of was that Claire had been trying to protect them.

Claire's dreams still puzzled her, though. Had she known she would die like that? Had she seen it and were the dreams the reason she saw through the trial so quickly? She rubbed her temples as the spiralling thoughts gave her a headache. It made her angry to think she would never get the chance to ask Claire about any of this.

~~~

At 1800 hours on the dot, everyone reconvened in the conference room. Dane stood at the head of the table with his hands on his hips.

The authority in his posture was evident. Lauren settled in on his left with Drew beside her and Nate and Lucy opposite.

"Okay what has everyone got? Lucy, you go first."

Lucy stood and hooked her laptop to the overhead projector.

"Well I did talk to a friend at GCHQ and he said that the Divine Watchers have been on the radar more and more of late but every time they seem like they are getting somewhere, someone from SIS shuts it down. They don't know who or if they do, they aren't saying. Just that the order is coming from somewhere inside SIS."

"Sorry what's SIS?" Lauren asked.

"It's the Secret Intelligence Service formerly known as MI6."

"Oh, I see."

"Anyway, as I was saying," Lucy continued "I did find out a few important details and a few names that have been linked to the Divine Watchers." She clicked a button on her laptop and a picture of a distinguished looking man came on the screen. He had to be in his early fifties but was tall and lean with dark hair slightly greying at the sides.

"This is Elliot Henderson. He owns Omega Pharmaceuticals, which on its own means nothing, but after trawling through loads of data, I found a link to a shell corporation called Redcast. Redcast seems to own a few different companies, one of which is Pure Living. Pure Living are the people offering the trials for the Divine Watchers. He has also been linked as a Divine Watcher himself but always denies it."

"Shit, so there could be some big players then?" Nate asked.

"Looks like it and that, along with the fact that GCHQ keeps having any chatter shut down, is worrying," Lucy said grimly.

"Good job, Luce."

"Nate, what have you got?" Dane asked.

"Well, nothing like that but my contact is gonna give us backdoor access to the CCTV in the county for the foreseeable future. He went to school with Claire too, so he wants to help."

"Who is it?" Lauren asked.

"James Stevens, do you remember him?"

"Oh yes. He was such a sweet guy."

Dane tamped down the jealousy. He didn't like hearing her talk about men he didn't know and trust as sweet, but he wasn't enough of a tool to say anything. The last thing she needed was him getting all possessive and jealous especially after what she had endured with Jeff the jerk.

"Did you manage to get that extra CCTV around the area sorted?"

"Yes, Drew helped me and it's already working."

"Great thanks."

"Drew—have you got that list for me?"

"Yes, and I wrote down as many contact details as I could remember. The security code for the property gets changed weekly so I don't know what it is now, but I have written down what types of security he has. Some of it can be accessed by computer so it's quite easy to get around. I've done it more than once and he never found out."

"What about the hack?" Dane asked.

"I got in and downloaded all the files, but they're all in some sort of ancient script that I can't read."

Dane looked at Lucy "Luce, can you read it?"

"No, this is way over my head. You're gonna need to get a specialist in for this."

"Okay, I can talk to Zack about that. Thank you, Drew," Dane said taking the paper from him.

"I have spoken to a few contacts and they have offered their assistance should we need it," he finished.

Dane stood up. "It's late and I'm tired and hungry. Let's meet back here tomorrow at o-eight-hundred hours and decide what we should do next."

"What about Daniel?" Nate queried.

"Well, he was passed out when we left him yesterday. He was pretty upset about the photo and the note and he would have probably felt even worse when he woke up," Dane said.

"Do you want me to check on him?"

"Yeah, that would be good, thanks."

"Lauren, you can stay at my house if you would like or would you prefer to stay at home? Either way I'm not leaving you on your own. Not with two maniacs on the loose."

Lauren was happy to concede to that. She wasn't stupid and had no ideas of bravery.

"Mine please."

Nate looked at Drew "You can crash at my place."

"Thanks," Drew answered looking pleased that he was being treated less like an enemy and more as a member of the group.

"Everyone, stay sharp. Any one of us could be a target as we were all close to Claire." He turned, looking at Lucy.

"I know, I know," she said laughing. "You do remember I know how to shoot a gun and have black belts in karate and jujitsu, right?"

"Shut up, bratfink," he said ruffling her hair. "You're still my baby sister."

"I know," she said with an affectionate smile hugging him.

~~~

He could be an overprotective jerk sometimes but Lucy knew it was only out of love even if it was annoying. Lucy gave him grief about it but she loved that her brother was so protective. She often wondered if she would have been the same with her little sister had she not been taken. She'd been so young when it happened that she hadn't been able to comprehend it. Thinking about it now, she still couldn't. How does a baby simply disappear from a secure hospital wing without a trace? Maybe when this was finished she would open up her old files and start looking into it again.

Chapter Thirteen

Driving back through town, they drove past Irish pubs and modern dance clubs. Thai restaurants, Italian restaurants, Chinese, everything you could think of were all nestled together. The town was humming with life but they drove past all the takeaway chains as well. Dane obviously had somewhere specific in mind to eat.

Lauren leaned her head back against the headrest and let her mind wander. She smiled to herself as they passed through the town centre and the life-sized bronze statue of the famous Hereford Bull. She and Claire had sat astride it last New Year's Eve while Daniel took pictures. They had all been slightly tipsy. She and Claire had been giggling as they tried to climb on. It was a wonderful memory. How had life gone from that to weird cults and stalkers? It was so hard to wrap her head around.

Dane broke through her reverie. "I thought we could get some Italian take-away from the place on Church Street if that's ok?"

"Perfect, I love that place. I definitely need comfort carbs and maybe even some Tiramisu for after. I'm sure you're not used to a woman who can eat their body weight in carbs," she said self-deprecatingly.

"Actually, it's very refreshing not to have to be the only one eating. I hate it when a woman orders a salad and then spends the whole meal looking like they want to devour my food," he laughed. Just as well, thought Lauren because when she was stressed, she ate, unfortunately.

Pulling up to the curb, he came around and opened her door, careful to put his body between her and anybody that might be watching from across the road.

"Come on, I'm not leaving you alone," he said, scanning the area as he spoke.

"Do you think he's watching us?"

"Well we weren't followed but we have to remember he knew you were at Fortis earlier so I'm just being careful."

Their senses were assaulted by the amazing smells of garlic, tomatoes, and oregano as they walked into the restaurant. Coming to meet them was a tall mountain of a man who clearly loved his job. In his fifties with a gentle face and dark slicked-back hair that was greying at the temples, he was a handsome man who oozed charisma. Lauren could practically smell it from across the room. He had a white apron on and a pad and pencil in his hand.

"Dane!" he boomed in a strong Italian accent. He grabbed Dane around the shoulder in a fatherly hug. The affection between the two men was evident.

"So good to see you. And who is this beauty?" he asked, grasping her hand.

"This is Lauren Cassidy, a very special friend of mine. Lauren, this is my good friend Andreo Barsetti."

"A pleasure," he said kissing her hand, making her blush. "Ah and she blushes. What a wonderful woman. What can I get you? Do you need a table?"

"No, we've had a really long day and would love some of your wonderful food to take away."

"Ah of course. I will have the chef make you some of our wonderful Insalata di Pancetta with Penne Biondi for main and does the lady have a sweet tooth?"

Lauren blushed again "Yes," she sighed "I fear I do."

"Wonderful. I will make you Torta al Cioccolato to finish."

"That sounds like heaven."

Andreo beamed at her words.

"Take a seat; I will bring you something to soothe you while you wait." Ushering them into a table in the corner, he disappeared and quickly returned with a dry crisp Pinot Grigio for her and a bottle of Bulmers Original for him.

"Ah it pains my heart to serve cider in my beautiful bistro but alas we are in the home of cider."

Dane laughed at the expression on his friend's face. He had heard the same comment since he had been able to drink. "Well you can't grow up here and not drink the drink that has made it famous, my friend," he replied as he always did. It was a trusted routine and it always helped to ground him.

"Alas this is true."

"Well I'm a wine girl, I'm afraid," she interjected.

"Ah. A true find, my friend. I will leave you now. Maria will bring your food over soon". He kissed her hand and clapped Dane on the shoulder.

"Make sure you come and see me soon." Then he was gone like a whirlwind zipping between tables.

"What a lovely man!" she exclaimed.

He nodded. "He is. We met when I was fifteen and looking for a Saturday job. I strolled in here looking like shit with my trousers hanging around my arse and my long hair hanging over my eyes asking for a job. He told me to come back looking like I deserved it and he would consider giving me one. I was very cocky, thinking I would smarten up and he would give me a cushy job."

"What happened?" Lauren asked, enjoying the insight into him.

"I put on some smart trousers and got a haircut and went back. He gave me a job washing up for one pound twenty an hour. I worked my arse off that summer. I thought it would be a good way to pick up chicks. But instead I learnt about hard work and respect. I did a lot of growing up that summer.

"Do you know he can look at almost anyone and know what they want to eat or drink? It's amazing. I've seen him do it hundreds of times. I asked him once how he did it and he just said you could tell by their face and body language. I can't do it though, and I've been trained by the best to read body language. I tried it once when I was about seventeen. I was on a date and thought I would impress her and order for her."

"What happened?"

"She ran out crying when her rare steak arrived. I didn't know until after that she was a vegetarian. She never did call me back."

Lauren laughed, feeling relaxed for the first time in weeks. This all felt so normal, almost like a real date. "I wondered about that when he didn't ask what we wanted to eat or drink and got it spot on. He seems like a lovely man."

"He is. He and my dad have been my biggest champions," he said taking a sip of his cider. "They were so proud when I joined the army and when I made Special Air Service; they wanted to shout it from the rooftops. Luckily they suppressed that feeling and were extremely discreet. Nobody had a clue what I did except my family and I still don't really talk about it." He went quiet then. "Except with you. I have this habit of running my mouth when you're around," he realised aloud and frowned.

"Ah, saved by the waitress. Thank you, Maria," he said, standing to take their food as she came over to them. He went to hand her his credit card and she pushed it away "Andreo says it's on the house."

"Thank him for me please," Dane said graciously.

Chapter Fourteen

Bridport Dorset

Marcus threw the glass decanter at Michaels' head, causing him to duck. He was apoplectic with rage. How could that stupid fuck miss such an easy shot? All he had to do was follow that pathetic excuse of a son of his and make sure he brought his lovely Lauren home.

He'd been furious when he found out Drew had betrayed him. After everything he'd done for the boy. He shouldn't have been surprised though, as Drew had always been a disappointment to him.

He'd ordered Michaels to kill Drew for his betrayal. Simple, or so you'd think, but 'NO'. Michaels had failed to kill his pathetic excuse for a son. He was tired of being surrounded by people who were just not worthy. He felt like he had to do everything himself.

The only upside to this was that now he knew for certain that his little girl had incredible abilities. The only reason Michaels was still breathing was that he had stuck around afterwards and gotten that vital information, otherwise he feared he would have killed him in a fit of rage.

"So, tell me again what happened after you *failed* to kill the boy," Marcus said as he clenched and unclenched his fists and tried to remain calm.

"I watched as the guy and the woman helped him back inside. About ten minutes later, Lauren and that Dane guy pulled up in a hurry and ran inside. I decided to stick around and see what transpired. I kept out of sight, so nobody saw me. Around seventy-thirty, the guy and Drew walked out of the building and he had no sign of the injury at all. He even jogged to his side of the vehicle. I'm telling you there's no way he would have been walking properly let alone jogging after that injury unless he had been healed somehow."

Marcus was quiet while he processed the information. He had known she could heal as a child, but to learn that she could heal something as significant as a gunshot wound was exciting. He wondered what else she could do. Her powers would be invaluable when the end came, and the new beginning began. They would need healers in the new world, and her ability would give him great standing among the hierarchy of the Divine Watchers.

Resigned to the fact that he was going to have to bring his daughter back into the fold himself, he gave orders to Michaels. "Bring the car around. We're going to go get my daughter."

Michaels ran to do his bidding. Marcus sneered as he walked to the window and looked out on the beautiful lawn and flower-beds. Pathetic man; Michaels had been entertaining for a short while, but he'd exceeded his usefulness. He would have to be dealt with after all this was sorted out. The higher-ups would not accept failure or weakness and that was what Michaels and Drew had become—weak failures. Marcus watched as the gardener trimmed the hedges on the borders. He felt energised by the thought of getting his daughter back and it made some of the bile and anger in his gut ease.

This was the reason the superior ones had to rid the earth of these lower intelligence types and start the world again so that superior beings could lead it.

His second mobile phone rang; it was the phone that only 'they' called him on. He'd never met them face to face but had been dealing with them for over two years now and it felt that he was finally proving himself.

It had taken him years to prove he was a devout follower, worthy of contact with the leaders of the group. Marcus had been a follower of the Watchers for over twenty-seven years but, because he himself was not gifted, it had taken him a lot longer to climb the ladder to where he was now.

He did regret telling them about Lauren, though. She could have been his ace in the hole. He should have just waited until he actually had her before telling them, instead of informing them as soon as he found her, but he'd wanted to impress upon them how important he could be to the cause and secure himself a place in the new world.

He answered on the next ring.

"We grow increasingly impatient, Marcus," the robotic voice said. "You vowed that you would have your daughter brought to us by now. There are some among us that think you may have been lying to us. You have, after all, known of her whereabouts for some days now and still you have not retrieved her."

Marcus tried to swallow but his mouth had gone dry. The last time he heard of someone disappointing them, they had wound up hung from their arms and disembowelled. The picture had been sent to all followers as a warning of what would happen if they felt people were not trying hard enough.

"I've found her," he said quickly. "I'm just on my way to get her now." His voice came out weaker than it should and that made him furious with Drew and Michaels for putting him in this position.

"Ah good you have seven days to deliver her to us. We will contact you with instructions." The line went dead. Marcus fought the temptation to throw the phone. He needed to stop this fucking around and retrieve his daughter.

~~~

Looking out over the Thames from his corner office, the distinguished looking man disconnected the phone and turned to his colleague.

"We will have her in seven days, my friend," he said, addressing the perfectly tailored man next to him.

The man nodded and smiled.

"I will contact the international clinics and put them on standby." Turning back to the window, he let the satisfied smile tilt the corner of his lips.

Soon the end would begin, and he and his associates would watch as governments fell, and the world was returned to its perfectly natural state with the Divine Council ruling.

It had taken more than fifteen years to put the wheels in motion and assemble all the weapons they would need. It had taken longer than that to get the correct people in place but now it was all coming together. Soon the Divine Ones would show the world how things should be. He placed a call to the Divine Ones to let them know.

Chapter Fifteen

Clearing the plates away after the most amazing dinner she'd had in a long time, Lauren placed her hand over her full stomach. She felt full to bursting and strangely content considering everything that had happened in the last few days.

Pulling her down onto his lap, Dane nuzzled her neck.

"Come on, let's get you to bed. You must be beat." And she was. She felt all relaxed and floppy partly due to the food baby she was having and partly due to the wine earlier. Coupled with doing a healing and the stress, it was a wonder she could keep her eyes open.

But no matter how tired she was, she couldn't stop that tingle of awareness that shot through her every time he touched her, even when it was in a non-sexual way.

She felt him lift her into his arms and nestle her against his chest as he carried her to her bed. She enjoyed the heat of Dane's body and luxuriated in his rich spicy masculine scent. The hair on his chest tickled her nose as he moved.

~~~

Dane pulled the covers back and gently laid Lauren down and began removing her clothes. He knew she was tired and tried to keep it as non-sexual as his body would allow, even though it was causing him to grind his teeth into dust. Being a gentleman sucked sometimes. He left her in just her underwear so as not to tempt his control to the breaking point when she was so exhausted. He turned to go back out to the living room and she reached for him.

"Stay." Just one word but it betrayed such vulnerability and trust.

"Of course, honey. I'll stay." Stripping down to his boxers, he climbed in beside her and cuddled into her back. Spooning, they called it. He had never really been into cuddling; all that clingy stuff made him feel itchy on the inside, but this felt nice—natural. He could hear her breathing even out as she fell into a deep sleep. His last thought before sleep claimed him was that he could do this forever.

~~~

Lauren woke to the sound of the birds and bright sunshine filtering through the pale-yellow curtains.

She stretched and felt a hard-male body pressed up against her. Propping herself up on her elbow so that she could see him better, she saw Dane lying on his back with one arm thrown behind his head and the other wrapped around her thigh.

Her leg was thrown over his muscular thighs. She should have felt embarrassed or shy that she had been so brazen in her sleep, but she didn't. Lauren took the time to enjoy looking at his body while he was sleeping. She let her gaze roam from his beautiful face and past his strong jaw shrouded in dark stubble. Her eyes moved lower down over the graceful curve of his tanned neck to his muscled shoulders and large biceps. She continued her visual journey over his highly-defined pectorals with the sprinkling of dark hair and down to his ripped eight-pack. Her gaze continued towards his happy trail to his… She gasped. *Oh my God!*

"What did you expect?" a gruff voice said. "You were devouring me with your eyes."

"I can't believe you let me do that. I thought you were sleeping," she said, embarrassed to have been caught looking.

"I was," he said, "until you started eye-fucking me."

Lauren laughed and poked him in the side playfully. "I was not."

He laughed as he sat up and grabbed for her, tickling her ribs unmercifully. She wriggled, trying to fight him off. Tickling was her weakness; she was the most ticklish person she knew. Before she could catch her breath though, things turned from playful to hot.

One minute he was tickling her, the next he had flipped her on her back and was lying between her thighs with the ridge of his hard erection pressed against her core.

~~~

 He looked down into her eyes. Her beautiful breasts heaved as she tried to catch her breath. *God she was beautiful* and she was killing him. He could feel the heat of her through his boxers.

"Make love to me, Dane," she said in a voice made husky by arousal.

"God, I thought you'd never ask," he replied thickly.

He quickly stripped his boxers off and settled back between her soft thighs. He could feel the wetness of her arousal through her panties as she rubbed against his straining cock. He leaned forward and trailed kisses along her collarbone. Moving down, he slowly peeled the shoulder strap of her bra down and, with quick fingers, reached around and unclipped the back. He pulled the lacy bra away and allowed his eyes to feast upon her breasts.

He captured one sweet pink nipple in his mouth and sucked it into a hard peak, before moving across to the other to give it the same attention. Slowly walking his fingers down the soft skin of her quivering stomach, he slid her underwear down her legs.

Finding the hot wetness of her core, he slid a finger into her heat, shocked at how wet and tight she was. He felt her arch towards him and loved that she was so responsive. Withdrawing his fingers, he brought them to his lips; she tasted like heaven.

He could see her eyes dilate as she watched him suck the taste of her from his fingers. Just watching her face made his dick jump and he could feel the pre-cum leaking from him and coating her stomach.

"Please Dane, now!" She pleaded as she gripped his shoulders.

He'd wanted to go slow but slow was going to have to wait. Lining his swollen leaking cock up with her tight entrance, he drove into her hot tight body right to the hilt in one smooth stroke.

She was so tight he shook with the strain of keeping still. She pushed against him and his control broke as he pulled back and started pushing back into her wet heat. He felt her body squeezing his cock so hard he could hardly think straight.

Dane fought the rising tide of his orgasm. He hadn't been this out of control since he was sixteen and making out down by the river with Karen Somerby. He tried to slow down and get a slower rhythm, but she wrapped her legs around his waist and met him stroke for stroke.

He needed to go deeper—he needed to consume her. Lifting her leg, he hooked it over his arm so that it changed the angle. He could feel himself hitting her inner walls and it made her clench around his sensitive cock.

He could feel her climax building. He was so deep, and his pelvis rubbed against her clit every time he drove into her and he soon felt the first few pulses of her orgasm building. He reached down and pinched her clit and she shattered like glass into a thousand tiny pieces. The sensation was overwhelming.

Her body felt like it was squeezing him to death, and he loved it. He pumped into her as she rode the wave of her release and it triggered the most powerful climax of his life. He pumped the last part of his seed into her womb before he realised what they had done.

Panting, they both slowly came down to earth. Leaning on his forearms so as not to squash her with his weight, he looked into the eyes of a thoroughly-ravaged woman. One who was smiling a sappy smile of contentment.

"Honey, we didn't use protection," he said tenderly.

"It's okay. I'm on the pill and I'm clean." She sounded so relaxed and the trust she put in him humbled him.

"Me too, honey." He leaned down to kiss her. He couldn't figure out why, but he was slightly disappointed. He liked the idea of her round with his child. Rolling off her, he grabbed her hand. "Come on, Miss Sleepy, we have to get to the office, and we need a shower."

"No, don't want to."

"Come on." He scooped her up, tossed her over his shoulder and carried a giggling Lauren to the bathroom where they discovered that showering together was definitely the way forward.

Chapter Sixteen

Lucy pulled her beloved Mazda up to the front of Fortis. She got out and tried to balance her handbag with all her essentials in it— lipstick, phone, gun—with the coffee tray and the bag of pastries she had bought for everyone. She loved mothering people. She knew it didn't gel with her kick-ass persona but that was half the fun.

Putting the box of pastries on top of the coffee, she hauled her handbag, which was more of a mini suitcase really, over her shoulder.

Walking to the front door she nearly tripped over the pink gift box that was sitting on the doorstep. Shit! This could not be good news! Pink boxes left in the night were never a good thing unless it was from Santa.

Stepping around the box with her precious coffee, she unlocked the door and disabled the alarm. She locked the door behind her before striding into the tech room. She decided to deposit her pastries and coffee in the conference room first. Will Granger, their resident geek, was away on assignment in Paris, but he would kick her ass if she brought food near his equipment and she didn't trust him not to have the room bugged.

She ran the security footage from overnight and stopped it at 0330 when she saw a figure walk into the shot and leave the box. Their equipment was the best but if someone hid behind a hat and dark glasses, it was very hard to see enough to run facial recognition software.

Going back out to the front, she was about to examine the box when Nate and Drew pulled into the car park. Nate got out with his usual smile and swagger and Drew just grinned at her shyly.

"What's this, Luce?" Nate said, pointing at the box.

"I don't know. It was here when I arrived, but it can't be good. I was just checking the security footage before I came to get it." She knelt to take a closer look.

"NO!" Nate yelled at her causing her to jump. "Don't touch it; we don't know what it is."

"God damn it, Nate. I was just looking at it. I'm not a bloody novice, you know," Lucy said indignantly. She loved these guys, but they sure could be overprotective sometimes.

~~~

Nate just frowned and stepped closer kneeling down to inspect the box carefully and putting his ear to it. He looked closely around the edges and then gently lifted the lid.

Nate swore viciously. Inside was a picture of Lauren and Dane sitting in the local Italian bistro. The picture was grainy and looked like it had been taken with a long lens. Scrawled across the picture was RIP. Nate lifted the picture with the tip of a pen Lucy handed him. Underneath it was another picture, this one of Lauren on her own. This one had been mocked up to look like she was in a coffin. Sick fucks!

Leaning back so Lucy and Drew could get a look, he took out his mobile phone and shot off a quick text to Dane informing him of the situation. He quickly got a text back. *Secure the box. Be there in five.*

"They're on their way. Let's get this box inside."

"I'll get some gloves," Lucy said and rushed inside.

"Who the hell is doing this?" Drew asked nobody in particular.

Nate shook his head.

"I have no idea, but we will find out," he said as Lucy returned with latex gloves. Taking the gloves, Nate picked up the box and followed Lucy and Drew into the conference room.

Going to the coffee, Lucy handed one to Drew. "I wasn't sure how you liked it, so I just got everyone cappuccino," she said.

"That's perfect, Lucy thank you," he said formally.

"There are pastries over on the side if you're hungry," she said indicating the box of fresh pastries. In a move typical of a man his age Drew went over to the food and had soon wolfed down two of the decadent pastries.

~~~

Lucy smiled as she watched him; she had always wondered what it would be like having a little brother or sister. Lucy always felt a pang of pain in her chest when she thought of the baby sister she had lost and often wondered how different her life would be if she hadn't been taken.

She knew she was lucky to have had such a wonderful father who had been both mother and father to her, but she'd missed her mother every day. She still couldn't smell Chanel No. 5 without thinking about her. She'd never talked to Dane about it, but she knew Lizzie felt the same. Maybe if things went as she hoped with her brother and Lauren, she would get another baby niece or nephew to spoil. The thought cheered her up.

Dane and Lauren came into the room ten minutes later, holding hands and whispering to each other. Lucy raised a perfectly arched eyebrow. Well, she liked this development. This was what she'd hoped would happen when she saw them holding hands yesterday and, if the flushed look on Lauren's face was anything to go by, then things were going great. Catching Dane's eye, she winked, and he smiled back at her.

Sitting at the table, Dane handed Lauren a coffee and a pastry and got one for himself.

"Okay, what've we got?" he said addressing the team. He looked much more relaxed and happier than Lucy could remember ever seeing him. Lucy just hoped it would last after this latest development.

Lucy told him what she'd found when she arrived, and Nate then explained what had happened when he and Drew had arrived. Lauren remained very quiet throughout, only perking up when Lucy started to play the security footage.

"He could be the man from the photo," Lauren said excitedly. Maybe this would help them. Everyone nodded in agreement.

"Nate, can you contact Sly and see if he can get any prints off this or the photos? Lucy, can you see if you can get footage from any cameras in town and see if we can figure out who took this picture of us from last night? They must have been across the road so check all the CCTV in Broad Street and Kings Street." Dane was all business now—this was where he excelled.

"Is Sly back then?" Lucy asked, trying her best to sound nonchalant even though her heart had sped up.

"Yeah, he's home at the moment but he's due to start his last tour later this year, although I'm not sure when," he replied.

Sly was an old friend of her brother from the SAS and was still on active duty. Lucy had known him since they'd gone through selection together and Dane had brought him home for the weekend.

At the time, Lucy had been just a teenager and far too young for a man like Jace or Sly as he was known to the rest of Fortis to notice, but she had noticed him anyway and her young heart had fallen hard. Even then, she had known that she needed to wait until the time was right before she told him how she felt. Maybe her time was coming. She couldn't help the little bit of excitement that coursed through her at the thought of seeing him again.

Shaking off her thoughts, she realised Dane was waiting for an answer.

"Yes, of course. Is this Andreo's place?"

"Yes, we stopped for food before going home last night around eight thirty."

"Okay, I'll see what I can find."

"What are we going to do?" Lauren asked, turning to him.

"We're going to the Gloucester Royal Hospital."

"What about me? I really want to help," Drew said determinedly.

Dane looked at him thoughtfully. "See if you can find out where your father is, I want to know where at least one suspect is."

Standing, they all started to head off on their various missions.

"Stay alert, people," Dane shouted as they all left the conference room.

"Yes, dad," Nate and Lucy chorused making Lauren laugh and Dane chuckle and shake his head at their antics.

~~~

"Are you okay?" Dane asked Lauren, who had been very quiet until then.

"Yes, I guess I'm just spooked that someone has been watching me."

"I'll keep you safe, I promise you that." She looked up at him then with so much trust that he knew he'd done the right thing not telling her about the bug. He couldn't bear the thought of anything else scaring her. He was humbled to see the belief she had in him but was seriously starting to wonder if it was warranted. How had he not seen a tail? He had never suffered from self-doubt before, but he was getting a giant helping about now.

"I know you will," she said with so much faith in those few words that he vowed to himself then and there that he wouldn't let her down no matter what it took. Taking a step back was going to be hard though, especially with her looking at him like that. He focused on the here and now and concentrated on the job.

"I just want to stop by Daniel's on our way. He knows nothing about any of this and it's only fair to keep him apprised of things."

Lauren agreed. Daniel had been through enough already and she wondered how he would react to the latest developments.

~~~

It made her slightly nervous about how he might react and she hated that she felt that way. She didn't fear Daniel but she had felt a bit unsure of herself since the previous day. She made sure to school her features so that Dane wouldn't pick up on her feelings. The last thing she wanted was to cause angst between the two friends.

Chapter Seventeen

When they arrived at Daniel's place, he was in the garage getting the mower out. He stopped and watched as they climbed from the truck and came to a stop in front of him. "I thought I'd get the garden tidied up for Paige," he said. He looked contrite and self-conscious. Lauren looked at him closely, noting that his eyes looked clearer. Even though he had showered and shaved, he still had dark circles under his eyes but he looked better.

Lauren decided she had to make the first move and get this awkwardness dealt with. She stepped forward only slightly hesitant and hugged Daniel. He accepted her embrace and held her tightly and she felt him relax. She stepped away and assessed him.

"You look better. Have you eaten?"

"I had some coffee earlier."

"Come on, I'll make you something. You're no good to Paige if you waste away." Tugging his arm, she pulled him into the house. She felt instantly more at ease now that things had gone back to normal. Dane followed behind.

She sat Daniel down at the counter and set about pulling out all the things she would need—bacon, sausage, eggs, mushrooms and hash browns.

"I need to talk to you," Dane declared, sitting down across from Daniel. He then set about telling him everything that had happened in the last two days. When he finished, he sat back to let his friend process it all.

"So, Claire was sick. Did you know?" he said looking at Lauren as she placed a full English breakfast in front of him.

She tensed slightly. "No, I had no idea and it kills me that she didn't tell me."

Daniel nodded slowly "Sometimes I think this is all a horrible nightmare and I'm going to wake up and she's gonna laugh at me. It's like I didn't know her and the thing that makes me the angriest is

I can't confront her about it all and then I feel like a bastard for feeling that way."

"I know what you mean," Lauren said thoughtfully "but we just have to believe that the important stuff was all real. Her love for you and Paige was real, of that I have no doubt. You were her life!"

Daniel just nodded; he looked like a lost little boy. He changed the subject then as if he wasn't ready to confront what she was saying or perhaps he didn't believe it. She knew he would need time to come to terms with all the secrets Claire had kept and the brutal way she had been taken away from them. She just hated to see him hurting so much.

"Are you okay?" Daniel asked, looking her over as if looking for a physical injury. She knew he was referring to what had happened with them yesterday and she could see the guilt in his eyes.

"Yes, I'm fine, Daniel. Dane's been wonderful and he knows everything that happened with Jeff." Daniel looked at them both then.

"So, you two are together?" She looked at Dane, waiting with a nervous stomach to see what he said.

"It's early days," he said, "but we're seeing where this goes." He looked at Lauren who smiled tentatively.

~~~

Dane could see the slight confusion on her beautiful face but he knew he was doing the right thing, holding back from her a bit. As much as he wanted to shout for all to hear that she was his, his first job was to keep her safe. The only way to do that was to pull back a bit so that he could think clearly. The thought of losing her kept tugging at him like a pain and he rubbed his chest to ease the feeling.

"Look after her, man. Don't let anyone hurt her. I'm happy for you guys and Claire would've been dancing around the kitchen," he mused. "Make it count though; don't think bad things won't happen to you because you never know when you could have it snatched away."

Lauren leaned forward in her chair and wrapped her arms around Daniel, and Dane reached over and squeezed his shoulder.

Dane was well aware that life could take unexpected turns and horrible things could happen. He had lived through that and still watched his father live through it.

"We will, man," he stated solemnly.

Daniel seemed to shake off his melancholy and then tucked into the breakfast Lauren had made. While the friends caught up, she busied herself making up a quick salad, which she left for Daniel and Paige in the fridge.

"I have to pick up Paige at eleven from her grandparents. They've been wonderful," Daniel said, "I honestly don't know what I would have done without them but it's time I got on with being a dad."

"Okay, we'll leave you to it then, but we'll keep you in the loop," Dane said to his friend.

Daniel walked them to the door and kissed Lauren's cheek. "Thanks for breakfast."

"You're welcome; give Paige a kiss from me."

Driving away from Daniel, Dane was satisfied that his friend would come out on the other side—definitely not the same, but he would survive this somehow.

Chapter Eighteen

Walking towards the Gloucester Royal Hospital always made Lauren feel slightly sick. She'd spent the worst days of her life there when she'd lost her mum and the smell of strong cleaning products always brought back the feelings of helplessness and despair.

The building was airy and modern, but it didn't seem to matter how good the architecture was or how clever the art was, it still felt cold and sterile to her. It was strange she didn't feel like this when she visited the Paediatric ward at Hereford County Hospital. Maybe it was because this was the hospital where her mum was treated or maybe it was that she could actually offer some help when she went there and didn't feel so useless.

Putting his arm around her like he'd been doing this for years instead of two days, Dane hugged her to him, offering comfort as if he knew that she was upset.

"Okay?" he inquired.

She nodded. "Yes, I just hate this place—too many bad memories." She shuddered as if the feeling of being here made her skin crawl. He squeezed her tight and dropped a kiss on her head. They stopped outside the front doors of the hospital so that he could retrieve his ringing phone from his pocket.

"Hey, what's up?" He listened intently, anger darkening his expression as he nodded. "Okay listen, you should take Paige and go to your parents for a while until this is over." He nodded. "Ok call me when you get there and make sure you're not followed. Yeah, yeah. I know. Okay, bye."

Swiping his phone to end the call, he looked up at Lauren. "Someone left a gift on Sylvie and Malcolm's front doorstep for Paige. It was signed by Claire. Daniel's going to take her to stay with his parents in Scotland until things are sorted here."

"God, when will this stop?!" she exclaimed.

"Come on, let's go see if we can find out and see if anyone recognises the man in the photo."

~~~

Approaching the reception desk of the Oncology department, he flashed his private security badge at the woman and asked to speak to the head of Oncology. The matronly-looking receptionist sniffed and looked over her glasses at them.

"Mr Hale is a very busy man. Do you have an appointment?"

"No, but can you please tell him Dane Bennett and Lauren Cassidy are here to see him about Claire Thompson?" He used his polite 'don't fuck with me' voice that he normally reserved for the tax office.

Paling slightly, Miss Congeniality picked up her phone.

"Mr Hale, there is a Dane Bennet and Lauren Cassidy here to see you about Claire Thompson. He insisted it's important. Yes, okay I will tell him." She practically purred the last sentence, causing Lauren to giggle. Turning back to them, all signs of the simpering sex kitten were gone.

"Mr Hale will be with you shortly. Please take a seat." She indicated the chairs by the elevator.

"Thank you, Miss Tate."

"Wow, that was some transformation from Miss Trenchbold to Miss Simpering Sex Kitten and back in twenty seconds," Lauren whispered, causing him to laugh out loud. They went to sit down but before they had settled in their seats the elevator pinged open.

A tall thin man with salt and pepper hair smoothly styled with gel and a designer suit under his white coat came out. Miss Tate indicated Dane and Lauren all the while smiling and preening. He swivelled to meet them and put out his hand to shake Dane's hand; he then turned to Lauren and shook hers too.

"I'm Edward Hale, head of Oncology. What can I do for you?" he asked, getting straight to the point. Dane looked at him and disliked him on sight. He had clammy hands and a weak handshake. His father had always told him never to trust someone who had a weak handshake. He seemed nervous too. His eyes kept moving around the room as if scared of something. Lauren didn't seem to recognise him, so he'd obviously not been here when her mum was ill, thank goodness.

"Could we maybe go somewhere more private. Do you have an office?" Dane asked.

"Yes of course, but we can't use my office. It's being set up for a meeting." Turning, Doctor Hale walked off. "Follow me, we can use this empty exam room," he continued as he entered it. "Please have a seat," he said sitting behind the desk and leaving them to sit on the lower plastic chairs. It was an age-old power play to put him in a position of authority. If he thought Dane would be intimidated, he was wrong. You didn't pass SAS selection to then be intimidated by a squirt in a suit. He knew every trick in the book about intimidating people. Shit, he'd practically written the book.

Straightening and fixing Hale with his interrogator's face, he proceeded to ask about Claire. Mr Hale confirmed that she had been a patient but that he could not say anymore and hid behind the patient confidentiality excuse.

"This is a murder investigation, Mr Hale, and anything you say could help us." Hale squirmed slightly in his seat and sweat broke out on his upper lip, but he was either too stupid or too scared to say anything else.

"I'm sorry. I really can't help you but if you would like to come back with a subpoena then I can release her records to the courts." Dane went silent for a minute and then pulled a copy of the picture sent to Daniel from his wallet.

"Do you know this man?" he asked, pushing the picture across the table towards Hale.

He looked at it quickly and then shook his head. "No, I've never seen him before."

"Are you sure?" Lauren stated. "It's very important and this was taken at the hospital."

He looked again "No. No I don't. Now if you'll excuse me, I have patients to see."

She felt like screaming at him "Liar, liar pants on fire", but of course didn't. Hale stood up then to indicate the meeting was over and they followed suit.

"Thank you for your time." Dane said not bothering to offer his hand. The man was lying, and he had no interest in playing games with him. He watched as Hale quickly disappeared back into the lift.

~~~

Hale quickly punched in the number for his employer. He was agitated and nervous. He couldn't afford for anyone to find out what he had been doing or his reputation would be finished. Then his ditzy wife would find out and leave him. He didn't love her but she was the perfect trophy wife and her family had the money and backing he needed to keep him in the life he had become accustomed to.

"Yes," the terse voice answered. It made Hale grind his teeth having to deal with Marcus Preedy.

"I just had a visit from a Dane Bennett and a Lauren Cassidy asking about Terry Griffiths and Claire Thompson. They were flashing pictures around of them together."

The line went quiet.

"Did you find out who they worked for?"

"No, but I don't think it's the government."

"Okay, I'll have Griffiths dealt with. Meet Michaels at the usual place to give him the flash drive. How did she look?"

"Who?" Hale asked confused.

"Lauren Cassidy. How did she look?"

"Um fine. Normal, I guess. Why?"

"Don't question me, just answer the fucking question."

Hale hated this man so much and cursed inwardly at his own stupidity for getting involved with him. "She looked… well healthy."

"Good."

The line went dead, and Hale raced to his car to make the drop.

~~~

They walked outside into the beautiful sunshine and quickly walked to the truck. Stopping next to the car, Lauren turned to him.

"He's lying," she said in frustration.

"Yeah he is."

"So, what now? Shouldn't we show the picture around the hospital?" Lauren asked, planting her hands on her hips.

"No, now we wait. I want to keep an eye on Hale and see what he does next. We can come back later and show the picture around."

"Ugh.,I'm rubbish at waiting," she complained and threw her hands up.

Dane took her hand and pulled her to him, dropping a kiss to the crown of her head. He loved the feel of her against him. He couldn't wait until all of this was over and he could just immerse himself in her without the threat to her life hanging over them.

He hated feeling as if he was putting his life on hold, but he had no choice but to put the brakes on. For now, he would just have to take stolen moments like this and make them count. He was finding it harder and harder with every minute to keep that distance from her emotionally. It was as if she was burying herself in his heart. A floodgate had opened, and he was having trouble stemming the tide of his emotions but knew he had to for her sake.

Lauren was facing away from the hospital with her head on Dane's chest and her arms around his waist, so she didn't see Edward Hale scurry to his Jaguar XE, but he did.

"Come on, let's follow the *good doctor* and see what he's up to." They jumped in the truck and Dane pulled out a few cars behind

Hale. They followed him for about five miles before they saw Hale turn into The Badger's Arms pub. He drove past and then turned around in a layby and drove back to the pub.

He parked near the front exit so that he could see who came and went and made sure Hale couldn't leave without them seeing him. Hale still sat in his car, which was parked at the furthest end of the car park. Hale appeared to be waiting for someone or something.

"So, what's the plan now?" Lauren inquired excitedly.

"I want to see who he's meeting so we wait."

She groaned "More waiting!"

Dane laughed "Is someone enjoying the adrenaline of the chase? Cause I gotta say I can think of better things to chase than this idiot." He trailed his fingers over her thigh, causing her to shiver.

Just then a big black SUV pulled into the pub. It parked two cars over from Hale and a stocky man in his forties who was wearing a dark t-shirt with combat trousers got out. This guy had mercenary written all over him. He scouted around to make sure nobody was watching and then approached the Jaguar. Dane had made sure he positioned his vehicle so that anybody looking wouldn't be able to see her past him. It was unlikely because of the tinted glass but he didn't want to take any chances.

"Do you recognise him?" Lauren asked as she watched the man intently.

"No. I'm gonna get a couple of pictures and send them to Lucy." Using his phone, he snapped a couple of pictures and quickly sent them. They weren't the greatest quality because of the distance but he hoped Lucy could clean them up enough to get an ID.

Hale hadn't gotten out of his vehicle but had just rolled down the window. He and the mystery man were in a heated exchange of words by the look of their body language. Dane was pissed that he couldn't hear them. Maybe if they could get an ID on this man it wouldn't be a total loss. Hale seemed to hand something to the man through the window, but it was too small to identify. Maybe drugs, he thought. The man got back in his vehicle and left a few minutes later.

Lauren turned in her seat to look at him.

"So, what was that all about?"

"Not sure, but if I had to guess I would say some sort of drop."

She nodded her head "Yeah, I wonder what he gave him?"

"You saw that, huh?" She nodded.

"You have good instincts. What's your take on this?"

She snorted "Yeah right. Of course, I do."

Dane frowned then "I'm serious," he said feeling a bit annoyed.

"I think it was a drop of some sort, maybe drugs or information."

"See good instincts. I thought the same." He smiled then and he could tell she was pleased by the compliment.

They followed Hale back to the hospital then and nothing of any interest happened. "Come on, let's head home. I know the perfect little pub in Ross-on-Wye right by the river and they make the best ploughman's lunch ever," he said. He knew he probably shouldn't, but they had to eat. *Right?*

~~~

On the drive to lunch, Dane called Lucy and asked her to get a tap put on the doctor's home and work phones and run a background check on him. He also asked her to make the picture of the mystery man a priority.

Sitting on a wooden table by the river in the sunshine with a soda and lime watching children play on the park nearby, Lauren realised that she had really needed this bit of normal today. She and her mum would often spend a Sunday afternoon in a beer garden in the summer just having lunch and catching up.

It wasn't fancy or anything but sitting with a cold drink and listening to children play in the play area and families having fun was nice. She hadn't done this since her mum died and she missed it.

She was glad he'd suggested it. It balanced her equilibrium and gave her a minute to just sit and think.

Dane had been wonderful since all this had started. She was shocked at how quickly things had moved between them but when you knew you knew, and she had known he was special for a long time.

He did seem a little pre-occupied today though. It wasn't anything obvious just subtle nuances like his reserved response to Daniel about their relationship status. Maybe he was just in combat mode. She would try not to over-react to it though. It was normal for people to have things on their mind; she couldn't be the centre of his attention all the time. Maybe she could distract him from whatever had caused the quietness on the drive over.

"Tell me something that you've never done that you would love to do," she asked him.

Dane looked at her "That's tricky. There isn't much you don't do in the Special Forces. Um, okay." He sat quietly while he gave it some thought. Lauren liked how he took her seriously, even silly questions like that one. His eyes lit up then. "I've never seen the Mappa Mundi in the Cathedral and would love to." The 13th-century map had been exhibited in the Cathedral since before 1855 and was the largest medieval map known to exist.

She sat forward abruptly. "How is that possible? You're thirty-eight years-old and live in the city where it's exhibited. Most of my year one class has seen it! We need to remedy this first chance we get," she said, using her teacher's voice.

He laughed and held up his hands in defeat. "Okay what about you? What would you love to do and have never done?"

"Oh, that's easy, drive an articulated lorry." Ever since she was a little girl, she had loved Lorries. Not cars but Lorries. Her mother had taken her to The Three Counties show in Malvern and she had been smitten ever since. She even had a small collection of special edition models. All her girlfriends thought she was mad; it had perplexed even her mum. Lauren was so girlie in every other way.

He burst out laughing then. "That's hilarious. You're the biggest contradiction, all feminine and soft and then you go all trucker on me."

She tried to look indignant but failed and ended up laughing as hard as he did.

"I guess I should probably learn to drive a car first, though."

"That would definitely be a good place to start." He laughed then.

The server bringing the ploughman's lunch to them interrupted their discussion. He was right, it was the best she had ever eaten. There was home-baked ham, three different cheeses, freshly baked bread, farmhouse chutney and pickles. Lauren tucked in greedily, only stopping when she looked up to find Dane looking at her.

"You're stunning," he said with what she thought looked like regret in his eyes. She blushed and looked away

"Uh thanks," she said feeling a little self-conscious and unnerved by what she saw in his eyes. What could he be regretting?

~~~

Finishing their lunch in silence, each was lost in their own thoughts. They had both finished their lunch when the young server brought them over a bottle of champagne and two glasses.

"Sorry, we didn't order this," Dane said kindly. The poor girl was rushed off her feet; she must have gotten the wrong table.

"No, the gentleman over there sent it," she said pointing to an empty space. "Oh, I can't see him now," she said looking around.

He was instantly on alert. Standing, he placed himself between Lauren and the way the young server pointed.

"What else did he say? What did he look like?" he asked, his voice rising.

"Um, just that you were newlyweds and he and his wife—Claire, I think he said—wanted to congratulate you."

"What did he look like?" Dane practically growled.

"Um, normal, average height, blonde thinning hair, pale looking with big glasses."

Throwing two twenty-pound notes on the table, he grabbed Lauren's hand.

"Thanks," he said to the startled girl and pulled Lauren quickly towards the car.

Putting his body in front of her and holding her close to his side, he constantly scanned their surroundings for threats. Practically throwing her into the truck, he jumped in after her and floored it out of the car park. He reached over and unlocked the glove box, pulling out his Browning and placing it in the centre console for easy reach.

"It was him wasn't it? The man from the picture?" Lauren asked him, already knowing the answer.

"Yes, I think it was. We are going to have to seriously limit your exposure until he's found," Dane stated almost angrily.

"Did I do something?" she asked, hating that she sounded so weak.

"No, you didn't do anything," he stated, gentler now. "It was me; I should have been doing my job not having romantic pub lunches."

Lauren flinched at his tone.

Dane had no sooner finished berating himself for losing focus when the black SUV they had seen meeting Hale came barrelling down on them. It came out of nowhere. Dane cursed and grabbed for his firearm.

He could see her looking frightened as she realised what was happening.

"Is it the man from the car park?" she asked and he could hear the fear in her voice.

"I think so. Just keep your head down and hang on, it's gonna get a little bumpy."

Lauren immediately tucked her head against the seat and ducked down as far as she could. She wasn't ready to die. She could feel the calm come over him as he went into mission mode. Dane was completely focused on what he was doing. She didn't feel an ounce of fear or uncertainty, just complete surety in his ability to get them out of this.

Dane swerved as the SUV behind them tried to ram them off the road. The vehicles were matched for weight and power and he felt certain that he wouldn't be able to push them off the road as long as he kept up some evasive manoeuvres. This prick was good, but he was better.

He heard her let out a scream when the back windshield exploded as a bullet hit. This guy couldn't hit a barn door with a tractor. Dane decided to opt for a move his old CO had shown him during training.

He swerved the car to the far side, making sure to keep Lauren the furthest away from the other vehicle. Then, when they were side by side, he slammed on the brakes. His vehicle came to a thundering stop as the other carried on going. In the blink of an eye, he shot out the back tyre of the SUV, causing it to swerve dangerously towards the verge. It rounded a corner and he lost sight of it.

He turned then to check Lauren, who was still ducked down with her hands over her head. He could see that she had little cuts on her arms from the glass windshield.

"It's okay, you can sit up now. Are you okay?" His words were gentle and his gaze assessing as he let his eyes wander over her as if to reassure himself she was okay.

"Yes, yes. I'm fine." Despite the shaking he saw the determination in her eyes and gratitude.

"Come on, let's get back to Fortis."

"Shouldn't we go see if we can catch him?"

"No, it's too dangerous. I've already nearly gotten you killed twice today. I'm not taking any more risks."

Lauren could see that he was blaming himself for this but couldn't figure out why.

"This isn't your fault, Dane."

He rounded on her then and she could see he was furious not with her but himself.

"Of course, it's my fucking fault. I'm meant to protect you, not get careless and put you in danger. I've been selfish and it nearly got you killed. It won't happen again," he said with an air of finality.

With that, he put the vehicle in gear and drove back to Fortis.

The drive home was tense and silent. He was pulling away from her and she could feel it.

Dane mentally chastised himself for allowing this to happen. He should have been on guard at all times. His job was to protect her. He'd been followed twice but how? He might have been distracted but he had been watching for a tail, as it was almost second nature. Then it clicked. His truck must have a tracker on it. That was the only explanation.

He banged his hand on the steering wheel in frustration, causing Lauren to jump. "Sorry," he said, quickly regretting scaring her. Driving straight to Fortis, Dane jumped out of the vehicle and came around to Lauren's door before she got her seatbelt off. Positioning his body in front of her, he helped her from the car and ushered her inside constantly alert. Walking into the tech room, he yelled. "Lucy, Lucy!"

"Yes," she said poking her head up from a computer hooked up to multiple monitors.

"Get Drew and Nate back here now." She raised an eyebrow. "Please," he said.

Chapter Nineteen

Pacing the conference room, Dane tried to calm himself but he was so angry. How had he not noticed him? He was fucking trained for this, for God's sake. Best of the fucking best and he couldn't spot someone watching them.

Zack should kick his ass up and down the 'Pen Y Fan' for this. He was going to have to stay away from her, even though it broke his heart to do it. He had to have a clear mind if he was going to keep her safe and the only way to do that was to keep his distance.

Nate could take over her close protection. He trusted Nate with his life and hers. Calmer now that he had made his decision and had a plan, he looked at Lauren and knew he would have to be brutal to make her accept this was happening. God, he didn't want to hurt her, but he couldn't lose her to a madman. If he broke her heart, at least he could go on knowing she was okay and living a happy life and wasn't dead.

"Dane, please sit down, you're making me nervous." He took a seat opposite her. He knew she would see it as a rejection, but he had to start pulling back from her. He was conscious of her uncertainty in the car and his heart ached. He would prefer it if she was angry. This wasn't her fault, he was the one being a jerk even if it was for her own good.

Drew walked into the conference room and, as if sensing her pain, sat next to Lauren. He frowned, noticing the obvious tension in the room.

"What happened?" he asked Dane in a not too friendly way.

"Let's wait for Nate," Lucy said, trying to diffuse the atmosphere in the room. "Pepsi anyone?" she asked, reaching into the fridge at the back of the conference room. Dane just shook his head no. Drew and Lauren nodded and Lucy brought them around to them, seating herself on the other side of Lauren, smiling and winking.

"Ignore Grumpy," she said in a stage whisper, causing her brother to give her a filthy look. Lauren tried to smile at her, but it came out more of a grimace.

Lucy was gonna kick his ass if he kept this up.

Nate strode into the room. "What's happened?" he asked, echoing Drew. Grabbing a bottled water from the fridge, he sat down next to Dane, completely oblivious to the dirty look Lucy was giving him.

Dane stood up and started pacing again as he explained to the rest of them what had happened at their meeting with Edward Hale and then what had happened in the pub and on the drive back.

"I think my truck has a tracker on it. I want all the vehicles, company and personal, checked."

Nate nodded "I'll make it a priority."

"I also want to know if there is a connection between Griffiths and this mystery man Hale met. There is no way this is all a coincidence."

Dane looked at Lucy "Tell me you got something?"

"Well, I looked into Edward Hale. He has a nasty gambling habit and was up to his eyes in debt until eighteen months ago when all his debt was cleared. He now has ten thousand pounds deposited into his bank account every month from an off-shore account. I'm still trying to trace it, but I think it's linked to Redcast. Also, interestingly I managed to get some security footage from the burial ground, and look." She clicked a button on her laptop and an image came on her screen. "The man from the photo was at Claire's funeral."

"Fuck fuck fuck" Dane swore. "He's everywhere."

"Well, I talked to Sly," Nate said "and he's gonna get a friend of his in the forensic team to try and get some prints off the photo or box. But he thinks it's unlikely as too many people watch CSI these days. He said to say 'hi' by the way, and that you still owe him a round of golf." Sly was always busting his balls about golf when he was home.

"I'll call him soon as this shit is done," Dane said.

Everyone turned to Drew.

"Well, bad news. I talked to Rose, who works for Marcus, and she said he left late last night on a business trip with Michaels in tow. He told her to ready one of the spare rooms because his daughter was coming to stay," he said the last with an apologetic look at Lauren. "I'm so sorry."

"Stop stop. This is not your fault you're as much his victim as I am." Everyone went quiet while they all processed the new information. Dane rubbed a hand over his face tiredly.

"So, we're assuming that Marcus and Michaels are already here given the drive is only one hundred and thirty miles or so," he said to no one in particular.

Drew nodded. "Right. Did you have any luck with the identity of the mystery man from the car park?" Dane asked, turning back to Lucy

"Not yet but I'm working on it."

"Okay, I also want you watching all surveillance in and around Lauren's place and anywhere else you think pertinent."

"I want to help," Drew said. "You know I'm good with computers."

"Fine, help Lucy."

Lucy looked at Drew, noting that there was more to him than met the eye and he had an innate sense of right and wrong, even if he had been brought up by a bastard.

"Nate, I want you to stay with Lauren twenty-four seven. Do not let her out of your sight," Dane said with authority.

"What are you going to do?" she interrupted.

"I need to see some friends of mine who might be able to help," he replied vaguely. He hated the censure he could see in her eyes but hardened his heart and just looked at her.

"I never had you down as such a jerk," she said angrily. She looked at him with hurt-filled eyes. "But you run along to your friends. I can take a hint. You had your fun and now it's back to business." Each word was said with more and more anger. "Well, fuck you. Fuck you very much. I had a blast." With that, she turned and stormed from the room.

"You bastard," Drew said angrily. "How could you do that to her?" Dane gave him a look that would scare most grown men and, to his credit, Drew never even flinched.

Lucy started clapping "Well done bro. When you fuck up, you do it properly."

Dane turned his gaze from Drew to Lucy.

"Bloody hell, Lucy! I'm trying to protect her, and I can't concentrate properly around her. It's better I hurt her feelings than get her killed."

Nate shook his head. "God, I thought I was green with women, *hermano*, but you take the prize."

"Just do your fucking jobs and let's get these bastards dealt with," Dane said in frustration.

~~~

Lucy found Lauren in the bathroom wiping her eyes. "You okay?" she asked, putting her arm around her.

"Yeah, I guess. I can't believe I got so angry. That's not like me. I just thought he would be different, you know? But that was naïve of me. Men are all stupid idiots," she spoke with conviction.

"You know he really likes you, sweetie." Lucy said gently. "I've never seen him like this. He's being a complete dumbass at the moment. Don't worry, he'll see reason soon. Just hang in there."

She gave Lucy a watery smile "Thanks, I appreciate it, but I think I'll just leave relationships to other people. They don't seem to work for me." Washing her face and the little cuts on her arms from the glass. Lauren straightened up and smiled. "See, all better. Who needs men?" she said in a slightly shaky voice.

Lauren came out of the bathroom to find Nate waiting for her.

"Your chariot awaits, Chiquita," he said, offering his arm in a flamboyant gesture. She curtsied daintily.

"Lead the way, kind sir," she said, playing up to him and knowing Dane was watching through the glass window of the conference room. Well, screw him. She wasn't gonna let him see how much he'd hurt her. With a big smile, she allowed Nate to lead her to his car.

He watched his surroundings and put himself in front of her, but he was much less intense than Dane had been. Shaking that thought off, she settled into the soft leather of Nate's Porsche Cayenne and listened to the mundane chatter of the radio.

~~~

Walking back into the conference room, Lucy looked from the hole in the wall to her pacing brother who was rubbing his bloody knuckles.

"What the hell!" she exclaimed with some frustration.

"I had a little accident," he said, shrugging. "It seems I can't control my temper any better than I can do my job."

"Stop being an idiot and come and sit down. I'll clean that up and put some antibiotic cream on it."

"Its fine—I'll clean it in a minute."

"Sit!" she said in a tone that brooked no argument.

"God, you're so much like mum," he said. "Well, at least what I can remember."

"Really? You never told me that before," she said quietly as she reached for the first aid kit in the cupboard.

"I don't normally think about it, to be honest."

"Why did you hit the wall?" she asked while cleaning his hand with an alcohol wipe.

"Cos, I fucked up and I hurt her after promising I wouldn't." He looked at Lucy then, with genuine regret on his face. "I know I have to put her safety before my feelings for her. I'd rather hurt her now than get her killed because I wasn't concentrating."

"Could you not just have explained that instead of going all cold, hard, uncaring bastard on her?"

"Apparently not," he said with a chagrined smile. "Seriously though, Lucy, I care about Lauren a lot and I can't do my job properly if I'm not concentrating fully. I'd never forgive myself if something happened to her because of me. This is for the best."

The last was said with such conviction that Lucy decided to let it go for now.

"So, what's your real plan? Are you going to see the guys at the camp or are you doing something else?"

"I'm gonna go see Tucker, Sly and Smithy and see if they can lend us some help. I'm also gonna put a call into Eidolon and see if they can help. There are just too many variables now, and with Zin and Zack away and Daniel and Will out of the picture we're spread too thin."

Lucy nodded in agreement bringing in Eidolon would be a big help.

They were a very secret Black Ops Ghost squad and had helped Fortis out on multiple occasions. Zack and Jack Granger's Eidolon team lead had done some missions together in the past and the two remained good friends. It also helped that Jack was also Sly's cousin. Lucy finished cleaning Dane's hand quietly.

"So, the whole unit's back?" Lucy asked, thinking about Sly's team.

"Yes, they re-deploy in a few weeks."

Lucy hoped they could help. Her brother was right, They were spread thin and there was nobody she would rather have around than the guys from Dane's old unit.

~~~

Marcus let himself into Terry Griffith's old dilapidated farmhouse and looked around with disdain. *How could anyone live in such filth?* The orange and brown patterned wallpaper was faded and peeling. There were water stains all over the ceiling and down the walls, and the carpets looked like they hadn't seen a vacuum in years.

It made his skin crawl. He decided to wait for Griffiths to come home; he wasn't going to kill him yet. The man had an uncanny ability to find out information that others couldn't. But he wanted to scare him a little and let him know that getting too close to the subjects they were trying to recruit was forbidden.

A short time later, he heard Griffiths arrive in the rusty old Jeep he drove.

He walked into the house, muttering to himself about caring and being a family and stopped in his tracks when he saw Marcus Preedy.

~~~

Preedy was a tall man with wiry muscles and not an ounce of fat on him but that wasn't what made Griffiths nervous; it was the man's eyes. He had the coldest eyes he'd ever seen and it was as if he could see straight inside your soul.

Griffiths hated being surprised and hated feeling scared even more. He straightened his spine and, in his best show of bravado, said, "What the hell are you doing in my house?" Before he had a chance to finish that thought, Preedy had him against the wall with a knife to his throat.

"Who do you think you're talking to?" Marcus was angry now and was trying to stop himself from just slitting the man's throat then and there.

~~~

He could feel Griffiths' stale breath on his cheek and see the sweat that had popped out on his forehead. The feeling of having power over him gave Marcus a rush like no other. Tilting the knife so it just nicked Griffiths' neck, he asked again "I said who do you think you're talking to?" Griffiths gulped causing the knife to nick him again.

"I'm sorry, Mr Preedy. I didn't realise it was you. Please forgive me." Griffiths hated apologising to this man, but he was smart enough to know that he couldn't outmatch him in fighting skills. No, he had to out-smart him. Marcus stepped back and dropped the knife from his throat.

Who the fuck had he thought it was, the stupid fuck?

"Sit," he sai,d motioning to the chair with the knife. Marcus walked around the chair he had placed in the centre of the room. He could see it was making Griffiths nervous. "Now, do you remember our rule about not getting involved with subjects?"

"Yes, Mr Preedy?"

"So why then are there people wandering around with pictures of you and Claire Thompson and asking questions?"

Griffiths swore inwardly. He'd been careless about his pursuit of her friends and now it was coming back to haunt him.

"It's not what you think. I was just trying to talk her into the trial, that's all."

Marcus walked around Griffiths trying to decide if he believed him. He didn't trust the man, but Claire was dead now so as long as he got the message not to do it again that would do.

"Well, that's not your job. From now on, stay away from the subjects and just be a good little boy and gather the information or next time…." he let the sentence tail off knowing that imagination was worse sometimes than actual threats.

~~~

Griffiths had never hated anyone as much as in that moment. Not his parents who ignored him, his grandparents who had treated him with contempt, Daniel Thompson, not even that weasel of a teacher that thought it was ok to abuse young boys. No, at that moment he wanted to kill Marcus Preedy with a need so strong he could hardly breathe.

~~~

Marcus could see that Griffiths was trying to control himself and found it rather funny that this pithy little man thought he was any competition for him. Taking a few deep breaths, Griffiths gained control of his temper and nodded.

"Yes sir."

With a final stroke of the knife down Griffiths' neck, Marcus left.

Quickly rushing to lock the door, Griffiths slumped down behind it breathing hard. He loathed feeling weak, and vowed that Marcus Preedy would rue the day he had ever met Terry Griffiths, and his payment would start with the lovely Lauren.

Chapter Twenty

Lauren decided that, as she had missed her visit with the kids in paediatrics on Saturday, she wanted to go today. She couldn't believe it was only Tuesday. She felt as if weeks had gone by but it had only been three days since this had started.

Nate had agreed to drive her and said he'd like to stay and watch her with the kids. She suspected that it was because he had to stay with her for security, not because he wanted to spend the day with sick kids.

Walking up to the nurse's station at the start of the corridor, she greeted the nurses on duty and asked about some of the kids. She was relieved to hear that some of the children she had spent time with last week had gone home after huge improvements over the weekend.

She then inquired about Noah Mitchell. Noah was a seven-year-old boy suffering from leukaemia. She had met Noah and his mum Skye in the early spring. He had only just been diagnosed, and they had struck up a firm friendship. Lauren suspected that Noah had special abilities but hadn't broached the subject with Skye yet.

Noah had been responding well to treatment at the beginning, but the last test had shown that the treatment was no longer working, and he needed a bone marrow transplant.

"How's Noah?" she asked the nurse in charge.

Casey Bridges shook her head. "Not so good."

It broke her heart to hear of the lovely little boy's plight. He was such a sweet child with a wonderfully upbeat attitude. It frustrated her that her gift would allow her to heal certain things but not others. She could heal a wound or cut, or even a gunshot wound, but illness that involved cells was different. She could slow them down or alleviate some of the pain, but she couldn't fully eradicate the disease. It didn't help that he was a rare blood group so finding a donor was proving difficult.

~~~

Nate stood quietly at her side, strangely upset hearing that a little boy he didn't know was so sick. He'd always been a sucker for kids and wondered if there was anything he could do. He'd ask first chance he got. They walked down the corridor towards a side room, knocking before stepping in.

~~~

Entering the little hospital room, Lauren looked at Noah in the bed and then went over to hug Skye who she could see had been crying. Noah was asleep but she could see from the hollows in his cheeks and the dark shadows under his eyes that he was deteriorating.

Walking to the child, she lifted his little hand in hers while his mother did the same on the other side. She let some of her healing energy leave her body and infused Noah with as much as she could. Her body soon became weak and so she stopped. For some reason, this kind of healing weakened her quickly. She looked down at the boy. His colour seemed better for now and his face seemed more relaxed.

"I swear your very presence is good for him," his mother commented.

Lauren sat down on the chair opposite. "I'm sorry, Skye. This is my good friend, Nate Jones," she said indicating Nate.

He offered her a shy smile "Ma'am," he said.

"Oh, please call me Skye. I'm pleased to meet you," Skye said with a shy smile of her own.

~~~

Nate had never felt anything like it before. The minute he had walked in the room it was as if he had been sucker-punched. Seeing the boy looking so fragile in the big hospital bed had caused an ache in his chest, then Skye had turned around and his world had tilted.

She looked so hauntingly beautiful with her big brown eyes surrounded by the longest lashes, made all the more poignant by the glistening unshed tears. He'd felt the overwhelming urge to go to her and comfort her and offer his protection to her and Noah. He hadn't. He didn't reveal any of what he was feeling; just smiled and kept his mouth shut. He didn't want to come across as crazy and she could be married for all he knew. Although he didn't see a ring.

Turning back to Lauren, he noticed that the boy—Noah—was awake and was looking at him as if he could see into his soul.

"Don't mind him," Skye said, "he does that sometimes."

Then the boy offered him the biggest smile and said, "I knew you'd come. I've been waiting!"

Nate didn't know what to say to that.

Turning his head to his mother, Noah said "He's the one, Mummy, he's the one I told you about. It's going to be okay now he's here." With that, he closed his eyes and fell back to sleep.

Lauren and Skye looked at Nate with looks of complete awe and wonder on their faces. Nate just shrugged feeling awkward and slightly unsettled by the incident,

"Cute kid."

They sat with Skye for a little longer, making small talk before saying their goodbyes.

~~~

When they reached the car, Lauren looked at Nate. He seemed shaken by what had happened with Noah and Skye and honestly, so was she. She'd spoken to Skye about Noah's dreams but Skye had never wanted to believe in them as she couldn't bear the disappointment if it didn't happen. Nevertheless, Noah had been having dreams for the past two months about the big superhero man who was going to fix his blood and make him all better. He'd even described the man but she'd never made the connection to Nate; of course it was obvious now. She wondered if she should tell Nate everything but feared it might scare him away. His next question soon made her realise how she had underestimated this man's compassion.

"What blood type is Noah?"

"He's AB negative." She didn't expand as she wanted what would happen next to be organic. She instead watched as a massive sigh of relief flowed through Nate's body.

"I'm AB negative too," he said in a near whisper. "Can I be tested to be a bone marrow donor?"

Lauren nodded trying not to show her excitement. "Yes, I can call the hospital and get them to set it up."

"Okay do it."

For the first time in days, she felt hope. Hope for a little boy that had never done anything bad to anyone.

"Thank you, Nate. You have no idea how much this will mean to Skye."

He looked at her funny then. "You know I think I might." He turned back to concentrating on the road then. Lauren decided not to confide in Nate about Noah's dreams; she didn't want to put undue pressure on him.

Chapter Twenty-One

Dane felt like crap. He'd hardly slept for thinking about the look on Lauren's face when he'd rejected her. He had spent the rest of the previous day trying to follow up leads on Hale and searching the CCTV recordings for signs of Preedy.

Thanks to Drew identifying the mystery man as Michaels, they now knew that Preedy was close. It had been the first bit of luck they'd had when Drew had seen that photo on Lucy's computer and identified Michaels. That still didn't explain how he had found them at the pub, and made him suspicious that he and the man from the pictures were linked. There was no way that they both just happened to be there at the same time.

He had worked until the clock read 0200 and then headed home, hoping that he would be tired enough to sleep. He had driven past Lauren's place twice just to check that all was quiet before eventually going home.

He'd tried to sleep but every time he closed his eyes, he heard her call him a jerk. She was right, he was a coward. But he wasn't scared of his feelings for her. He recognised that he had strong feelings for her—hell, he was half-way in love with her and wasn't scared of that. He was scared stupid that he would lose focus again and get her killed and he couldn't bear that. He just kept going back to that last mission in Afghanistan when his unit was ambushed and two of his team—his friends—had been killed and all because he had missed the signs.

He allowed his mind to drift back to that day two years ago when everything had gone to hell. The sights, the sounds, everything about it was still fresh in his mind.

He hadn't talked to anyone about that day—not even Daniel, his best friend. In fact, the only person who knew was Zack and he wasn't sure how he knew. Shaking off his horrible trip down memory lane he instead thought about Daniel.

Dane had thought he understood how Daniel felt when Claire was killed but if it was even a fraction of what he had felt yesterday in that beer garden and in the car then he didn't have a clue.

In his life, he'd seen the two men he was closest to in the world—Daniel and his dad—have their hearts ripped apart when they lost the women they loved, and he couldn't face that happening to him. Yes, it was selfish. He knew that. However even if they got through this and he had managed to protect Lauren, there was no guarantee she would stay.

Look at his mum; she'd had a loving husband who she professed to love and children who had loved and adored her and still it wasn't enough to stop her from driving drunk. If he hadn't been enough to stop his mum leaving him, how could he expect another human being with no ties to him to stay?

Knowing that he would not get any more sleep, he threw off the sheet and got up. He went into the conservatory he used as an office. At four in the morning, the sky was starting to lighten, and the birds were about to start their dawn chorus.

Normally he loved it but today he just found it irritating. Taking his stale coffee to his desk, he sat down and opened his laptop. Will had set the system up so that he could log into the secure network from home and access files that had already been downloaded, including the CCTV ones.

An hour later, Dane pushed back from his desk and scrubbed a hand down his face in frustration. Deciding to take a shower and see if that cleared his mind, he headed upstairs to his luxurious bedroom. He had bought the old detached cottage at auction three years ago. It had been derelict and in need of some serious TLC. He had had the cottage renovated and extended before he'd moved in.

It was now a modern four-bedroom home with all its original features still intact, including the dark exposed oak beams and the well at the bottom of the garden. The well had also been restored and now gave him fresh water.

A large oak bed and oak wardrobes and drawers dominated his room. The en-suite bathroom had a luxurious claw-foot bath on a raised dais and a double-width shower. He hadn't realised until recently that he had built a family home.

He could have had that with Lauren but no, he'd behaved like an insensitive dickhead and ruined what could have been his future with a family. All because he was scared of losing her. Better a coward than a broken man.

Dane had always known that he wanted a family and, although he had enjoyed his days playing the field, he had always known he wanted to settle down one day.

Stepping into the shower, he let the hot water spray ease the tension and weariness from his muscles. He couldn't help but think of the shower he had shared with Lauren and how she had felt all slick and hot as he had taken her hard against the shower wall.

Inevitably, his body started to respond but he ignored his errant cock and turned the water dial to cold. He didn't deserve any relief. His body jumped at the shock of the cold water, but it refreshed him and cooled his body. Towelling off quickly, he dressed in old worn jeans and a white t-shirt.

Feeling more human, Dane brewed some fresh coffee and went back to his laptop. Ten minutes later, he couldn't believe that he hadn't made the connection sooner. There was CCTV of Preedy captured on a traffic camera going north towards Kingsland and an hour later footage of the man from the photo with Claire. Bingo!

The images were grainy, but he was sure it was them. This footage was from yesterday, so he knew they needed to move fast. He didn't believe in coincidence and he had to find out where they had gone. Could this man work for Preedy? Was that the connection they were looking for? His veins buzzing with energy, he called Lucy.

"Lucy get up; meet me at Fortis in thirty minutes. I think I've found something." He hung up before he realised he hadn't even given her the chance to speak. *Ah well she'd get over it.*

~~~

Arriving at Fortis twenty minutes later, Dane was pleased to see Lucy and Drew pull in behind him. They had loaned Drew a company vehicle since he had taken the train from Bridport. The lack of a car was just another way his father had controlled him.

Nate had checked all the vehicles for trackers. They had found one on each of the private vehicles. Dane had immediately told everyone that their vehicles had to be checked before every use. It was a pain, but worth it to keep them safe. It did mean that everyone's home security was now compromised though, so they were going to have to be even more vigilant at home until this was finished.

Swinging his legs from the truck, he jogged to the front door and punched in the security codes. Wrenching it open, he waited for Lucy and Drew to proceed him. Striding through the security doors, he watched Drew and Lucy banter and felt for the first time that perhaps they were getting somewhere with all this. Shaking off his thoughts, he went looking for coffee in the kitchen.

"I'm making coffee you guys want some?" He shouted from the kitchen. Lucy just poked her head around the door and looked at him like he had grown horns. *Yep she wanted coffee.*

"Yes please." This from Drew. He was starting to warm to the boy.

He was glad Drew had agreed to stay with Lucy until things were sorted out and, knowing that he had someone there to watch her, helped give Dane one less thing to worry about. He was very protective of his sisters, especially Lucy. Drew had also agreed to a personal tracker if he left the building so that they could find him if something happened. Dane knew he was still in danger from his father but also knew if he wanted to keep him around the best way to do it was to offer him some freedom. He was almost certain now that he wasn't a threat to them.

He would ask Lucy if she had done any more digging into Drew's background. If Drew was hiding something—and he found himself hoping that he wasn't—then Lucy would find it. Though it pained him to say it, the kid was growing on him.

Ushering them both into the tech room, he explained what he had seen. Lucy and Drew both agreed that it wasn't a coincidence.

"The only thing that's troubling me is if this guy knows where Lauren is, and he works for Marcus, why hasn't he told him?" Drew asked. Dane was impressed. Drew was showing immense insight; he had definitely underestimated the kid.

"We're assuming because nothing has happened yet that he hasn't told him or maybe it's a power play. By withholding information, he thinks he has control and we both know he wants to see us suffer for our supposed bad treatment of Claire," commented Lucy.

Lucy was right, Dane thought and nodded his head in agreement.

"I agree. I think it could be a power play. Marcus wants Lauren unharmed and clearly this guy doesn't. But why hasn't he made his move yet? He's had ample opportunity to do so and hasn't."

"Maybe it's all part of his sick twisted game," Lucy suggested. "He builds it up in order to make her and us suffer more."

"Agreed—but," Dane said, "that is also a huge risk and the more time he wastes, the more time we have to find him."

"I've seen this before though," Lucy interrupted. "I think this guy thinks he is superior to us and so we won't catch him. We can use this; if we can get Marcus to believe that this man means his daughter harm, he might give us information on him."

Dane wondered what Lucy meant by that comment. When had she seen this kind of behaviour? *She had been an analyst at GCHQ, hadn't she?*

Drew's excited voice broke into his thoughts. "I'll do it. I can contact him and speak to him and see if he will take the bait."

Dane agreed. "Fine. I'm gonna run some searches and see if we can find any properties out towards Kingsland that link to Preedy."

Dane felt more positive than he had since all this started. They all set about trying to gather more information.

Three days later, they weren't any closer to Preedy and they hadn't found any links to any properties in the area. Preedy had apparently dropped off the grid. Nobody could find him, and he wasn't answering Drew's calls.

Chapter Twenty-Two

Lauren was beginning to get antsy. Everything was quiet. There were no new developments on Preedy or the mysterious stalker, and she knew she must be driving Nate mad asking him every few hours.

She slumped on the couch and tried to read but her thoughts kept drifting. She had been thinking of her mum the last few days and what she would make of all this. She couldn't think of Marcus Preedy as her father, it just provoked too many feelings of "What if". What if he had found them years earlier? What would her life have been like? What if he had been a good man? How would her life have been different? Would she want to change things if she could have? Urgh, it was too complicated. It was easier to think of him as Marcus Preedy—the man that was responsible for the death of her friend.

Jumping up from the sofa, she wandered around her flat that she was beginning to hate because of her enforced house arrest. Nate walked out of the bathroom in only his running shorts, whistling some happy song and that made Lauren want to throw something at him.

"Do you have to be so happy?" she snapped. He stopped in his tracks.

"Someone woke up on the wrong side of the bed," he said looking wounded.

"I'm sorry." She instantly regretted her outburst. Nate had been such a sweetheart and she was being a bitch.

"No worries, Chiquita. I know it's frustrating for you." He ruffled her hair affectionately as he went past her on his way to the kitchen.

She'd grown close to Nate over the last few days and felt that they had formed some kind of bond after their visit to the Paediatric ward. She hadn't told him about Noah's dreams and wondered if that was best left for Skye to do. Nate had been true to his word and the blood tests had been set up for next week.

She had called Skye after setting up the blood tests and told her that Nate had asked to be tested. She had been over the moon and insisted on talking to Nate. Nate had blushed as he had spoken to Skye and she knew that they had spoken on the phone a couple of times since. It made her happy that Skye and Nate were forming some kind of friendship; that Skye had someone to talk to and maybe just maybe there would be some hope for Noah.

She still missed Dane though and she felt like a horrible selfish cow for begrudging others their happiness. How was it possible to miss someone that had only been in your life for such a short time? Putting her thoughts of him aside, she realised Nate was waving a hand in front of her.

"Hey, earth to Lauren."

"Sorry I was miles away. What did you say?"

"Dane said they should have some more info on your father's whereabouts soon. In fact, I must go into the office today so you can catch up with Lucy if you want while I do a few things".

Her heart jumped—would Dane be there? Did she want him to be? Hell, when did she become such a basket case?

"Sounds good," she said, plastering on a bright smile and trying not to look too eager. She ran her hands down her denim shorts and pulled at her old soft Levi vest top. Maybe she should change. But she didn't want to look like she cared. Oh well, stuff it.

When they arrived at Fortis, she wasn't sure if she was relieved or upset that Dane's truck wasn't there. Opening her door, Nate escorted her into the building and down to the tech room where Drew and Lucy were working.

Drew lumbered over to hug her. They had taken to chatting every night and had developed a closeness that surprised her, considering she'd known him less than a week. But maybe it was a sibling bond? They shared so many interests and if anything good had come from this mess, then he was it. Her little brother... she didn't think that would get old any time soon.

Nate went over to talk to Lucy.

"So, what we got, Luce?"

"Well we have a name for our stalker." That got Lauren's attention and she went over to join Lucy and Nate. "He's forty-two-year-old Terry Griffiths and he's a porter at the hospital. He lives alone. His mum died last year. He was her caregiver.

"His mother had a hernia operation and a district nurse had been coming in daily to change the dressings. There's a bit of a question mark over her death. Apparently, she fell down the stairs at home, but she wasn't very mobile so as a rule didn't go upstairs. All her things, including her bedroom, were downstairs so I'm not sure about that. Anyways, one of the district nurses found her.

"The Coroner ruled it an accidental death. Griffiths also has a history of mental illness including Schizoid-affective disorder, which means he's prone to mood swings and psychotic episodes."

"So, we know how he came into contact with Claire but not the nature of their relationship," Lucy added.

Lauren, who had perched on the edge of the desk beside Lucy, bristled at this.

"Easy tiger!" Lucy said, catching Lauren's hand and squeezing. "I didn't mean anything by it, just that he may have thought it was romantic not that it was. We all know Claire adored Daniel."

"Any news on Marcus?" Nate broke in.

"Yes, actually," said a deep voice from the door. Her heart jumped to her throat.

Dane strode into the room but wouldn't look her in the eye. She didn't know if she wanted to throw herself at him or punch him. Either way, her stomach went all fluttery and her heart beat faster.

She needed to get a grip, but it was so hard when all she wanted to do was run to him. He looked tired, with bags under his eyes, and had at least two days worth of beard. He still looked like the most gorgeous man on the planet to her, though. She hated that he wouldn't look at her and wondered if he just couldn't stomach the thought of her or if it was guilt from him being a douchebag.

"Marcus is in Southampton," Dane went on. "Looks like he has some kind of shipment coming in. I have surveillance on him now, so we'll be able to watch all his movements. Nate, can I have a minute please?" Nate followed him out of the room.

"I'm sorry, Lauren. I'm gonna kick his ass for behaving so rudely."

"Don't worry, Lucy. It's probably for the best anyway," she said bravely while her heart continued to break.

~~~

"What do you want?" Nate said tersely.

Dane stopped and turned "What's with the attitude?" he demanded.

"Really? You're asking me that after the way you just behaved? I hear her crying herself to sleep at night over you, *hermano.* You're fucking breaking her heart, you prick." Nate paced and brushed a hand through his hair and blew out a breath. "She's trying to be brave, but you really hurt her and now you're ignoring her. I never would have believed that you could be deliberately cruel."

"It's for the best," Dane said coldly. "I'm trying to protect her. I can't protect her if I'm not objective and I can't be objective around her. When I'm with her, all I can think about is her," he finished uncharacteristically.

Nate could see the strain on his friend's face.

"Just do your fucking job and protect her," Dane grated out.

"Fine. If you don't care maybe I'll take her out and show her some fun." Before Nate could finish the sentence, he found himself up against the wall with a forearm to his throat.

"You stay the fuck away from her, you hear me?"

"Yeah exactly, man," Nate said shoving him off. "You don't care, do you?"

"Of course I care. That's why I must stay away from her," he said sounding defeated. "Why can't anyone see that?"

"You better wise up quickly, *hermano*, and tell her you love her cos if you don't, you're gonna lose the best thing that ever happened to you." Nate slammed from the room.

"Everything okay?" Lauren asked when Nate returned.

"Yeah fine, let's go," he said tersely.

~~~

Back in the conference room, Dane paced. Was he in love with her? He knew he had been falling for her but was that what this was? Love? He sat at the table and put his head down for a second. He thought about the time they had spent together recently and in the past, and the emails they had sent.

It was true he cared for her deeply and he admired her. Her bravery and courage, her wit and humour, and her sharp intelligence. She made his body burn and he wanted to be with her all the time. He sat up suddenly as an epiphany hit him. *Yes!* He was in love with her. He loved her! He didn't know when it had happened, but it had. She was it for him.

That was why he knew he was doing the right thing by leaving her protection to Nate. Nate was objective when he wasn't. However, his loving her didn't change anything. Just because he loved her didn't mean she would stay with him. *No, this was the right thing. Wasn't it?* He was beginning to wonder.

~~~

Moving unseen through the hospital, as if a ghost, was a blessing for Terry Griffiths. All his life, people had ignored him. At school, he had never been picked for team sports, prefect, or pupil council, and his parents had been no better. They had been so involved with each other that they had just ignored him and allowed him to do his own thing. It used to upset him.

But when he had gotten older, he had realised that walking around unseen was a good thing. He could go places other people couldn't, and do things and nobody would know.

He would often listen in on conversations and no one realised he was there. This was the very thing that had allowed him to get close to his beloved Claire. He had always been socially awkward, and people shied away from him, but he knew they were just scared of his superior intelligence. She hadn't been, though. She had smiled at him.

He'd heard her talking to her consultant about her diagnosis and heard her telling Mr Hale how she couldn't tell her family and friends about it. He'd thought nothing of it until she had come out of the room and he saw her beautiful face.

She had noticed him as she came out of the room and smiled tentatively. He knew at that moment that they were destined to be together and that she felt the same way.

He'd made a point of looking out for her over the next few months. She'd sat and chatted with him in the hospital cafeteria and he'd known then that she would be his and he would love her forever.

Then she was taken away from him. Just like that she was gone. That bastard, Hale had tried to get her to talk with his colleagues about that medical trial. She'd been right not to trust him though and as soon as he'd made her family and friends pay for neglecting her, the Consultant and everyone on the Divine Watchers would be next.

Then he and Paige could be a family. He would treat her like a princess and tell her all about the love he and Claire had shared. But first he had to set tonight's little performance in place so that he could get near that bitch Lauren. He tittered to himself as he scurried down the corridor, he couldn't wait to see them all suffer—especially that bastard Preedy.

~~~

Dane left Fortis and went to meet with Sly at the golf range. Sly was in his usual spot near the end of the range with his back to the wall when Dane arrived. He knew the position was defensive and knew his friend had taken it as naturally as his next breath.

He wondered why it was so hard to be like that around Lauren. Shit, he didn't wonder, he knew. She consumed him—his thoughts, his feelings—and being away from her wasn't helping. Dane looked at Sly as he approached, and knew his friend had seen him. He watched as Sly adjusted his stance and took a swing that sent the golf ball flying. Sly looked up at him then.

"Hey man, long time no see," he said, giving Dane one of those half shoulder man hugs.

"Hey Sly. How long you back for?"

"We're bugging out end of July so not too long. Gonna do my last tour then I'm done."

"Good, you can come work with me; business is really taking off what with all these home-grown terror threats. Zack would love to have someone with your training and experience."

"Yeah, maybe I will. So, I got a partial print from the box that was left outside Fortis. I had a friend run it through the database and it came back to a Terry Griffiths."

"Yeah that's what I thought, but it's good to confirm it."

"What's going on, man?"

Dane told him everything they knew so far leaving out his disastrous attempt to protect Lauren.

"Shit, that's fucked up, man. I start a training exercise next week but if you need anything before next Friday, just call."

"Thanks, Sly. I have Tuck and Smithy doing some surveillance for me in Southampton, but could you put the rest of your team on standby for me? Strictly off-the-books, though. Also, can you maybe put a call into Jack and see if Eidolon could be on standby?"

They were funded by a private organisation that nobody except maybe Jack knew about.

"Yeah, sorry I wasn't around this weekend or I would have done it. As for the rest, it's already done. Jack says he's monitoring the situation and is on hand for any back up you need. I'll speak to the rest of guys on the team later, but it won't be a problem."

They shook hands "Stay safe, bro."

"Yeah, you too, man."

He was nearly to the gate when Sly shouted "Give my love to Lucy," and winked. Dane gave him the finger and carried on going. He could hear Sly laughing as he left. Sly had always had a soft spot for Lucy and never missed an opportunity to rib him about it. Dane had been very vocal about his teammates staying away from his baby sister but in fact Sly was a top bloke.

He'd always had an uncanny ability to find things out. He was very guarded about how, but there was nothing he couldn't get info on eventually. Dane suspected it had something to do with Jack. He was also a good man to have your back in any situation and he really hoped he would come work for them after he got his discharge.

～～

Dane decided to take a drive to see his dad. The investigation had come to a standstill and they were waiting for leads to come back with information. He'd called ahead and his dad was in.

He'd taken to sitting outside Lauren's flat in his car from midnight until four in the morning since Nate had been protecting her. It wasn't that he didn't trust Nate—he did, but he just couldn't shake the feeling that it was his job to protect her. It wasn't like he was sleeping anyway. He normally went home as it started to get light and crashed for a few hours before going back into Fortis.

Dane pulled up to the old barn conversion just outside Weobley. The place looked the same as when he was a child. The rope swing still hung from the massive oak tree in the garden and the wooden den that his dad had built for them when they were kids was still in the corner. It all looked a little worse for wear, but he found it comforting that it was still there. Maybe if he got a chance this summer, he would repaint the den for when his nephew came to stay with his dad. The idea of the next generation playing here made him smile.

Colin Bennet walked out of the side door towards his son. He was a tall lean man who was still in great physical shape. He still had a full head of hair even if it was all grey, and tan leathery skin from working outside as a carpenter.

Dane looked at the man who had raised him, as he came towards him with a big smile, and wondered how he had ever thought his dad was broken. He looked so strong and robust. Colin was only an inch shorter than he was, but his shoulders were wider even now.

"Hey, son, what brings you out to see me on a weekday?" he said as he hugged him. Colin had always been an affectionate dad and, although it embarrassed the hell out of him when he was younger, he appreciated it now. He had thought that one day he would be that kind of dad, but he doubted he would even get the chance now.

Thinking of Lauren made him long for things that he couldn't have, at least not without risk. Was he willing to take the risk? He wasn't so sure anymore.

"Just thought I'd come for a visit and a chat," he replied. He didn't know why he'd sought out his dad now, but he always had in times of inner conflict. His dad had always been there for him with solid advice and patience. Were those the actions of a broken man? Had Dane been unfair to his dad to think that? Looking back, his dad had only ever been a wonderful father—strict, but kind and he had never let them down.

He had even joined the school board of governors so that he could stay very much involved with his kids' schooling and education. The thought that he had somehow inadvertently wronged his dad upset him.

~~~

Colin looked at his son and didn't like what he saw. He looked exhausted and very troubled. Dane had always been a good son. Oh he'd gotten into a few scrapes with Daniel but nothing truly awful, just boyhood hijinks. Nevertheless he looked upset now and Colin hated to see any of his adored kids hurting.

"What's the real reason?" he asked in a firm but kind voice. Dane had never been able to get something past him.

"Come on, let's get something cold to drink and you can tell me." He walked back around the side of the house and into the large kitchen with his son beside him.

~~~

The room still had the same oak cabinets that Colin had hand built and painstakingly carved all those years ago. His mum's favourite china was still displayed on the dresser and her cookbooks still in the bookcase. It made Dane's heart ache with the loss. How could you love someone and hate them at the same time? It was strange but that's how he felt about his mum.

"How do you do it?" he asked his dad as he turned and faced him. "How do you stay surrounded by all of her stuff after everything she did?"

His dad looked shocked and hurt but then he smiled sadly. "Is that what this is about? Your mum?"

"I just can't understand how you can still love her knowing that we weren't enough for her."

"Is that what you think? That we weren't enough?" Colin sat down at the table suddenly looking every one of his sixty-three years.

"Yes," Dane ground out, sounding frustrated and angry. "How could we have been? She claimed to love us and yet she effectively killed herself and left us." He felt his throat close around the last words. He slumped down into the seat at the table.

"Your mother loved you with everything that she was. You were her life," Colin said softly. "When we lost Megan, she was beside herself; she blamed herself and couldn't get over her belief that she hadn't protected her. I never blamed her, and I told her that hundreds of times, but she just couldn't get over it. All she had ever wanted was to be a mum and she was the best." Dane nodded his head in agreement. She had been before.

"She was, until we lost Megan," he murmured.

"She started drinking to dull the pain in the beginning," Colin explained. "But over time, it became an addiction. She knew she wasn't doing right by the rest of you. Lucy came up to her one day sat on her knee and begged her not to leave you all as Megan had. That about broke your mum's heart. She cried for hours, but in one way it had been a good thing. It woke her up and she decided to get some help.

"The next day she drove to the doctors to get some help with her depression. On the way home, she had the accident."

Dane looked like he'd seen a ghost. He hadn't known any of this.

"But she was drunk, wasn't she?"

"No, she hadn't had a drop—her blood showed no alcohol. She was just unlucky. Lights from an oncoming vehicle had blinded her and she lost concentration for a fraction of a second. In that second, the wheel clipped some mud on the embankment and flipped her car into a tree."

"Why didn't I know this?" Dane asked, feeling sick. All his life he thought his mum hadn't loved them enough to stop drinking and had been selfish but in fact that wasn't the case. She was the loving mother she had always been. She had chosen them in the end.

As he'd grown up, he'd realised that the drinking couldn't be controlled, and it was grief, but he had never forgiven her for deliberately getting in a car drunk when she had other children who needed her.

"You were a child. How could I have explained it better? I told you about the accident, but I don't know where you got the idea that she was drunk."

"Kids at school told me." He felt foolish for not asking his dad before now, but the other kids had been vile, and he had gotten into a fight. His dad had punished him for fighting and he had decided to believe the worst.

Colin pulled his son towards him for a hug.

"I'm so sorry, son. I never knew. If I had, I would have set you straight sooner. I guess this explains why you were always so angry about your mum's death."

"But it broke you," Dane said in a voice clogged with emotion. "I saw you. You were heartbroken."

"Of course, I was. She was the love of my life and yes, I was devastated for a while, but I realised I had three children to take care of and that gave me the strength to go on and make your lives better. I slowly came to terms with everything and it helped me to move on.

"Don't get me wrong, I was still heartbroken and to a degree I always will be, but I don't regret loving her. We had so many good times together before and after you kids came along, and I wouldn't trade that for never having known her."

Dane sat quietly for a while, processing everything his father had said.

"I'm sorry. You're right. Looking back now, it was only just after she died that you seemed so grief-stricken." He swallowed to loosen the knot in his throat caused by tears. How had he thought this man was broken? How had he gone through life having it so wrong? He was not an overly emotional man. Oh, he had cried in his life, but he was not the type to be open about his emotions, but he was damn near to blubbering like a baby right now.

"So, what or should I say whom has prompted this?" Dane laughed then and felt the tension ease; he never could sneak one past his old man.

"Her name's Lauren. We met a few years ago through Daniel and Claire. She was Claire's best friend."

Colin shook his head. "Terrible business."

"Yes. The thing is the person we think killed Claire is stalking Lauren. I love her, Dad, and I was so scared and cowardly about my ability to protect her and so frightened of losing her and getting my heart broken that I pushed her away and I've hurt her."

Dane hung his head in shame.

"Well faint heart never won fair maiden son. So, what you gonna do about it?"

"I'm gonna throw myself on her mercy and beg her to give me another chance," Dane answered, becoming animated.

"That's my boy. So why are you still here? Go get her."

He stood up and hugged his dad tight.

"Thanks, Dad. You're the best."

"Love you, son."

"Love you too, Dad. I gotta go. I'll call you later."

"Okay and I want to meet her soon," he shouted at his son's retreating form.

"Yeah, no problem, just as soon as I get her to forgive me."

Dane ran to his car eager to get to Lauren and beg her forgiveness. Clouds had started to turn black indicating an approaching storm.

Chapter Twenty-Three

The sky had turned a very nasty grey colour with clouds rolling in. Lauren's mum had always used the saying "It's black over Bill's mothers." She wasn't sure of the origin of that particular saying but she remembered most of the sayings her mum had used. Her mother had always been coming out with things like that, and it made her smile to remember.

Everything was so quiet tonight; even the birds had gone quiet as if they sensed the storm coming. It was early—only seven—but with all the clouds, it was dark and seemed much later.

She heard the first few spots of rain hit the balcony and could hear the thunder in the distance. Rising to close the balcony door, she was stopped by Nate. "I'll do it," he said, motioning for her to sit. He'd been very quiet since they'd returned from Fortis, which wasn't like him.

"You hungry?" she asked as the first flash of lightning lit up the room. Lauren stopped and counted five seconds before the boom of lightning nearly deafened her. That must mean the storm was only a mile away.

"Yeah I could eat," replied Nate.

"Pizza?" she suggested.

"Sure, why not."

"What do you want on it?"

"Not fussy," he said distractedly. "Whatever you're having." *Well wasn't he just Mr Chatty tonight?* She dialled her usual pizza delivery service and ordered a large Texas barbecue with chicken.

"Should be about thirty minutes," she said, settling down to watch the storm from the couch. Nate nodded distractedly. "Sure."

Lauren loved thunderstorms and always had. Even as a child, she had loved the flash of the lightning, the sound of the rain pelting the roof, and the cosy feeling of being inside safe and warm. When she was a child, she and her mum used to snuggle on the couch and watch them. She loved how the sky changed colour and how wild and untamed it was and yet how safe she felt wrapped in her mum's arms.

She wondered if she would ever experience that feeling of safety again. She had for a few days with Dane but then that was gone too. Maybe things weren't meant to last for her. She would be okay—she always was—but it was a different thing to be just okay as opposedto being happy and fulfilled. Lauren watched as the lightning flashed again, lighting up the room around her and pondered what would happen next.

~~~

Twenty minutes later, as the storm reached its peak, the door buzzed. Lauren jumped up to answer it.

"Hello!" She shouted through the intercom.

"Pizza delivery!"

"Okay, just a sec." She grabbed her purse off the entry table and was about to open the door when Nate nudged her aside and grabbed his wallet.

"Stay there, I'll get it." Nate approached the door checking the peephole to see who it was. Satisfied the person with the Presto Pizza jacket on was out there with their pizza, he opened the door.

Nate reached to take the pizza with one hand while handing over money with the other and, as he did, he felt fire burn through his upper thigh. Dropping the pizza to the floor, he realised he'd been shot and reached for his gun. Before he could react, the pizza guy stepped forward and shot him again—hitting him in the shoulder.

Nate crumpled to the ground, blood soaking his white t-shirt.

He heard Lauren scream "NO!"

She rushed to him and was about to crouch down next to him when someone grabbed her by the hair and yanked her up painfully—almost pulling it out by the roots.

Nate struggled to get to Lauren, but the pizza guy had a gun to her temple and an arm around her neck and was now backing away towards the door.

"Don't be clever. I'll put a bullet in her," the man said.

Nate knew that if he made any sudden moves this psycho would shoot her in a heartbeat. His vision was going hazy from blood loss, but he tried to reassure her as he saw the fear in her eyes.

"Don't worry, *Chiquita*, we'll find you," he said confidently. The man tightened his grip on Lauren's neck, putting her into a rear naked chokehold. Stupid prick was gonna kill her with that move. Nate saw her go slack as she started to lose consciousness. She tried to fight but Nate saw her slump as she fell unconscious.

Nate watched with despair as they left—he'd failed her. He tried to twist so that he could reach his phone from out of his back pocket, but pain lanced through his leg and shoulder, making him nauseous. Falling on his side, he managed to grasp his phone and hit Dane's number. He needed to get help.

"Hey, Nate." Dane said sounding relieved.

"Dane… Lauren …. Gone… Griffiths has her… he shot me," he managed to say, before passing out.

~~~

"Nate! Nate! Fucking answer me!" Dane shouted through the phone as he pushed the accelerator on the truck up to eighty miles an hour. He quickly called an ambulance and then called Drew and Lucy, who were still at Fortis, and told them to meet him at Lauren's ASAP. Ending that call, he then called Sly.

"Hey buddy, twice in one day."

"Sly, I'm gonna need that help. Nate's been shot. I'm not sure how bad yet and Griffiths has Lauren."

"I'm on my way, bro. Text me the address."

"Thanks, Sly," he said and hung up as he careened into her street. The paramedics had just arrived, and Dane raced up the stairs in front of them. Nate was on the living room floor, just inside the door in a pool of blood. Dropping to his knees, he checked for a pulse and held his breath. It was weak and thready but there.

The paramedics pushed him out of the way gently and set about quickly stabilising Nate as he watched on, praying to God and anyone else who would listen that his friend would make it and Lauren would be okay until he could find her. And he would find her!

Lucy and Drew pushed through the door and Lucy looked in horror at Nate.

"Is he…?"

"No, but it's gonna be close," Dane said matter-of-factly as he crossed to her and enfolded her in a hug.

"Where's Lauren?" Drew asked, looking around the room and sounding panicked.

Dane's voice shook slightly as he said, "Griffiths has her."

Drew went pale and then stormed outside. Lucy went after him and found him punching a wall and swearing.

"We'll find her, Drew," Lucy said softly, rubbing his back in a comforting gesture.

The paramedics raced past with Nate on a gurney and he looked pale and still.

"Come on, let's go to the hospital and see if Nate's gonna be ok."

Drew shook his head. "You go. I'm gonna find my sister," he said and walked off.

"Let him go," Dane said behind her. "He needs to let off steam. Lucy, can you please go and speak to Mr Aden and reassure him everything is okay. I'm not sure I would sound very reassuring right now." He motioned to the old man who stood at his door looking frail and worried.

"Yes, of course," she said, walking towards Mr Aden.

Dane texted Sly to meet him at the hospital. Lucy was back a few minutes later.

"He's fine—a little shaken but resolute. He's going to stay with his son for a few days until things settle down."

~~~

That had been easier than he thought. All the hours he'd spent watching Claire's friends had paid off. He'd bugged her phone on Saturday while she was out with that security guy. It had been so easy… and they called themselves a security company. *Ha, none of them were a match for him.* He had just had to wait for the right moment.

When he had heard her order pizza, all he'd had to do was intercept the delivery guy. He was now dead in an alley behind the houses. He did regret killing an innocent but he was collateral damage in the war he was waging, and so he had made it quick and painless.

The goon looking after her had gone down like an elephant; brawn did not beat brains this time. Griffiths knew Lauren would be out for a while. After that chokehold had put her out, he'd given her a little something to keep her that way. When she came around, she would have an awful headache. Ah well, that was just the start of her suffering and nothing compared with what his Claire had gone through all alone except for him. Yes, this was just the beginning of the pain they would all feel at his hands.

~~~

At the hospital, Dane watched as they wheeled Nate through to Resus. He'd tried to follow but was stopped by a nurse.

"You can't go in there; just let the doctors do their jobs. Can you give me some details please?" She put a hand on his arm and steered him in the direction of the reception desk. He wanted to ignore her but knew the only way he could help Nate was by giving them as many details as he could.

Lucy sat down in the relatives' room to wait for news; she looked up as the door opened.

"Jace, what are you doing here?"

She was the only one to call him Jace other than his mum but Sly liked it when Lucy called him by his name. In fact, he liked everything she did.

"Dane called me for some back-up. Is there any news on Nate yet?"

She shook her head no. He grasped her hand as he sat next to her and, as if that opened a damn, Lucy burst into tears.

"Hey," he said putting his arms around her and letting her cry. "He's gonna be fine. It'll take more than a couple of bullets to kill Nate." She sniffed and pulled herself together. Shit, she even looked beautiful when she cried—he was done for.

"I know. It's just he looked so pale and still and there was so much blood and I'm so worried about Lauren. I'm okay really," she said sitting up and moving away from him slightly. Jace hadn't realised Nate and Lucy were so close but Lucy hardly ever cried, and he felt jealousy burn in his throat at the thought, but it was his own fault—he should've made his move, not fucked anything that looked like her just to try and get her out of his system.

Nate was a good guy and if, God willing, he came through this, Jace couldn't think of a better man for Lucy even if it did eat him up inside.

Dane walked in and sat next to them. He leaned forward, rested his elbows on his knees and put his head in his hands—he looked completely shattered. They sat like that for a few minutes before a nurse came in and said the police were here and wanted to speak to them.

"Okay," Dane said visibly pulling himself together. "Just give me a second please." To Lucy he said, "Call Zack and let him know what's going on. Please see if he can get the locals off our backs."

Lucy nodded. "Sure, I'll do it now."

"Afterwards I want you and Sly to go back to Fortis and see if you can start running the CCTV and facial recognition software around Lauren's flat. Also hack into the ANPR cameras and see if you can get any details on the vehicle used. It's been thirty minutes since she was taken," he said looking at his watch. "There must be something, and we can't afford to waste any time on this. Sly, can you contact your cousin and see if he can lend us some manpower?"

Sly nodded. "Of course, I already texted Jack to give him notice that things were heating up."

"Thanks."

~~~

He got up to go and explain what was going on to the police. This was not gonna go down well with the locals. Luckily, Zack had some contacts in high places that could hopefully pull some strings. Walking into a side room, he was greeted by two detectives. He put on his professional persona and stuck out his hand to shake the hand of the closest officer.

"Detective, I'm Dane Bennet from Fortis Security." The older detective took his hand.

"I'm Detective Rogers, and this is my partner, Detective Parry. Can you tell us what's going on please, from the start?"

Dane explained nearly everything, leaving out the bit about the Divine Watchers and their earth cleansing plans and finishing with how Lauren was missing.

The detective looked shocked. "Well that's quite a tale."

He was getting pissed. This was not a tale. Just as Rogers was going to start giving him the 'let us handle this spiel' he got a call. Dane observed as the man straightened to his full five feet ten inches and sucked in his rotund belly.

"Yes, yes sir… oh okay, sir yes, of course, yes we will." He hung up looking beetroot red and like he was gonna blow a gasket.

"That was the police commissioner. We've been told that you're handling this, and we'll supply back up and support as necessary. Please let me know if we can be of any assistance," he said offering his card. DS Parry looked like he was going to argue but Rogers cut him off with a glare.

"Thank you, detectives, we will."

Dane returned to the relative's room and called Lucy. "Lucy— updates?" he asked curtly.

"I spoke to Zack and he said he should be back by next Friday and to keep him in the loop." Lucy told him. He was glad his boss would be back soon.

"Thanks, Luce." He wanted to be out there looking for Lauren, but it was his job as team leader to wait for Mr and Mrs Jones to arrive so that he could explain in part what had happened to their son. This is why he fucking hated being in charge. He wanted to go all 'Hulk' and start smashing things up until he found Lauren, but he knew that a calm head would be what got him his girl back.

"Put the phone on speaker so I can speak to Sly please, Luce. Sly, have you started checking the surveillance in the city? See if we can pick up Griffiths. Start from Lauren's place—he must have had a vehicle to move her in. Call the rest of the guys and ask them to come back. We need them on this. No point watching Marcus. It's not like he can get near her right now."

"Sure, I'm already on it."

"Don't you want to leave them on Marcus so that you can put that plan we talked about into play? Maybe he can find her quicker than us?" interrupted Lucy.

Dane nodded. "Yeah, good call. Leave Smithy and Tuck."

"Let me know as soon as you hear anything, okay?" Lucy said quickly

Dane agreed and hung up when a harried-looking doctor walked in.

"Are you the family of Nathan Jones?" he inquired.

"Yes," he said not bothering to explain that Nate was not blood but was family. "His mum and dad are on their way. They live in South Wales so won't be here for a while."

"Well, Mr Jones has been very lucky. We're taking him into surgery now. It looks like both the bullets missed all the vital arteries, but he's lost a lot of blood and this has made things very tricky. He's AB negative and that blood type is not held in the hospital, so we had to wait for some to be sent over before operating. Mr Jones did come around and was adamant that he did not want to receive anything but AB negative as he is scheduled to be tested to be a bone marrow donor and didn't want to jeopardise that. That said, he's fit and strong and should make a full recovery barring no complications in surgery. But he's going to need to rest."

"Don't worry, Doctor, he'll get rest," he said thinking of the formidable but lovely lady that was Mrs Jones.

The doctor nodded gruffly and turned to go but stopped. "What regiment are you, son?" he asked.

Dane looked at him appraisingly—they didn't talk about this.

The doctor eyed him seriously and held up a hand. "Don't worry, I understand. My son is in the parachute regiment and you Special Ops boys pulled his regiment out of the mire more than once, so for that I thank you."

He stepped forward and shook the doctor's hand. "Our pleasure, Sir. Nate is ex-parachute regiment," he said.

"We'll take very good care of him, I promise." With that, the doctor smiled, then turned and left.

Dane sat and waited for Nate's parents and wished now that he had taken the time to find out what Nate had wanted to talk to him about that night at Lauren's. He'd been so wrapped up in things, he'd forgotten. He was going to apologise and find out what Nate had wanted the first chance he got and apologise for the incident earlier.

God, just thinking about how scared Lauren must be twisted his insides. He had to find her and fix this. She couldn't be dead, he just wouldn't accept that. He would find her and fix the mess he had made of things. Resolved, he phoned Lucy to see how things were going.

Chapter Twenty-four

Oh hell, why did her head hurt so much? Lauren tried to roll over and realised that her hands were secured tightly in front of her. Opening her eyes, she slowly blinked and tried to remember where she was. Then it all came back to her. *Oh God! Nate! He'd shot him. Was Nate dead?*

Tears burned her eyes as she tried to remember. Terry Griffiths had grabbed her. She struggled to sit up, but her hands were cuffed to some sort of post and the movement caused nausea to roil through her stomach and bile to burn up her throat.

Moving slowly, she realised her ankles were bound with rope but not bound to anything. She wiggled her toes, trying to get rid of the pins and needles feeling. Through the small high window in the top of the wall, she could just make out the light from the full moon and realised that she was in a large cellar with just a bed and a side table.

Wriggling as best she could to sit up, she looked behind her. She could see a door above some steps and, on the walls, she could see pictures. While she couldn't make out who they were of, she could see that there were hundreds of them.

Oh, how she wanted Dane. He might not want her, but she would give anything to see him and tell him she loved him and that it didn't matter if he didn't love her, she just wanted him to know.

She lay there feeling so scared and sorry for herself for a minute. He would find her; she knew he would, even if he didn't love her. He was a warrior and he'd take it as a personal failure.

Taking some deep breaths, Lauren tried to get control of her fear; she was no good to anyone if she just lay here and didn't help herself. She had never needed a man to fight in her corner before and she wasn't gonna start now!

"Ah, you're awake."

She turned towards the sound of the voice and blinked furiously when a light came on. Her eyes adjusted and she watched with her heart banging as Terry Griffiths came down the steps. He was dressed in chinos and a purple paisley shirt, and had a black armband on his upper arm.

He stopped as he moved closer to her and she felt the hatred coming off him in waves. He was truly a very twisted and sick man, and she needed to get away from him as soon as she could.

"Are you hungry?" he asked suddenly. "You missed dinner," he continued, with a sinister laugh. She said nothing, knowing that whatever she might say could set him off.

"Don't look so worried, Lauren. I'm not going to hurt you … Yet. We're going to get to know each other first. You're going to tell me all about my Claire and why you neglected her and let her suffer all alone." He said the last with so much anger and menace that she shrank back, as spittle flew from his mouth. He had gone a puce red as he'd looked at her and then he turned and fled up the stairs, muttering as he did.

She heard the door lock and her shoulders slumped. She needed to get out of there. He was unstable and she was not gonna die in some damp cellar at the hands of a madman. Wriggling back onto her other side, Lauren drew in a shocked breath as she faced the wall with all the pictures. Every picture was of Claire and all taken without her knowledge, by the looks of them. On every single one was a cut-out picture of Terry Griffiths. She felt sick and could feel bile burning her throat again. She dry-heaved for a few minutes while trying to get control of herself by taking deep breaths.

Lauren looked around for something to help her break the cable ties on her wrists but there was nothing. Feeling defeated, she slumped back down to conserve her energy. She would rest up and wait for an opportunity.

~~~

Terry walked around his kitchen trying to get control of his temper; he hadn't meant to snap at her. He planned to be nice so that she relaxed her guard but seeing her there alive and breathing while his beautiful Claire was dead and buried just made him lose his grip for a short time.

He pulled out the picture of Claire in the park that he'd taken two weeks before she died. In it, she was looking up at the sky with a beautiful smile on her face and he'd known that she was thinking of him. He felt the first stirrings of desire as he looked at the picture and rubbed a hand along his erection. He quickly stopped and put the photo away. Now was not the time and, unlike some men, he could control his body's animal urges.

He decided that he would leave Lauren alone overnight and take her a nice breakfast in the morning. He hoped this would gain her trust and then, maybe, she would tell him all about his Claire. He gave an evil twisted smile as he thought about what fun he would have with her over the next few days.

~~~

Drew really didn't want to do this but they needed all the help they could get to find Lauren, and his father had contacts everywhere. His connection to Terry Griffiths would give them even more of an advantage. If it meant a beating from his father then so be it. He would take anything his father dished out if it meant getting his sister back safely.

It wasn't the thought of the beating that made him apprehensive. No, he'd had so many of those he'd stopped caring. But going behind Dane and Lucy's back when they were just starting to trust him bothered him a lot. But if it meant helping Lauren, he would do it anyway. Calling the familiar number for the hundredth time this week, he waited to see if his father would pick up. He doubted his luck would turn now but it was his only hope.

"Drew, what can I do for you my traitorous child? Are you calling to apologise for your betrayal or are you going to help me find my daughter?"

Drew was so shocked that he'd answered that he paused before stating "Lauren's gone!"

"What the fuck do you mean gone?" His father bellowed down the phone.

"Terry Griffiths took her; he shot the man guarding her and took her. I need your help!"

"So, let me get this straight—first you try and hide her from me and now that she's gone you want me to help?"

"Yes, I do."

"And what do her friends think of this?"

"They don't know," Drew replied. There was silence on the line while Marcus thought; Drew knew there was no point in rushing him as it would only take longer. He bit his tongue to stop his impatience from causing him to say something he shouldn't.

"Well, I am going to help, but by help I mean I will get my daughter back safely with me where she should have been for the last twenty-six years. I need all the information you have on what happened. Meet me at her house; I want to see where she lives. Text me the address," Marcus said thoughtfully.

He wanted to know everything about her gift and maybe her home would give him some clues.

"Fine," Drew said. "When?"

"I should be there by midnight," Marcus answered, and then hung up before Drew could speak. Drew had serious reservations about this and knew Dane was going to kick his ass, but if they could use Marcus's connection to Griffiths to find Lauren, then maybe they would be in a position to capture Marcus too. It was time to face the music and tell Dane and Lucy what he'd done.

~~~

Marcus punched the dashboard of the car. How could he have been so stupid? He'd known that Griffiths was a psycho but how had he found Lauren? It must have been the Thompson woman—everything kept coming back to her.

"Michaels, Griffiths has my daughter," Marcus stated without emotion, speaking to the man in the seat beside him. "I don't think he will kill her straight away but eventually he will, and I still need to deliver her to the Watchers in one piece. Have everyone, and I mean everyone, checking Griffiths' background. I want every rock uncovered." Michaels nodded like the dutiful little minion he was. "Do a good job and I will reward you later," Marcus said, running a hand along the bulge in Michaels' trousers, causing the man's hands to tighten on the steering wheel. He loved manipulating people and he always found Michaels worked better with an incentive.

~~~

Dane was leaving the hospital when he got a call from Smithy, who had been watching Marcus, letting him know that Marcus was headed Dane's way, and that they were tailing him.

"Okay, change of plan. You and Tucker stay on him, and Sly will pull the rest of the team in to help me." Dane hit the disconnect button and immediately it rang again.

"Yes," he said abruptly.

"It's Drew," a voice said. "Where are you?"

"I'm just leaving the hospital; Nate is going to be okay after a lot of enforced rest."

"Well, I've done something and you're not gonna like it. I need to see you. Can you meet me at Fortis?"

Dane paused this, knowing this did not sound good. "Yes, okay. Ten minutes?"

"Yes, that's fine. See you then."

They both hung up.

~~~

It had been two long hours since Lauren had been taken. Dane could feel his stomach twist at the thought of her in the hands of that lunatic for even a minute. He'd made a complete mess of things and needed to put it right, starting with getting her back home. Maybe then he could fix some of the damage he had done by being such an ass.

He loved her. She'd somehow slipped under his skin like she belonged there, and he didn't want to know what it would feel like without her in his life now. *Oh, please God no! Please let her be okay.* He would spend every day for the rest of his life making it up to her if she would just be okay. She was his soulmate. Dane drove quicker now as if his revelation made everything more urgent.

Fortis was lit up like Christmas as he entered. Sly and Lucy, their heads close together, were hunched over the surveillance computers that were hooked up to the city. Zack operated a 'don't ask, don't tell' policy with Will Granger, their tech guy. He carried on past, leaving them to concentrate and went into the conference room.

Crossing to the back, he got a cold bottle of energy drink from the fridge. It was gonna be a long night and he needed the caffeine. The temperature had cooled slightly after the storm, relieving the muggy feeling in the air and Dane felt better for it. He sat waiting for Drew and wondered what the hell the kid had done now. He felt sorry for him and admired his computer skills, which had turned out to be just as good as he had said, and would in time rival Will's, but he didn't trust him fully. He had a slightly wild untamed streak in him that could be either very good or very bad. Drew walked in a few minutes later and sat down catty-corner to Dane. He looked like he was about to face his executioner and Dane figured out why when he spoke.

"I got a hold of Marcus and told him what happened and asked for his help," Drew said in a rush.

"You did what?!" he exploded, at the top of his voice.

"He has contacts everywhere and he already knows Griffiths. You said yourself this plan would work," Drew defended as Lucy and Sly came running into the room.

"What the hell, bro?" his sister said.

"This moron has contacted daddy and told him what happened," Dane said, his voice dripping with scorn as he pointed a finger a Drew. Lucy looked at Drew and shook her head.

"Jesus, Drew, I like you, but you really have a gift for winding him up," she said, jerking her thumb at her brother. "Okay tell me everything."

Drew explained the conversation with Marcus, finishing with when they were meeting.

"This could work in our favour," Sly said. "The kid's got a point about his contacts and his connection to Griffiths. We've had some run-ins with the Divine Watchers and from what we could ascertain they have people from all occupations as members. If we were to get ears in her flat and maybe bug Marcus, this might help us bring them both in."

"I agree," Lucy said and then turned to Drew. "But you're putting yourself in an awfully vulnerable position, Drew. Marcus won't trust you now and you could be in danger."

"I don't care," he said with all the nonchalance of a twenty-one-year-old. "And anyway, he'll only rough me up, he won't kill me."

"What about Michaels? He's already shot you once."

"Yeah I've been thinking about that and I think it was a test to see if Lauren could actually heal me."

"That's quite a risk though, don't you think?" he said unsure and knowing Lauren would never forgive him if he got her brother hurt.

"No, he only nicked my leg; I don't think it was meant to kill me. Please guys, let me do this?"

"It's our best chance." Lucy surmised.

Dane paced the room. "I don't know. This plan was good before Lauren was taken, but now we could be putting her right in the crossfire." After another minute of pacing, he sat down again.

"Fine. But I want eyes in there in case something goes wrong, and you'll need to get him to make calls to his contacts before he leaves. That way, we'll get the help and then we can pick him up. We don't have long so let's get moving."

Everyone started gearing up with comm-units, bugs, and weapons and were on their way twenty minutes later.

~~~

Pulling up around the corner from Lauren's house the team, which now included Drew, approached the flat from the back in case anyone was watching the front. As they approached, Drew tripped over something.

He reared back and had to stop the bile that rushed up into his stomach. In front of him were the open sightless eyes of a young man. He was missing his shirt and had a bullet hole in his chest. The others rushed up to him. "Shit!" exclaimed Sly as he bent over the body. "This must be the original pizza delivery guy."

Dane swore. "Fuck, this is the sick son-of-bitch that has Lauren. We'll put a call into the locals as soon as this has gone down with Preedy. We can't afford for them to come waltzing in now and fucking this mission up." Lucy and Sly nodded their agreement.

Drew stepped away and followed them up the back fire-escape to Lauren's flat. For the first time since this started, he was scared. Seeing his first dead body didn't help and the realisation that he might never see his sister again almost made him drop to his knees. For the first time in his life, he felt like he belonged, but he knew he had a way to go to convince Dane. Nevertheless, he still treated him with respect. Fortifying himself for the coming confrontation, Drew vowed to himself that he would do whatever it took to get his sister back.

Entering the flat, they could see the crime scene techs had left, and all that remained was crime scene tape and blood by the door. The room looked normal except for the small amount of white dust used by the forensics people, but it looked like they had been hastily pulled away before finishing the job, as there was only dust by the door. Drew watched Lucy as she went around the flat, sweeping for bugs just in case and was surprised when she found one in the phone in the living room. She crushed it under her high-heeled boot and swept the rest of the house.

"I found one bug by the phone over there," she said, indicating the living room side table. "But the rest is clear; it was pretty basic—but would have done the job."

"I guess we know how Griffiths knew they were having pizza then," Sly said.

"How was it missed on the other sweeps?" Dane queried. "And how for that matter did they miss the dead body in the alley out the back?"

"Not sure. Thebug could be a new plant and maybe the crime scene techs came through the front. It doesn't look like they did much before they were pulled away. Could be they hadn't got that far," she said shrugging. "We'll have to ask Nate when he's up to it." Quickly Lucy planted her much more sophisticated bugs around the flat and tested the feed.

"I can probably get one camera in by the DVD player, but it means you'll need to try and keep him in here as much as possible," she said to Drew, who nodded. Fifteen minutes later they were all done and quietly left, leaving Drew alone to wait for Marcus.

~~~

Dane, Sly and Lucy quickly ran over to the hotel on the corner where Sly had secured them a room.

"Wow!" Lucy said walking into the plushest hotel room she had ever been in. "This is amazing. What a waste to come here for this. I'm definitely coming back here when I get married," she said breezily, causing Sly to grind his teeth imagining her with Nate. Tamping down his jealousy and his vision of Lucy crying over Nate, he abruptly started putting all the gear together so that they had sound and visual in Lauren's living room.

~~~

What's got his panties in a twist? Lucy thought as she came over to stand next to him. Honestly, men were a complete mystery to her. They watched Drew pace on the live feed. Dane was watching the window intently for any sign of Marcus. His phone pinged with a text. He had texted Tucker earlier and told him to let him know when they were five minutes out and then to pull back.

"Okay, heads up. He's on his way," he said to Lucy and Sly.

"Sly, get yourself into position by the bedroom window; it has a better angle. Tuck's team is already in position on the other major exits. And Eidolon is covering the wider perimeter."

"Thank you, boss. I have been the sniper on the team for nine years, you know." Sly said dryly.

"Yeah sorry. It'sjust that this is really important to me."

"I know, man. I got ya back, don't worry."

Luckily, being close to the Cathedral meant that this was a dead-end street for vehicles, but they could still have someone run and didn't want to let this chance to capture Marcus go. Sly set up his scope and L96 sniper rifle from the bedroom window. Then they all sat and waited.

Chapter Twenty-Five

Drew couldn't hear them but he was sure that they could hear him. They decided not to put a receiver on him in case Marcus noticed and realised it was a trap. He didn't know why he was so nervous. He'd faced Marcus a thousand times and each put down or beating had just made him hate him more, until all he felt now was loathing for the man that had spawned him.

Maybe it was because so much was riding on this. It hadn't always been like that, though. When he first went to live with him after his mum died, he'd constantly sought his father's approval—he'd wanted to please him.

He had quickly realised that Marcus only tolerated him because he was blood and, as soon as Drew had started to have an opinion or push back against anything Marcus wanted him to do, Marcus would lose it and hand out one of his beatings.

The only people who had shown him any kindness were the staff, except Michaels. Michaels hated Drew and was jealous of him. Drew suspected that Michaels' feelings for Marcus were not exactly that of a boss. He'd seen Michaels leaving his father's room one night at three in the morning—clad only in his boxers. Not that he'd cared what they got up to.

Drew's musings were interrupted by the sound of several vehicles stopping outside in the quiet street. Crossing to the window, he watched Marcus and Michaels get out of the big Land Rover, and then Michaels said something to the four goons in the second vehicle.

Drew walked to unlock the door and opened it to let Marcus and Michaels come in. Drew watched Marcus as he stepped over the threshold with Michaels behind him, careful to avoid the blood. He was dressed in his usual bespoke black suit and designer shirt, his shoes highly polished. He looked around with disdain clearly written all over his face and walked around, going into each room and checking that nobody was there.

"So, this is how my baby girl has been forced to live." Marcus said, mainly to himself, with a sniff of distaste. Drew didn't respond, knowing that one wasn't required. This was not a social call and he had no interest in catching up with his father.

Marcus had come to stand in front of Drew with Michaels beside him. He knew what was going to happen next; it was the standard procedure.

Michaels grabbed Drew by the arms, forcing them behind his back. Marcus removed his jacket, folded it neatly and placed it over the chair. Turning back to Drew, he let his fist fly, splitting Drew's lip with the first punch. He then kneed Drew in the stomach, causing all the air to leave Drew's body. He followed this up with an uppercut to the jaw. Blood was flowing out of Drew's mouth and he spat it out as Michaels dropped him to the floor. Marcus stepped back, rolled his shoulders and continued pacing around the room.

"I can't tell you how disappointed I am in you, Drew. I have given you everything and all I have gotten in return is betrayal, lies, and bad attitude."

"You have given me nothing but abuse," Drew spat. "You have put me down, beaten me and used me as your free muscle, not ever giving me the love and care of a parent."

"Love?" Marcus laughed. "Love is for the weak. It makes you trust people who don't deserve it. The only person I ever loved betrayed me and when she left, she took my daughter."

"What about Lauren?" Drew asked.

"What about her? I don't know Lauren to love her, but she is mine and her place is with me. That is why I have called all my contacts to find her." Marcus had still not given away his association with Griffiths and Drew knew this could be the last time he saw Marcus. He didn't feel any pain or hurt from that, just relief, but something had always bothered him and now seemed like a good time to confirm it.

"Did you kill her; did you kill my mother?"

Marcus laughed. "More like put her out of her misery. That whore helped my Martha leave me and then insinuated herself in my life and gave me you," he spat. "I did you a favour when I had her killed."

Drew felt rage like nothing he had ever felt before and, in a show of complete adrenaline, lunged at Marcus, pummelling him with his fists. He managed to get some hard blows in before Michaels hauled him off with a gun to his head. They then proceeded to kick the crap out of him. Drew lay there, not feeling most of the blows that rained down on him. He had done all he could now.

~~~

Watching through the camera and listening on the coms, Dane was disgusted as he listened to Marcus talk about Lauren as if she were a possession, and hearing how he had treated Drew sickened him. It made him thank God for his own father and gave him a lot more sympathy and understanding for Drew.

As soon as he heard that Marcus had called in his contacts, he yelled "go go go" into the comms. Tuck's team moved in to secure the four goons by the entrance while Sly and Dane moved towards the flat.

When they burst in the door, Marcus was so engrossed with beating Drew that he and Michaels never saw them coming. Yanking Marcus off Drew, Dane landed a few vicious blows before putting Marcus in a back hammer-lock and zip-tying his wrists. He turned to Sly, who had easily subdued Michaels.

"Let's get these two to Fortis and get Marcus's phone to Lucy so she can monitor it." Preedy had gone deathly calm now.

"You have just signed your own death warrant, boy," he aimed at Drew. Dane pushed him towards two of Tuck's team members.

"Take this trash to Fortis and hold him until I get there." He knelt next to Drew. The kid was a bloody mess, his face already swollen from all the damage inflicted on it, His lip was split open and bleeding, both his eyes were swelling shut and he probably had a few broken ribs. Dane was glad he'd managed to get a couple of blows in on Marcus and wished he'd landed a few more, but time was not on their side unfortunately.

"Hey, kid, can you sit up?" he asked. Drew groaned and tried to move. "Lucy," he said into his comms, "get a medic up here."

"No," groaned Drew. "I've had worse. Just get me some ibuprofen and I'll be fine after a few hours."

Dane paused. "Okay, let's see how you are in a few hours then. But I want Sly to check you over when we get to Fortis." He gripped Drew's shoulder tightly. "Well done, Drew. Your sister would be very proud of you. It was incredibly brave. You really proved yourself tonight. I'm sorry for not trusting you sooner."

"Thank you. I just hope it helps find her. You will find her, won't you?" Drew said sounding young and frightened for his sister. Dane nodded, hoping like hell that he was telling the truth.

~~~

Lauren woke up as she heard Terry come down the steps.

"Ah, you're awake. Good. I have some food for you. Firstly, though I would like to apologise for my reaction last night. I fear it was all the excitement of the evening."

"What time is it, please?" she asked politely, not wanting to set him off again.

"It's seven in the morning, my dear. Here, I brought you some breakfast. It's only toast and tea, but I don't want you spoilt. You are here to suffer, after all. However, my lovely Claire wouldn't understand so I will try and treat you well until it becomes time for this to end."

Lauren trembled. She knew that the end would probably involve her painful death. She accepted the toast and tea because she wanted to keep her strength up in case an opportunity to escape presented itself.

"Thank you," she said, nibbling on the dry toast as he held it out to her.

"I'm going to go out in a bit, but first I'll take you to the little girl's room to relieve yourself." He untied her legs from the bed but left her wrists bound in front of her. Taking her by the arm, he guided her up the steps into the main house, which was filled with old-fashioned furniture from the eighties. The walls were all mildewed and stained and it smelled damp.

"Here," he said, pushing her towards a small room that contained a toilet and sink. "Do your business and don't lock the door or I will punish you."

Lauren quickly relieved herself and washed her hands. Splashing her face with water, she eyed the stained towel and decided to air dry rather than catch something from it. She opened the door and Griffiths walked her back down to the cellar. He went to tie her legs back up.

"Please," she said, "please leave my legs untied. I promise I won't do anything stupid."

He looked at her, considering her request. "Fine. It's not like you can go anywhere or anyone can hear you," he said in his singsong voice. Lauren shuddered and decided that his high-pitched voice scared her as much as if he had been screaming at her. Griffiths then left her and went back up the stairs.

She heard the click of the lock and knew it was pointless to try the door. She wondered if anyone was coming for her and thought again about Dane. Would she ever see him again? Knowing that she couldn't and shouldn't rely on anyone else to save her, she tried to slip her wrists out of the zip-ties but only succeeded in making her wrists bloody and sore.

She then set about nibbling at the plastic with her teeth and, after what seemed like hours, the plastic gave way. Rubbing her injured wrists, she looked around again for something to help her escape. She deliberately ignored the wall of sickening photos. Lauren quickly realised that the only weapon she had was surprise. Sitting on the small bed, she waited.

Chapter Twenty-Six

Dane needed coffee. He went to the kitchen and found Drew already there—he looked awful. Both his eyes were nearly closed and his lip was all swollen. Sly had needed to put a stitch in it and Drew had shown again how resolute he was. He hadn't moved a muscle when the needle had gone in and had refused any medication.

"How are you feeling?" Dane asked, realising it was a stupid question as soon as he asked it.

Drew just lifted a shoulder in a shrug. "Been better and been worse. Has my father said anything?"

"No, he's a real piece of work. We've been questioning him all night and he's one twisted fuck. The worst of it is that he thinks he's the victim."

Drew shook his head, incredulous. "Fucking unbelievable."

"Michaels isn't much better. He has a serious amount of loyalty to Marcus and it turns out, they are having a relationship. Michaels told us how he and Marcus would be together openly after the world had been set back on track."

~~~

Drew wasn't shocked; he'd suspected as much but he had a feeling that Marcus had never intended for them to be together. Marcus had always been very vocal about his hatred of homosexuals and Drew knew he would never want to lose face by going back on that publicly; he was probably just using sex as a way to control Michaels. Either way he didn't care as long as they both got locked up and Lauren was returned unhurt.

"Michaels also bragged about how he had followed Hale back to the hospital so that he could talk to Griffiths and that was when he'd caught Griffiths following us. Pure damn bad luck for us. Not that it redeems my part in it."

So, Dane was still blaming himself, Drew thought sadly.

"Did we get anything useful on Lauren yet?" Drew asked as he sipped lukewarm coffee through his damaged lips.

Dane shook his head. "No, Tuck's team checked out Griffiths' place and found nothing but filth. He'd been living there until recently by the looks, but he's long gone now. We're gonna keep eyes on the place though in case he comes back. We do have a contact at SIS following a lead that we hope will pan out, and we have eyes on the burial ground in case he visits Claire there."

Dane paused as if he wanted to say something else. "I'm sorry about your mum, Drew. I know what it's like to lose a parent."

Drew looked up "You heard that?" he said with no real surprise.

"Yeah, we did."

Drew nodded. "She didn't deserve. That she wasn't perfect, but she was my mum, ya know."

"Do you need anything? Painkillers?" asked Dane, changing the subject.

"No, Lucy's been mothering me all night, waking me and giving pain relief and stuff. I think she likes me," he said with a smirk which came off more like a grimace because of his abused face. He was trying to lighten the moment by trying to wind Dane up. He didn't like talking about this stuff.

"Ha, I think that ship sailed, my friend." Just then, Lucy came careening around the corner. "Speak of the devil, here she is now."

"We've got something."

They rushed with her back to the tech room. Sly was already bringing up satellite images.

"Our contact at SIS found this. It's an old farmhouse towards Kingsland that used to belong to Gladys and Robert Price. They were Terry Griffiths' maternal grandparents. They died a few years back when their car hit a patch of ice, flipping them into a ditch and killing them both.

"They were estranged from Terry and his parents. His second cousin was the sole beneficiary in their wills, but he lives in New

Zealand, so the property was left abandoned. Sly is trying to see if he can pick up any heat signatures." They all turned to watch Sly while holding their collective breath. They could see two heat signatures in the house.

"Okay, let's check this out. Lucy, I need you to handle comms nearby. Sly, you're with me. Drew, help Lucy."

~~~

Dane was all business now. He had to go and get Lauren back. He and Sly loaded up on guns and knives, having learnt very early in their careers that you could never have too many weapons. Lucy gave them both an earpiece and tested the comms unit. It was almost invisible to the naked eye and could be used in two ways.

"Right now, you're ready to go bring our girl home." She leaned up and kissed both men on the cheek. "Stay safe."

"Always, baby sis." Dane replied.

~~~

It was a few hours before Lauren heard Griffiths come back; at least she assumed it was Griffiths that she could hear pottering around upstairs. It all went quiet again a short while later.

She decided to look at the pictures to try to determine where and when they were taken. They were all apparently taken without Claire's knowledge and the most frightening of all were the ones with Paige in them.

Griffiths had taken all those stolen moments of joy and freedom and made them something sinister and ugly by inserting himself into them. She felt her stomach tighten and roll as she realised what could have happened to Paige. She stopped as she heard running footsteps above her and got into position with her back to the wall.

Griffiths threw the door open and flew down the stairs towards her.

"What have you done?" he snarled.

However, he didn't get to finish that sentence because Lauren threw herself at him. She bent at the waist and ploughed her shoulder into his stomach. The momentum of them both moving in different directions caused Griffiths to go over her shoulder and land in a heap behind her. She didn't waste time to see if he was hurt, she just ran for the stairs.

She'd nearly reached the top when Griffiths grabbed her by her ankle and pulled her backwards, causing her to lose her footing. Lauren scrabbled to grab at the steps, ripping her nails back to the quick in her bid to pull away from him, but Griffiths kept dragging her back down. He grabbed her by her hair and pushed her back to the bed and with surprising strength.

She pushed away from him into the farthest corner of the bed, breathing fast from her bid for freedom. Griffiths stalked towards her with wild manic eyes. Grasping her arms roughly, he quickly zip-tied them in front of her pulled them high and attached them to the metal frame of the bed behind her head. She watched with heart-stopping fear as he took out a knife and started to run it down her cheek. Lauren was shaking and her breaths were coming faster. She needed to calm her breathing, or she was going to pass out.

"Now why did you do that, you stupid little bitch? I was trying to be nice, but you threw it back in my face. Now I'm going to have to show you what happens when people disobey me. Your silly little security boys just tripped one of my wires. But they won't reach you." he sing-songed in that repulsive voice. "I'm better than them. I have trip wires all over this property, They will probably be blown to smithereens soon," he said with an almost girlish giggle. "I can't figure out how you did it, but I know you tipped them off. They never would have found my connection to this place otherwise. I'm too clever."

He had his face so close to her that she could smell his rancid breath on her, making her feel nauseous.

~~~

Griffiths liked the look of wide-eyed fear on her face, and knowing he had put it there gave him a jolt of desire which he wasn't expecting. It had only been Claire for him. She was the true love of his life but maybe he could have some fun with Lauren before he killed her. The idea pleased him. He ran the knife along her neck and followed it with his tongue, enjoying the fear he could smell on her skin and the way her breasts heaved against him.

~~~

She was going to be sick; she was paralysed against this monster and what he was doing to her. Her very breaths went shallow when she felt the proof of his enjoyment against her leg.

Closing her mind to what was happening, she concentrated on her breathing—*breathe in and hold,, breathe out.* She had started to calm her mind when she felt him begin to cut at her top and saw the material in half. He nicked her skin with the knife causing her to flinch; she could feel the warm blood run down her stomach.

"Open your eyes, bitch," he said, squeezing her jaw between his fingers and shaking her. She opened her eyes and looked at him, letting all her hatred show.

"Ah you're a feisty little thing but I'll soon break you and make you beg for me to kill you." He used the knife to cut her shorts off, running his hands all over her body. So lost in his sick twisted games, he leaned away from her, giving her the opening she needed to bring her leg up and knee him in the balls.

He screamed in pain and reared back, holding his groin. Lauren scrambled back on the bed as best she could using her feet to push her into the corner and crunched into a foetal ball. Her wrists were twisted and aching from being wrenched above her head. If she was gonna die, she wasn't going to meekly lie back and die without a fight. She wasn't that person. She readied herself to kick out if he came at her again.

"You fucking bitch, I'm gonna kill you for that," he screamed with spit flying everywhere. He back-handed her, splitting her lip, the blow making her see stars. She refused to scream and show any weakness to this maniac; never again would someone enjoy her pain at least not if she could help it.

She ducked her head to try to avoid the next blow and kicked out with her legs, hearing him groan as she got in a good kick to his thigh. She waited for the next blow to come but it never did. She peeked at him and he had cocked his head and was listening.

"My alarms!" he screamed and ran for the door. Lauren sat up as best she could and tried to take stock of her injuries. The cut to her stomach was superficial and her face hurt like a bitch, but she was okay. She listened to see if she could figure out what had set Griffiths off. She could hear an alarm ringing and wondered what was happening, praying that it was Dane and the team and that they were okay. Whatever it was, she hoped it kept Griffiths busy indefinitely.

Her prayers weren't answered though as Griffiths reappeared a few minutes later and pulled the knife out again. He un-cuffed her from the bed and hauled her to him holding the knife to her throat as he backed her towards the steps. He nicked her neck again as he pulled her up the steps, causing her to flinch. Lauren could smell the metallic blood and swayed slightly, feeling light-headed.

~~~

Dane cursed when he heard the alarm; clearly they had the right place.

"Luce, what can you see?"

"We have two heat signatures moving close together towards the kitchen."

"Tango has some crude alarms set up on trip wires around the house; we must have set one off about five-hundred yards out by the start of the drive," he said, relaying the information to Lucy. "Get

Eidolon to send a team in; he might have bombs and traps set up around the area. Tell them to come in quiet; I don't want to spook this guy."

It was times like this when having a ghost op squad like Eidolon as allies was a Godsend. Dane approached the front door and Sly took the back. He peered through the front window but could see very little through the grime and dirt.

He walked towards the side kitchen window, keeping his head down, and his blood ran cold. Inside in profile to him was Griffiths, backing down the hallway to the rear of the house. He had a large serrated hunting knife pressed to Lauren's throat. She was only in her underwear and was bleeding from wounds in her neck and stomach. He needed to block out any fear and treat this like any other hostage situation.

"Sly," he whispered, "he's coming your way. He has Lauren with a knife to her throat and is using her as a shield. I don't have a shot."

"Roger," said Sly.

Going back around to the front door, Dane called out to the man inside. "Griffiths, come out. I just want to talk."

"Dane!" she cried, and he could hear the fear and hope in her voice.

"Don't worry, honey. It's all gonna be okay."

"Shut up!" shrieked Griffiths, yanking her back to him and catching her with the knife again. Dane was gonna tear this bastard's throat out with his bare hands for hurting and scaring her. Allowing his training to kick in, he shut his mind to Lauren as his woman and just allowed himself to think of her as a hostage again.

"Let's stay calm, Griffiths. Nobody needs to get hurt."

"I have nothing to say to you yet. It's not your time to suffer, it's hers. Don't worry, I'll send the neglectful bitch back to you piece by piece so that you can bury her."

Dane was struggling to keep his cool, he so wanted to wrap his hands around Griffiths' throat and squeeze until he had no air left.

"Stay frosty, man," Sly whispered in his ear. He stepped forward and slowly so as not to alarm him and pushed the door open.

"Stay back," Griffiths snarled, "or I'll slit her pretty throat in front of you."

The terror in her eyes would stay with him forever. Griffiths was getting even more anxious and unstable by the second and he needed to get Lauren away from him.

"Just let her go and we can talk. So, tell me, how did you meet Claire?"

"Don't you say her name. You didn't deserve her, none of you did. She was mine—she loved me. Her and Paige were gonna be mine," he said on a sob.

Dane took another step forward.

"No, stay back." Griffiths moved his arm so it was around her throat and put the knife to her left side digging it in and causing her to wince. Putting his hands up in a show of supplication, Dane stepped back.

"I have no shot," he heard in his ear. "If I shoot him now, he could stab her. Eidolon has Alpha team headed our way, but they're still five minutes out," Sly relayed to him. Dane knew they didn't have that long, but waiting for Alpha team, who would have a medic with them, was best for Lauren. Griffiths changed direction slightly as he started to back towards the kitchen door.

"Move in there slowly," Griffiths said, motioning to him to move into the kitchen. "If you move too fast, I will gut her."

Dane could see tears silently tracking down Lauren's beautiful face and blood dripping down her chest from the cuts in her neck. He was gonna send this sick psycho bastard to hell if it was the last thing he did.

~~~

Ushering Dane into a chair with the knife, Griffiths couldn't see a way out of this. If he let Lauren go to secure the hero then he knew he would rush him and he wasn't stupid. He knew he couldn't outmanoeuvre him physically, so that left using her as a shield. He backed towards the kitchen drawer where he kept his gun. Holding the gun in front of him, Griffiths felt euphoric because now he had the upper hand again. He would shoot the hero and gut the bitch, or maybe he would gut the bitch while the boyfriend watched.

Yes, that was much better—someone to watch his greatest performance. Holding the gun steady on the boyfriend, and with the knife to her rib cage, he slowly started to push the knife into her skin she flinched slightly but didn't scream.

~~~

She was so scared—seeing the calm face of the man she loved was the only thing keeping her steady. She could see the pulse in his neck and the way his body was coiled tight ready to move the first chance he could. That was going to have to be soon. Griffiths had lost it completely now. Lauren trusted Dane and the team to get her out of this though.

Lauren was determined not to show pain or fear because if she did, she knew Dane would tackle Griffiths and get himself killed. She had to fix this, or Dane was going to sacrifice himself for her. She couldn't let that happen. Then she saw Sly and knew what she had to do.

~~~

Sly knew the moment Lauren spotted him because she gave him a small smile and did the most heroic thing he had ever seen.

~~~

Dane sat watching Lauren and Griffiths not six feet away from him and his heart stopped. Everything went into slow motion. He knew she was going to do something by the smile that came over her face. He could see Griffiths pushing the knife into her skin—drawing more blood from her and his fists clenched. He had to keep a cool head or he would get her killed.

He had long ago come to terms with his own death but knew he would never survive hers. Never in his worst nightmare could he imagine what happened next. In a split second, several things happened. Lauren threw herself forward onto the knife, Sly took the headshot and Lauren crumpled to the ground with Griffiths landing on top of her.

With an inhuman roar, Dane threw himself towards Lauren, dragging Griffiths' dead body off her.

"Lauren, honey, can you hear me?" Blood was pouring from a wound in her side.

~~~

Reaching him in seconds, Sly took over and put pressure on the wound causing her to cry out.

"I know it hurts but I have to keep the pressure on," Sly said gently. Her breathing was rapid, and she started to cough up blood.

Sly knew it wasn't good. He'd seen it a number of times before; she apparently had a punctured lung and it was filling with blood.

He tapped his comms. "Lucy we need an Air Ambulance ASAP. Lauren has been stabbed and her lung is collapsing."

A calm voice spoke in his ear. "An Air Ambulance is already on route. I called one in as soon as I heard what was happening. They should be here any minute." God, it was no wonder Sly loved her. She was amazing, he thought, selfishly thanking God it wasn't Lucy in this situation.

"Hang on, honey. Help's coming. You're gonna be fine." Dane whispered to her as he held on tightly to her cold hand.

He turned to Sly "Why isn't she healing herself?" he asked, feeling despair in his words.

"I don't know, man. I have no experience with anything like this."

~~~

Air rasped in and out of her lungs and every breath was like being stabbed all over again except this time she could hardly breathe. She knew there was something she needed to do but was finding it so hard to stay awake; a blackness just kept pulling her into its warmth.

Her eyes flew open—Dane. She needed to tell him! She grasped at his shirt to pull him closer so that she could tell him. He bent his head close to hers.

"It's ok, can you hear the helicopter? You're gonna be fine." But she could see the tears running down his cheeks and glistening in his ink black eyelashes. It was funny the things you noticed when you were dying but he had the longest eyelashes she had ever seen, and she hadn't noticed before.

Struggling for breath now and fighting to stay conscious, Lauren declared in a quiet voice, "Love you," and then she coughed. "Wanted you to know," and then she let the darkness take her.

~~~

"Lauren, honey, no, don't go. I love you too. Please don't leave me."

He felt Sly pull at him. "Dane she's unconscious. Move out of the way and let the paramedics do their thing."

He hadn't even heard the Air Ambulance land as he was so focused on Lauren and making sure her chest rose and fell with each life-giving breath.

He let himself be pulled away as the paramedics gave her oxygen and put in a chest tube to drain her collapsed lung. Soon they had her stabilised and on a gurney waiting to be taken by air to hospital. Dane raced over. "I'm coming with you," he demanded.

"Are you next of kin?"

"I'm going to be," he said with as much conviction as Sly had ever seen.

"Okay, come on then," the paramedic said.

He turned to Sly. "Will you take care of things?"

"Yeah, of course, and actually Zack is back and is coming with Alpha team to clean this up before the police get here."

"Thanks, Sly," he said gratefully and squeezed Sly's shoulder.

Dane ran and jumped in the chopper as they were about to shut the doors. Lauren looked so pale and still. If it wasn't for the faint pulse in her neck, he would think he had already lost her. But she was a fighter and he wouldn't leave her side until she pulled through. He took her cold hand in his and rubbed her knuckles as he had after her scare with Drew. God, that seemed like a lifetime ago. He thought about what she'd said and wondered if she'd meant it or if it was the fear of dying making her think she loved him.

If she didn't then he'd just have to make her, because a life for him without her was inconceivable. He wanted them to get married and have children and grandchildren and grow old and learn to drive Lorries together and he hoped with all his heart that she wanted the same.

Chapter Twenty-Seven

At the hospital, the same doctors and nurses that had treated Nate met them. They crowded around her and quickly ushered her into the major trauma unit. Dane was left standing by the door bewildered. He had seen friends and colleagues shot and maimed, some losing limbs and even being killed and had never before lost his head.

He was always calm and in control. Now he just wanted to cry like a baby. He'd left everything too late. He slumped down onto the curb by the entrance and just sat and stared into space. What would he do if she died saving him? He couldn't live with it. What had made her do it? Why had she moved into the knife like that?

He felt a hand on his shoulder. Looking up, he saw Zack who sat down beside him.

They sat in silence for a while and then Zack turned to him "Like that, is it?"

Dane nodded solemnly. "She's it for me. I never saw it happening but that's the truth."

Zack nodded in agreement.

"I thought you were going to the scene?" Dane said.

"I was, but Sly said he'd handle it and that you could do with some support, so here I am. Come on, let's go see how your girl's doing."

They went into the hospital and up to the harried-looking receptionist. Dane managed to crack a smile as Zack charmed the older woman in seconds and had her eating out of his hand. That was Zack—007 smooth one minute and a cold hard killer the next.

"This lovely lady said we can wait back in the relatives' room while Lauren is in surgery." Sitting in the same room as he had when Nate was shot, Dane was glad for the quiet. Zack sat doing something on his phone and frowning a lot. He wanted to know what was going on with him but knew Zack wouldn't be pushed. He'd tell him if and when he was ready.

Letting his head fall back against the wall he kept replaying the scene in his head wondering if he could have known what she would do. Had there been a sign he'd missed but he kept coming back to the same answer of 'NO.' He never would have seen that happening no matter how many times it went down.

His head shot up when the doctor came in and he was relieved it was the same doctor that had treated Nate.

"Dane Bennett," he said, looking between him and Zack.

"Yes, that's me," he said, stepping forward.

"Miss Cassidy is in recovery. She had a punctured lung and her liver sustained some damage from the knife wound but she is very strong, and we managed to repair the damage. She'll need a lot of rest to allow her to recover properly and will probably need to stay in the hospital for a few days until we're satisfied that she is well enough to go home."

"Can I see her?"

"Yes, she was asking for you. Don't stay too long and try and keep her quiet; no upsetting her," he said, giving him a stern look. Dane shook his hand and thanked him again.

"I'm gonna get you guys a frequent flier card, I think," the doctor joked. Dane actually managed to crack a half smile at that before following him out. "Nurse Westerly will take you to her."

Following Nurse Westerly through to recovery, he was anxious to see Lauren and see for himself that she would be okay. Pushing open the door, he could see her tiny form lying in the bed. She had a drip in her arm and monitors on her fingers and upper arm. The white sheet that was pulled up to cover her chest made her seem deathly pale.

Pulling up a chair, he sat next to her and, taking her hand in his, he traced his finger along her pulse which was strong and steady. He felt hot tears fall down his cheeks and quickly dashed them away. Lauren was going to be fine; he needed to stop being such a cry-baby but God he had nearly lost her. He fell asleep like that until he felt her squeeze his fingers and looked up into the most beautiful face.

<p style="text-align:center">~~~</p>

Lauren felt like she had run a marathon and then been kicked by a horse. Everything hurt and it took her a minute to remember what had happened. Griffiths, the knife, *oh God Dane*. Struggling to open her eyes she nearly cried when she saw his head bent, holding her hand while he cried. Why was he crying? Was she dead? She didn't feel dead. She couldn't fight the sleep that was taking her back under though and closed her eyes.

She woke sometime later and looked down to see Dane asleep with his head on her hip and her hand still clutched in his. She squeezed his hand and then he looked up and she knew—she could see his emotions all over his face. He loved her.

"Dane," she croaked. He quickly got up and got her some water to sip.

"Small sips, honey." It felt like heaven as the cold water slipped down her throat.

"What happened?" she asked, and he explained what had happened after she was stabbed and how they had fixed up all her of injuries

"Can you remember what happened? Did he…?" God he couldn't say the words gulping he tried again. "Did he assault you, Lauren?"

Large tears filled her eyes as she shook her head "No, he touched me all over my body, but he didn't rape me. You got there before he had time to do anything else." She sobbed as she let out all the fear and pain she'd felt, as Dane held her and let her cry.

Dane wished Griffiths was alive so that he could kill him again.

After her tears and sobs had subsided, he could see her struggling to stay awake.

"Sleep now, Lauren. You're going to be fine. I won't leave you, I promise." And he meant it.

~~~

Over the next few days, people came and went, including Lucy, Sly, Nate, and her friend, Skye. Drew, who looked like he needed a hospital bed as much as she did, came every day. She'd been horrified when she'd heard what had happened with Marcus and scolded Drew for putting himself in danger like that. He had been unrepentant though and said he'd do it again in a heartbeat.

Lucy had brought food and clean clothes for Dane and he still wouldn't leave Lauren's side. Every time someone suggested he get some rest, he just growled at them and, in the end, they gave up. By day three, he was dead on his feet but still refusing to leave her. Lauren had tried to reason with him and convince him to go home and get some sleep, but he wouldn't hear of it.

She also tried to talk to him about what had happened, but he was stubbornly refusing to talk about it.

~~~

Dane was sitting looking out the window while Lauren slept when Zack walked in.

"A word," he stated, and it was clear it wasn't a question. Dane followed him out into the hallway, itching for an argument. Getting straight to the point, Zack continued.

"You need to go home and that's not a request." Zack gave him a hard look and waited for him to blow his top. He wasn't disappointed.

"Fuck you, Zack. You don't tell me what to do regarding this." Standing with his hands on his hips, Zack looked at Dane calmly. He was a good three inches taller and probably thirty pounds of muscle heavier than him, but he had no doubt that Dane would take him on pure adrenaline. Until of course that adrenaline ran out and Zack put him on his ass.

"Yes. I do. You work for me and you're exhausted. It's my responsibility to make sure you don't burn out. She's under Fortis' protection and also my responsibility." He knew it was coming so when Dane launched at him and got him against the wall, he wasn't surprised or worried.

"No, Lauren is mine. So back the fuck off, Zack. She is mine to protect." And just like that the fight went out of him.

Zack shrugged him off and watched as Dane slumped exhausted against the wall. "That is your one free one. If you ever do that again, I *will* kick your ass. Now go home and get a shower and some sleep. I'll watch over your Lauren for a few hours," he said emphasising the fact that he knew she was Dane's.

Dane knew he'd been played, but he also knew Zack was right; he was no good to anyone like this. He checked to make sure Lauren was resting and then left, taking Zack's Range Rover SVA. He loved this car but was in too much of a rush to get home to appreciate the luxury.

~~~

Lauren came slowly awake. She opened her eyes, expecting to see Dane sitting in his usual seat looking exhausted. When she didn't see him she looked around for him.

"He's gone home for a while," a deep voice said from the chair by the window. She turned to the voice and encountered a Norse God.

That was the only way to describe him. He had to be about six feet five inches with blonde hair and bluish grey eyes. He had the tanned complexion of someone who worked outside a lot and had broad defined muscles that rippled against his dress shirt as he walked towards her. He was all sleek powerful muscle and sinew without an ounce of fat anywhere.

He stopped a few feet from her with his arms crossed. He was dressed in a white shirt and dark grey dress trousers. The sleeves were rolled up on his shirt and that seemed to be the only concession against his sleek put together appearance.

"I'm Zack, owner of Fortis. I'm sorry I haven't been here to help with what's been happening, but I understand you've been taken care of," he said it like it was a reprimand. "I'll stay with you until he returns. I sent him home to shower and rest."

"Wow, how did you manage that?"

"I have my ways," he said with a sardonic grin. He seemed to study her then as if she was a bug under a microscope. "I consider Dane a friend. I won't see him hurt," he said bluntly.

Lauren felt her anger start to burn. "Excuse me?"

"I said I won't have Dane hurt by a SAS groupie."

Lauren felt like her head was going to explode with anger. If it wasn't for the fact that she was still weak from the attack and the obvious fact that this guy could snap her like a twig, she would kick his ass.

"Well, Mr High and bloody Mighty Fortis owner, I'm not a groupie. I love him with everything in me. If anyone wants to upset him, they're gonna need to go through me first, not that it's any of your goddamned business." All this she said from her prone position on the bed.

Zack looked at her, considering her, and then offered her a small smile that completely transformed his face but, despite all that hotness, he didn't stir her blood like Dane did.

But when he smiled, she could see how women would drop to their knees for him but not this woman. No, she had her man if they could just figure things out.

"So that was some kind of a test then to see how I felt about Dane?" she asked incredulously.

Zack nodded "You have to understand; he's my friend and I'm very protective of my friends," he said the last with a stern thoughtful face.

"Well I guess we're alike then," she said as he turned back to the window.

"I think I like you, Lauren, and I have just one question for you. Did you do it to protect him?"

She wasn't sure how to answer that. She knew what he meant but didn't feel comfortable telling him before she explained it to Dane. He turned and pinned her with a look that made most men tremble and the best he got was a raised pulse to show she was nervous.

"Don't answer that, I already know the answer," he said, turning back to the window again. "Yes, I definitely approve of you joining the Fortis family."

She snorted inelegantly. "Well the jury's still out on you, Mr Cockwomble."

Zack threw back his head and bellowed out a laugh.

"What did I miss? Did hell freeze over?" Lucy asked, looking confused as she strode through the door with Drew behind her. She smiled at Lauren and hooked her thumb back towards Zack. "Did he laugh? I ask because it's never been heard before. It's a bit like the Loch Ness Monster—it's been talked about but never proven."

Zack threw her a withering glare before returning to stare out the window. But Lauren could see that once you had Zack's loyalty you were golden. Coming over to the bed, Lucy bent down and hugged her and then moved back to allow Drew a hug.

"Are you okay?" she asked Drew.

"Seriously, sis, you almost died, and you keep asking me if I'm ok."

"Nah, it's all good. The doctor fixed me up fine," she replied shrugging it off. She knew it had been a close thing, but she didn't want to make too much of it in case it sent Dane into a meltdown. They still hadn't discussed what she'd done. She knew he was angry and, like the namby-pamby wimp she was, she didn't want to rock the boat.

"Drew's a Fortis guy now." Lucy said, proudly grabbing him in a headlock and knuckling his head.

"Get off me, you mad wench," he said, pushing her playfully. Lauren was happy to see that Drew had found another big sister. She looked at Drew for confirmation.

"Yeah, Zack's hired me as a trainee. I have a tonne of the tech stuff to learn still but Lucy and Sly have been training me in weapons and combat. It's gonna be a while before I'm ready to go out on any missions, but Nate has said he'll shadow me when he's back."

"That's wonderful news," she said, pulling Drew down for another hug. She looked at Zack. "Maybe you're not a Cockwomble after all."

He just nodded and chuckled in acknowledgement.

~~~

When Dane came back two hours later, he was surprised to see Lucy, Drew, Sly, and Zack all there.

"What's this?"

"Well we heard the guard dog had gone so we came for a visit," Lucy said, teasing him. "But it is time we left," she added, giving everyone pointed looks.

Everyone started to file out with hugs and kisses for Lauren, including Sly. Sly didn't surprise him but Zack, who was not prone to any outward sign of emotion, did surprise him when he winked at her and offered a small smile. It almost made Dane want to grab him by the throat again, but he managed to tamp down his jealousy.

He crossed to Lauren and kissed her cheek.

"How do you feel, honey?"

"Great—the doctor says I can go home tomorrow as long as I promise to rest," she smiled at him.

God, he loved her so much.

"That's great," he said. "Will you be okay on your own?"

Her face fell. "Well I was hoping you would be there to look after me," she said sounding uncertain.

He looked at her. How could she still trust him to look after her after he'd failed so spectacularly before?

"How can you trust me?" he asked simply.

"That's ridiculous. Of course, I trust you. I love you and I hoped that maybe you might feel the same?" She looked at him with such love and hope. Dane sat down next to her bed.

"God Lauren! I love you more than I ever thought it possible to love someone, but I failed you. You got stabbed because of me because I handled the situation with Griffiths all wrong."

"No, you didn't. I did that. I could see that you were going to tackle him and knew you would get shot and I couldn't let you. I threw myself forward to protect you because I love you and I knew I couldn't live without you."

"And yet you nearly sentenced me to the same fate, Lauren!"

He was trying to stay calm, but he felt all the helpless anger come rushing to the top.

"I died a thousand times while you lay there dying in my arms."

"I didn't know that you loved me. I thought perhaps you viewed me as a mistake." Dane felt his anger drain from him. This was his fault for being such an asshole to her and pushing her away. If he'd told her how he felt, maybe she would've stayed safe. Climbing on the bed and gently wrapping his arms around her, he held her for what seemed like an eternity.

"Honey, I'm so sorry. I pushed you away because I thought I would fail you and by doing so I did fail you." Lauren tried to speak. "No shush, let me finish. I did fail you but if you will let me, I want to spend every minute of every day making it up to you. I love you so much ,honey. You're the bullet to my gun, the Marge to my Homer, the gin to my tonic."

"Okay, okay, stop. I get it." She laughed but then stopped. "But really, you do?" She sounded so hesitant.

"Yes, I do. I want us to grow old together and have lots of kids and grandkids."

"Is that a proposal?"

"No, when I propose you'll know it," he said. "But if you ever pull a stunt like that again, I will blister your sweet little ass." He held her then as they talked about their hopes and dreams for the future. The nurse found them there asleep with her head on his shoulder.

Chapter Twenty-Eight

It had been ten days since Lauren had been released from the hospital and Dane had all but moved into her flat. They'd decided to stay at her flat while she recovered but would discuss other living arrangements in the future. She didn't care where they lived as long as they were together.

She'd been to his house once and had fallen completely in love with it. It was everything a family home should be; big spacious kitchen, large living room, four bedrooms and a massive secure garden. It even had a small guest lodge attached for when visitors came to stay.

They had settled into a perfect routine and she looked forward to his key in the lock every night. She wasn't unrealistic—she knew they would have disagreements, but she felt confident that nothing could tear them apart now. Dane had been wonderful, telling and showing her every day how much he loved her. Her confidence had returned, and she felt for the first time in years that everything would be okay.

She did however have one last hurdle to face and she had to persuade Dane to help her. She wasn't sure how she was going to broach this subject with him, but she wanted to meet her father. She knew he had been moved to a top-secret facility after he'd been detained. Dane had been so attentive and gentle and patient, but she needed to move on with her life and she couldn't do that until she'd faced Marcus Preedy.

She'd put in a call to Andreo earlier and had him deliver all of Dane's favourite foods. She'd showered and dressed in a soft pink off the shoulder top that hung to her thighs and a soft Jersey pencil skirt in cream. She wanted sexy but comfortable as her side was still tender.

Lauren wasn't used to being a 'femme fatale' but she was going to try and get around him using every feminine trick she could. She felt a little nervous but kept reminding herself that this was Dane—he loved her and would never reject her or laugh at her.

She set the cutlery and linens on the coffee table in the living room and waited. A few minutes later, she heard his car outside. Hearing his key in the lock gave her the biggest thrill and made her tummy twitch all at the same time. He came straight over and gave her a toe-curling kiss.

"Hey."

"Hey, yourself. I missed you!" she said silkily.

"I like this top," he said, stroking his fingers over her bare shoulder, making her all hot and tingly. He kissed her neck and bare shoulder before pulling himself away.

"Sorry, I can't seem to control myself around you."

"Don't *ever* apologise for that I love it. I asked Andreo to deliver us something for dinner. I thought maybe we could relax and just eat a nice meal."

"Sounds great. Let me get a quick shower first."

~~~

She was up to something, he just didn't know what, but Lauren didn't do subtle and she was definitely trying to butter him up for something. He didn't mind. In fact, he was just going to enjoy it and see what happened. Rushing through another cold shower, he hurried back to Lauren who was dishing up all his favourites from Andreo's.

They ate a beautiful meal of seafood linguine followed by Tiramisu. He could see she was nervous and although he was enjoying making her squirm, he felt kinda bad too.

"Come here," he said gently, pulling her onto his lap. "Now are you gonna tell me what this is all about and don't lie—I can read you like a book and you're up to something."

"Really, you knew, and you let me suffer?" she pouted.

"Well yeah," he said. "It was just so much fun. So, what's up?"

She looked at his handsome face with its five o'clock shadow and couldn't believe how lucky she was to have this wonderful man in her life.

"I want to see my father," she blurted out.

He looked at her. Considering everything she'd been through lately, he wanted to protect her but knew that sometimes the best he would be able to do would be to stand by her side.

"Okay, I'll arrange it."

"Really? Just like that you'll do it?"

"Yes, you need closure. But I want to be there. I don't want this bastard upsetting you."

She moved over him to straddle his hips and leaned forward to kiss him.

"Thank you."

"You're welcome," he said in a slightly strained voice.

~~~

Lauren could feel the strain of him holding himself in check; he had been so restrained around her since she was hurt. But she didn't want him to hold back. She needed to feel him moving inside her, showing her without words how he felt. She slowly started to grind her body into the hard bulge in his jeans and leaned up to feather light kisses along his jaw.

"Honey, what are you doing?" She almost laughed at the strained sound.

"Nothing," she replied. "Just showing you how much I appreciate you," she said with a grin. He placed both his hands on her hips to still her.

"Yeah well, you're gonna kill me." She got up off his lap and crossed to the other side of the coffee table.

"Well, if you're not interested, I guess I could just take care of it myself," she said while lowering the shoulder of her top more and bending forward so that he could see she was braless. She could see the fire in his eyes and his hands clenched on the arms of the chair. She lowered her hand and lifted the edge of her skirt slowly lifting it to reveal the black lace boxers she wore. "But if you're not interested, I can sort this problem out myself."

Lauren ran her hands over her legs and hips as she said it. She turned around and sauntered towards the bedroom, putting an extra sway in her hips, shimmying out of her skirt as she went. Before she made it halfway across the living room, Dane was on her. She squealed with laughter as he grabbed her by the waist, careful to avoid her injury as he twisted her so that she straddled his waist.

"Nobody takes care of this," he said running his hands over her breasts and mons, "except me and do you know why?"

"No, why?" God was that her voice? She sounded breathy like a virgin straight out of a Victorian romance novel.

"Because you're mine."

Lauren shivered at the commanding tone of his voice. He lifted her with one arm so that he could remove her top and settled her on the bed. He then proceeded to show her just how much he revered her body.

He blew on her aching breasts, then nipped at them and blew again causing them to bead tightly. Kissing his way down her body, he nipped at her hip and then, with so much tenderness that she almost cried, kissed the scar left by the knife wound that almost killed her.

~~~

Lifting her up so that he could remove her underwear and position his hands under the perfect globes of her ass, Dane settled himself so that he was kneeling between her thighs; he inhaled her heady scent and then rubbed his rough cheek against her soft thighs. He gently kissed her there and then, using the flat of his tongue, he licked her before plunging it inside her.

~~~

She held onto the sheets to keep herself anchored as she raised her hips, silently asking for more. As if reading her mind, he replaced his tongue with his fingers and slid them inside her as he sucked her clit into his mouth hard. She bucked off the bed as her climax shuddered through her; he continued sucking but gentled his touch and eased her down.

He crawled up her delicious body and she reached for him.

"You're over-dressed," she said huskily. He got up and quickly stripped his jeans and shirt off. Lauren's breath hitched when she realised he had been commando under his jeans. Crawling in beside her, he adjusted her so that she was lying atop him.

"I don't want to hurt you," he said with such love and passion in his eyes.

"I'm fine," she said and bent down to nip at his neck. As she raked her nails over his nipples, he gave a full body shudder, so she did it again and felt his hard cock twitch against her stomach.

"Lauren," he growled.

She took pity on him and ran her fingertips down his pecs and over his ripped abs until she felt the soft leaking tip of his cock. She scooted down him so that she was sitting astride his thighs. She looked at his cock; it was beautiful with veins running up it. He was circumcised and she loved the look and feel of it.

She licked her lips and he groaned again. Leaning down, she licked the tip, tasting the salty sweetness of him. It made her hungry for more, so she gently took the head in her mouth and twirled her tongue around before sinking lower. With each pass, she took more of him until she took him right to the back of her throat.

She continued to suck and lick and then added her hand and squeezed and twisted in a corkscrew motion at the same time as relaxing her throat and taking him even deeper. She felt his hands tighten in her hair and his hips start to buck as he tried to take control and she loved it. She was so turned on by his reaction, she could feel her desire slick on her thighs.

He was getting so close but he wanted to come inside of her body, not in her mouth. Not this time anyway. Pulling her off his now out-of-control cock, he pulled her farther up his body and positioned himself at her entrance.

"This is gonna be quick," he said. She lowered herself down onto his throbbing cock inch by delicious inch until she was fully seated. She stayed like that for a second until her body adjusted to him and then she started the slow rhythm that drove him mad.

Dane could see she was tiring and flipped her over onto her back so that he could do all the work. He tried to go slow, but his body just took over and soon he was pistoning into her like an animal. He could feel his climax start to build in his spine as her muscles started to contract around him. He reached between them and rubbed her clit how he knew she liked, and then she was bucking wildly underneath him. His body exploded in the most powerful climax he had ever had, leaving him spent and struggling to catch his breath.

Collapsing beside her, he dragged her into his arms and held her so that their bodies were still connected. It was only when he felt his seed start to leak from her body that he realised they had done it again.

"Honey, we didn't use anything again." She was silent for a moment and he wondered if he'd screwed up again.

"Would it matter so much if I did get pregnant?" she said, hesitantly.

Dane went quiet and thought about what she had said, and the more he thought about it the more he liked the idea of her rounded with his baby. He sat up on one elbow and leaned down to look at her. "No, not to me it wouldn't. I love you, Lauren, and would love for you to be pregnant with our child. The only problem is if we start this now, you're gonna have to marry me." As he said it, he reached over into the pocket of his jeans, which were carelessly thrown across the bottom of the bed and produced a small box. He slowly lifted the lid to reveal a beautiful platinum sapphire and diamond trilogy engagement ring.

"So, honey will you marry me and make me the happiest man alive?"

Lauren looked at the wonderful man who had stolen her heart and, with tears spilling down her cheeks, nodded. "Yes. Yes, I'll marry you." She kissed him as he placed the ring on her finger.

"I did have this whole romantic picnic planned but this just seemed right."

"It's perfect. I love it."

~~~

Lauren could feel nerves knotting her stomach as they approached the derelict buildings on an industrial-sized compound ten miles outside the city. It had only taken Dane a day to arrange the visit with her father.

They'd blindfolded her for the drive over as per the instructions from the covert agency now holding her father. They had let her remove it as they entered the compound. Zack had put in a call to some of his contacts to get her this meeting.

She wasn't sure what to expect from Marcus. Her mother had been terrified of him, but she knew that, at one time, her mother had loved this man. Surely, he couldn't be all bad. Drew was a wonderful man despite him. Confusion mixed with fear and curiosity and a small sliver of hope was giving her a headache. Beside her, Dane was like a growly papa bear, holding tight to her hand and offering support.

She knew he was worried about this meeting and if it might upset her, but she was made of strong stuff. If the last few months had taught her anything, it was that nothing people could do should be a surprise. Lauren squeezed his hand and offered a smile of reassurance for him that she was okay.

Pulling up outside the furthest building, they got out and she looked around. It might look derelict and abandoned but there were cameras following their every move and the razor wire around the perimeter fence proved it was anything but what it seemed at first glance.

With the butterflies from her stomach now making an appearance in her throat, she took some deep breaths as she followed Zack into the building. She had forgiven him for his rude behaviour in the hospital and found she quite liked him. Which surprised her. He was physically intimidating, cold and aloof. But when you got past that hard exterior, he was in fact the exact opposite. He was loyal and kind and had been very thoughtful towards her.

Three large men in black fatigues met them as they approached the door. They had large automatic weapons over their shoulders, and she could see knives sheathed in cases on their legs. The first man stepped forward to shake hands with Dane and Zack; he was obviously in charge here.

He exuded the kind of raw power and careful control that Zack did, but more than that it was the way he silently took charge and the other two looked to him for his reactions. He turned to Lauren next who was still tightly clutching Dane's hand.

"Miss Cassidy, I'm Jack Granger." He held out his hand for her to shake. He had a strong grip that she appreciated. Most men gave a limp handshake when greeting a woman and she hated it.

"Thank you for arranging this," Lauren said.

He nodded and turned, indicating they should follow him. The other two men fell in behind them, making her slightly twitchy. As if noticing her uneasiness, Dane rubbed her knuckles with his thumb.

"It's okay. They're the good guys, honey." It calmed her to know that he was relaxed; as relaxed as he and Zack ever got. They walked down a long corridor with white walls and artificial lighting before coming to a door with a keypad and a retina scanner. Stepping up to the scanner, Granger allowed the machine to scan his eye before keying the keypad. The door swished open and he ushered them in.

In front of them was another set of double doors with armed men on either side. What was this place? She hadn't asked Dane about it because she assumed it was some sort of government facility but now, she wasn't so sure.

"What is this place?" she asked Granger.

"This is our holding and interrogation facility."

"So, you're the government?"

He smirked then and gave a little chuckle. "Not exactly, Miss Cassidy"

She processed his non-answer as she followed them past the armed men. Granger showed them into a viewing room with seats and monitors and bulletproof one-way glass.

"I'll bring your father into this room so that you can see him first then Dane will let me know when you're ready and I will escort you in to speak to him."

She nodded at him. God, that's all she seemed to do these days, nod like a numpty.

"Does he know I'm coming?" she asked him then, feeling the nerves tighten her stomach.

"No, the prisoner doesn't know anything." He walked out leaving them alone.

"Do you want me to come in with you?" Dane asked while gently brushing his hands up and down her arms. It was warm outside but down in this underground whatever it was she was chilled and goose bumps had broken out on her skin.

"No. I need to do this on my own, but thank you." She leaned up to kiss him.

"Okay, but if he upsets you, I'm pulling you out."

Just then, the door to the interrogation room opened and one of Granger's men led a tall wiry man with greying blonde hair into the room.

They made him sit and then cuffed his wrists and ankles to bolts on the table and floor. He faced the glass and Lauren got her first good look at the man who had fathered her. She definitely had his colouring, but she had her mother's eyes and nose, as well as her face shape and build. Her father had a long thin face which was clean-shaven, and his hair was combed neatly to the side although it was definitely thinning. His eyes were the same colour as hers although his were cold and calculating and held no warmth or kindness.

"Okay, I'm ready," she said, straightening her shoulders and taking a deep breath. Dane knocked on the door and Granger opened it.

"Ready?" he asked in a calm voice.

"Yes," she replied, following him out and waiting for him to unlock the interrogation room door.

Before opening the door, he said, "If you want out, just say so. We have eyes and ears on you at all times."

Opening the heavy door, he allowed her to walk in on her own and then shut the door behind her.

~~~

She turned to face the man that she and her mother had spent nearly all her life hiding from.

"Lauren. God, you're the image of your mother." He looked shocked, shaken even. She crossed to the chair opposite him and sat down silently. She wasn't sure how long her suddenly weak knees would support her, and she didn't want to show any weakness in front of this man. Lauren could feel his eyes on her studying her intently.

"Why did you kill my friend?" She was blunt and she didn't care. She didn't know this man and felt nothing for him. She was waiting for some sort of love or recognition to kick in, but it just didn't come. All she saw was a cold man who had hurt people to get his way. He didn't answer her question.

"Did Griffiths hurt you?"

"Yes, he did. Why? Do you care?" she asked calmly

"You're my daughter, of course I care." They studied each other then, both silently trying to get a read on the other.

"Did she look after you? Your mother?" he asked instead.

She considered her answer while they studied each other. "She was the most wonderful mother anyone could ask for," she declared.

"Was?"

"Yes, she died a few years ago." She refused to give him details which he didn't deserve. He paled then and bowed his head.

"I loved her like no other. She was the love of my life—and she left me. I came home one day, and you were both gone." Lauren could see he was lost in his thoughts as he relived the past.

"She was terrified of you," she stated.

His head shot up then and he sneered.

"I only ever punished her for her own good to make her understand that she had to toe the line. She was so blind sometimes, she couldn't see the bigger picture of our ways."

"You don't punish people you love." she declared, incredulous.

He snorted. "Well I can see depriving you of a father left you undisciplined and insubordinate," he stated coldly. "She took you from me just because she couldn't handle a little discipline."

She could feel anger boil in the pit of her stomach. "You beat her; you were out of control with your obsession."

"You don't understand, Lauren; the gifted ones are the only ones who can cleanse the earth of evil and bring order to the world." He was a psychopath—he had to be. "She took you from me with the help of that bitch, Larissa. She helped your mother leave me and then took advantage of my pain to worm her way into my life and what did I get? That pathetic idiot Drew."

Lauren had never felt sorrier for Drew. He'd had the pain of being brought up by this man for seven years. She couldn't believe that he had remained so kind and pure when he was surrounded by such evil. She didn't try to defend Drew; she knew there was no point.

"Well, Drew is one of the best things that ever happened to me."

Marcus snorted at that, unbelieving.

"Tell me, Lauren, can you still heal?" He caught her off guard with his question. He must have noticed the flicker of unease that crossed her face because he smiled.

"Ah, you can. You'll be a wonderful addition to the Divine Watchers."

"You're insane. There is no way that I would help you or your sick friends." He smiled then, a sick twisted smile which made the bile rise in her throat.

"That's what your friend thought. She thought she was too good for us. But in this world, there are always ways to bend people to our will and we have some very powerful allies."

"Well, I guess we don't have to worry about you now, do we?" she said with false confidence. He laughed then, a chilling cold sound.

"You can cut the head off the snake, Lauren, but it will then grow two in its stead. I am but the tip of the iceberg."

"So why kill Claire?" she asked.

"She was being difficult and refusing to go to the clinic. She thought she was too good to help us and was going to start making a fuss. Then that idiot Terry Griffiths started fawning around her, so we had to dispose of her. I should have killed him then too, but he was a very handy person to have around the hospital, so I thought it was worth the risk. Your boyfriend did us all a favour when he killed him." Lauren didn't correct him that it was Sly that had killed him. Had they fed Marcus false information to trick him somehow? She didn't care either way; she just knew that he would never be anything to her but a monster from her past. Picking up the conversation, she continued,

"But Claire didn't know anything about what you did."

"No, she didn't know of our plans, but she knew enough to cause problems and threatened to go to the press. We couldn't afford the attention."

"But what did you want her for?"

"Ah Lauren, I can't tell you that until you agree to join us." He looked pointedly down at her engagement ring then, which she was twirling on her finger. "I'm disappointed he didn't have the decency to ask me for your hand in marriage, but no matter. I look forward to meeting my grandchildren and hopefully they will all have your gift." He leaned back in his chair then, looking relaxed like this was normal.

She was incredulous—he was mad as a box of frogs, he had to be. One minute talking about the world being cleansed and the next calmly telling her how he had her friend murdered. Lauren stood—she'd seen enough. This man was nothing to her and she knew that whatever happened to him she would feel no remorse. "You are nothing but a sick coward that hides behind strong people who are better than you." Then, head held high, she walked to the door that now stood open for her. As she walked through, Dane was there and she sagged into his arms.

"Take me home, please."

~~~

Lauren was very quiet on the drive back and Dane was worried about her. Several times Zack had been forced to restrain him so that he didn't go in there and drag her away from the sick evil that had fathered her. How could someone so kind and wonderful come from that much evil?

Thank God her mother had gotten her away from him or his evil would have swallowed her up. They'd decided to go back to Fortis before going home. They hadn't told Lucy or Drew about their engagement, wanting to get this meeting with her father over with first. Zack knew—of course he didn't miss anything—but he hadn't said anything to anyone else.

Arriving at Fortis was a relief. He wanted to get this done so that he could take her home—she was still recovering from her injuries and he didn't want to tire her out. It was all quiet in the outer office when they arrived. Zack and Dane had talked about getting a receptionist so that the outside world would believe they were a normal security specialists' company, not a specialist company that did government black ops jobs as well, but as yet they hadn't gotten around to it.

They walked hand in hand to the tech room were Lucy was showing Drew some of their new highly secretive surveillance equipment. Both looked up as Lauren and Dane entered.

Coming over, Lucy hugged her brother and then Lauren. Stepping back, she suddenly zeroed in on Lauren's hand as if she was some super-guided missile. Squealing like Imelda Marcos at a shoe sale, she started jumping up and down while holding Lauren's hand.

"Oh my God is that… did you?"

Dane laughed. "Yes, and yes."

Wondering what all the fuss was about, Drew came over.

Seeing Lucy's face, he asked, "What? What did I miss?"

Still jumping with excitement, Lucy grabbed Lauren's hand and shoved it in Drew's face.

"They're engaged."

Drew looked at them both. "Really? That's great! Congratulations." He hugged his sister and then pretended as if he was gonna hug Dane.

Dane stepped back "Hey man, we ain't brothers yet," he said laughing, but then grabbed Drew in a headlock and messed his hair up.

"God—why do you people keep doing that?" he asked, smoothing his hair out but secretly he liked it. He'd never had a proper family and loved having one now one that seemed to care about him.

Lucy was in heaven. "When are you getting married?"

Lauren and Dane looked at each other. "We haven't thought about it really," she said.

"Maybe early next spring?" He looked at Lauren for her answer. She gave him the most beautiful smile.

"Perfect."

~~~

By this time, Nate had hobbled in on his crutches and Sly came with him. It turned out the bullet had nicked Nate's femur and they had to put steel pins in it. She had offered to heal him but he had flat-out refused, saying she needed all her energy to help herself get better.

Lauren hated that she could only heal certain things and that she couldn't heal herself. However, she wondered if the ability to heal herself would have made her more flippant about life. She hoped not but it wasn't as if she could control it anyway, so she put it from her mind.

They came straight over to the group and, hearing the news, slapped Dane on the back and hugged her.

"If this guy doesn't treat you right, you let me know," Nate said with a friendly wink. Dane gave him a friendly punch on the arm and banter ensued. Lucy dragged Lauren over to the computer.

"We have so much to do; let's check out the wedding pages."

"Great. You know, I think I'm gonna like having a sister," Lauren said quietly and put her arm around Lucy for a hug. Lucy hugged her back and smiled and they sat down to plan.

~~~

Climbing into bed that night, Lauren was exhausted but had never been happier. She missed her mum and wished she was here but she'd found a wonderful man who loved her and was getting an instantly large family. They had skyped his dad, who was thrilled, and they had arranged to meet next week. The only person who didn't know was Daniel; they wanted to tell him in person.

She cuddled up to Dane's warm body and thought about the man who had fathered her. She found it hard to believe that they had the same blood running through their veins—or her brother for that matter. The only parent they shared was a maniac and yet they were normal.

She thought about Claire and still couldn't understand why she had kept so many secrets. She missed her so much. She felt herself drifting off to sleep and smiled she had her family and life went on that was all that mattered.

Chapter Twenty-Nine

Zack pored over the evidence that had been gathered when Marcus Preedy's house had been raided. Most of it seemed to be in a language that neither he nor his team recognised. Fortis had agreed to take the lead on this. The government would try Michaels for the murder of Claire Thompson, and Marcus Preedy would be kept out of it until they knew how far up it went.

The intel that they could decipher so far suggested that some government agencies had been compromised so, at the demand of the Home Secretary, this was staying completely off the radar until it came time for the praise. Then they would swoop in and take credit. Zack and his team preferred it this way anyway, as they weren't in it for the glory.

Looking again at the files in front of him, he sighed and rubbed his hand across his eyes. He was going to have to call her; they hadn't spoken in two years—not since that last mission in Afghanistan. She'd probably tell him to go fuck himself after the way he'd left things, but she was the best linguist in the world,. So, he was gonna have to suck it up and call her. A light knock on his door had him looking up.

"Sly, what can I do for you?" Sly looked tired; not regular tired but how he himself had looked before he quit the Special Forces.

"I wanted to let you know that I've decided to take you up on your offer to join Fortis."

Zack stood up and came around the desk; he leaned back against the desk and crossed his arms across his broad chest. "What made you change your mind?"

Sly paused. "I saw how quickly you got things done without the red-tape. I love what I do but everything is just so political now, it takes forever to get anything done." Zack nodded his head and held out his hand. "Welcome to Fortis."

Sly smiled. "I need to finish this last tour, then I'm all yours. It's an eight-month tour so I'll be free by the end of March."

"Be safe," Zack said and turned back to his desk, dismissing him.

~~~

Sly liked how no-nonsense Zack was and how he didn't speak just for the sake of it, he thought as he wandered down the hall. He looked up and found himself outside the tech room and, sure enough, there was Lucy. He watched her unnoticed. She was so beautiful with her long thick wavy chestnut hair pulled into a ponytail. She was concentrating really hard and doing that cute little thing with her tongue. It peeked out from the corner of her mouth, all pink and inviting.

She turned then and caught him looking.

"Sly!" She jumped up and ran to him. She was always like this—so happy to see him. It broke his heart that he had left it too late. She was Nate's now.

"Hey, I just dropped by to let Zack know I'd be accepting his job offer."

"You did? That's great. Are you bugging out soon?"

"Yeah, I'm heading back to base first thing."

She threw her arms around his neck and held on tight. He let his arms go around her and just held her tight, enjoying the feel of her pressed to his body and the scent of her tickling his nose. She leaned back and then kissed him gently on the lips and it was the sweetest kiss he had ever had—it was only a gentle meeting of lips, but it was the most intoxicating kiss ever and it killed him.

"You stay safe and come back to us, okay?"

"Of course, can't deprive the world of all this perfection," he laughed.

He pulled back before he embarrassed them both. "Say goodbye to Nate for me."

She frowned. "Okay, I will when I see him."

~~~

Lucy watched as Jace walked away and she prayed that he would come back to them. She had loved Jace since the day Dane had brought him home after they had passed selection. She had only been a teenager, but she had known even then. Of course he never saw her as a woman; he saw her as Dane's baby sister. She'd watched as, over the years, he had brought different girlfriends to their family gatherings, and bided her time. Well, that time was up. When Jace came back, she was gonna tell him how she felt and to hell with pride.

~~~

It was two weeks since Lauren had seen her father—or Marcus as she thought of him. She had thought a lot about her mum and Claire in the last few weeks, and the fear that both women she cared about had faced at the hands of that man. She'd arranged for everyone she loved and who had loved Claire to have a picnic and family day up on Hay Bluff on an August bank holiday.

They had arrived early so that they could all spend the day together. Everyone had brought some sort of food. Sylvie had brought her German potato salad and Lucy had brought enough cupcakes to feed an army. Lauren and Dane had brought meats and a portable barbecue that Zack was now dominating, much to Malcolm's annoyance.

The whole group was having a wonderful time. Even Dane's sister Lizzie, her husband and son Mateo had come. Paige and Mateo were getting on like old friends and Daniel looked a little better too. He had been relieved when everything had become known about Terry Griffiths but also horrified that Claire hadn't told him.

She had a feeling it was going to take a while for him to come to terms with everything that had happened, but watching him with

Paige now gave her hope. Seeing Dane playing tag with Mateo and Paige and throwing them up in the air had made her so broody and she couldn't wait for it to be their turn. He was going to make a wonderful father.

After everyone had eaten until they could hardly move, the group started to break up. Lizzie, Lucy, Drew, Daniel, and the kids went for a walk up the bluff. Sylvie, Malcolm and Colin—Dane's dad—just sat, enjoying the peace and tranquillity. Nate and Zack decided to test the new mini-drone they had acquired and went in the other direction. Taking Lauren's hand, Dane pointed around the bluff.

"Want to take a walk?"

"Yes, sure why not?" Walking along the bluff in the sunshine with a gentle wind tickling her neck, she felt happier than she ever hoped to be. She was all healed from her wound and physically was fit. She'd started having nightmares about her abduction and the attack by Terry Griffiths, and had agreed to see someone about it next week. Dane had wanted to go with her, but she didn't want him to. She needed to face this on her own, not have him save her.

Pulling her gently to a stop, Dane pulled out an envelope from his pocket.

"What's this?"

"Sit down and read it."

She sat down with slight trepidation; the feelings of contentment from moments ago gone. Sitting down next to Lauren, Dane put his arm around her back and gave her the envelope. Her hand shook when she saw the handwriting. Opening it slowly, she began to read:

My Dearest Lauren,
If you're reading this, then the fates have prevailed, and I am dead. I'm sure you have so many questions you want to ask. I will try to address the obvious ones. I did have a dream about my getting shot, but in my dream, Daniel always tried to stop him and we both ended up

dead. That is why I couldn't tell anyone. If he had found out, my beautiful Paige would be growing up an orphan and I couldn't let that happen.

Secondly, I knew Terry Griffiths had a crush on me, but it wasn't until the night I was to be shot that I realised how sick and dangerous he was. He had broken into my house and was going through my underwear drawer when I came home from work. I played it cool and told him we would be together soon, and he agreed to leave. I am writing this letter now as I know I don't have long left. The tumour is inoperable, and I knew if I told you, you would have wanted to try to heal me. We both know you can't heal this type of thing and that would have eaten you up inside. I decided on no treatment when I found out about the tumour being terminal. I didn't want Paige to remember me as sick and weak from chemotherapy or radiation, especially as it wasn't going to work. Please understand I didn't tell you out of love for you not for any other reason. Lauren, please be careful. The Divine Watchers are evil, and they are coming for you. My time is nearly up. Please know that I love you, my dearest friend. I am not afraid and when I die, it will be with happiness in my heart for all the love I have received from you all. Please take care of my Paige and Daniel for me.

All my love,

Claire

xx

P.S. I wish you and Dane as much happiness as Daniel and I had. (Yes, I dreamt that too).

Dane held her while she sobbed her heart out. He'd known the letter would be hard for her to read but also knew it would help her to heal. He had been shocked when Daniel had given it to him this morning. Daniel had found it tucked into the back of Claire's writing desk. There had been a letter for him and one for Paige too for when she was older. Lauren straightened up and wiped her eyes.

"Feel better?"

She nodded. "Strangely yes, I do."

"Ready to go back?"

"Can we just sit for a bit please?"

"Yes, of course." They sat like that with her nestled in Dane's arms for a while until Lauren felt composed and ready to face everyone.

"I must look a right state now."

He cupped her face. "You're beautiful even with red eyes," and he tweaked her nose.

When they returned, Lauren sought out Daniel, and Dane watched as they talked and embraced. She was so brave and loving and he still couldn't believe how lucky he was to have finally convinced her to be his forever. He felt someone come up behind him and turned around to see his father.

"Hey Dad, are you having fun?"

"Are you kidding? Running around after my grandson and spending time with my most wonderful children, of course I am." His father looked thoughtful then.

"I'm so glad you have found a love like your mother and I had," he said. Dane didn't want to talk about this his feelings. He still felt guilty about how unfair he had been to his mother and was about to say so when his father stopped him.

"I'm so glad you know the truth now after all these years. She was such a wonderful woman but after what happened, she changed—she just couldn't forgive herself and the only time she stopped hurting was when she drank. But she loved you all so much and would be so proud of you all."

Dane wasn't sure what to say. He'd adored his mother and had such mixed feelings about her. On the one hand, he still loved and missed her every day. On the other, he couldn't quite forgive her for not loving him enough to stop drinking earlier. He knew he was being unreasonable and childish but, after nearly thirty years of feeling betrayed, he couldn't just switch it off, although it didn't hurt thinking about her anymore

He didn't understand it either and knew he would never change, but he couldn't say that to his father. She had been the love of his dad's life and he wasn't going to upset him by telling how he felt, so he just said, "I know she did."

~~~

Colin Bennet watched his son walk towards the woman he loved and said a silent prayer of thanks. He loved and respected Lauren and could see how much she loved Dane. That was all he ever wanted for his children—to find a love like he'd had.

He watched as Lizzie sat alone, watching everything going on around her. He was worried about her; she had such sad eyes these days. Yes, something was amiss there, and he would have to keep an eye out. As for his baby girl, he knew she'd been in love with Jace for years and vice versa. If those two didn't figure this out soon, maybe he would have to do a little meddling.

Looking back towards Mateo being swung around by Dane, he felt excited at the prospect of more grandchildren to spoil and had a feeling he wouldn't have to wait long.

They all spent the rest of the afternoon playing games of French cricket, and flying kites. The day had been relaxing, cathartic and almost healing—just what Lauren hoped for a day for family and fun.

Epilogue

November

The room looked beautiful; Lucy had really gone all-out with it. She had white candles on every table and vases of cream roses dotted all around the entrances and exits. The entire ceiling had blankets of fairy lights, making it look like stars against the black fabric she had hung from the ceiling. She'd arranged for caterers to mingle with the guests and hand out canapés throughout the evening, and then a hot buffet would be set out around ten. Lauren was touched by how she had been welcomed into the Fortis family. She looked around at all the people who had come to celebrate her and Dane's engagement. The women were all decked out in party dresses and the men were handsome in shirts and trousers. She had come to love these people so much so quickly.

She hadn't stopped smiling since she'd left the clinic. Now that the shock had worn off and the fear over Dane's reaction, she was buzzing with excitement. Would they be early? Was it a girl and a boy or two boys or two girls, and did she want to find out?

What would they need to buy? Would she go back to work? So much to decide she couldn't think straight, but in the best way. She was having twins—two babies to love. She had to keep pinching herself to make sure it wasn't a dream.

Dane had already started the overprotective thing, even trying to help her dress earlier although that might have been a ploy as she hadn't ended up dressed—more like naked.

He hadn't left her side except to get her a drink and was constantly telling her to sit down and rest. She resisted the urge to berate him as she knew it was done with the best of intentions.

"I'm fine, Dane. I just want to talk to our guests." She laid a hand on his butt then, knowing it would distract him from his thoughts.

"You don't play fair, woman. I'll get my revenge when these babies are born," he threatened.

"Promises, promises," she laughed.

Just then, Skye and Nate walked in and for a second Lauren didn't recognise her.

Dane followed her line of sight. "Who's that with Nate?"

"That's Skye."

"Holy hell I didn't recognise her, poor Nate doesn't stand a chance," he said with a laugh.

"That was the idea." She winked at him.

"What have you been up to?" he asked suspiciously.

"Nothing," she said feigning ignorance.

"Um, why don't I believe you?"

She just smiled. "Dance with me?"

"My pleasure." He drew her out on to the dance floor as Ed Sheeran's "Thinking Out Loud" came on. He held her then as if she was the most precious thing on earth and as they danced to the song, he sang the words to her.

~~~

Dane couldn't remember a feeling like this. This right here was what it was all about. Life couldn't get better. He had the woman he loved and two beautiful babies on the way. He placed his hand on her still flat abdomen and chuckled at his earlier response. That was one for the grandkids and he was sure Lucy would take full advantage.

"What's got you laughing?"

"Just thinking about my unmanly reaction earlier."

"It was kinda funny in hindsight!" she agreed. The song ended.

"So, you ready to do this?" he asked.

"So ready."

They walked to the microphone the DJ had kindly set up on the stage. Dane tapped the microphone to get everyone's attention and the lights came up a bit.

"Sorry, folks. I don't want to take up much of your time. Lauren and I would just like to thank everyone for coming and sharing our engagement party with us, and a special thank you to my dad, Colin, and my pain in the butt, I mean lovely baby sister, Lucy. They've worked so hard and we really appreciate it. If it doesn't work out at Fortis, you've always got a job as an events planner, Luce." This was met with nods of agreement from some and laughter from others.

"What makes you think I can't do both?" Lucy shouted with a smile.

"This is true, bratfink, but anyway back to me." Dane said, making everyone laugh. "We have however decided to put the wedding on hold for a while." He paused then as murmurs started up. "We are going to postpone," he continued, "as we are going to be busy becoming parents." There were shouts of glee from their friends and family, and high-fives from some. Dane frowned; he hadn't expected that.

"Come on, Drew, pay up," shouted Nate.

"You guys knew!" he said looking from them to Lauren.

"They guessed weeks ago," said Sly. "Nate here's been running a book. Come on, you don't honestly think you can keep anything from us, do you?"

Recovering himself, Dane said "Well," and he looked at Lauren who winked, "did we mention its twins?" The room went quiet for a second and then erupted with noise; everyone was coming over, congratulating them and hugging them. Colin had tears in his eyes as he hugged them both.

"I'm so happy and proud right now. I think I need a whisky to calm me down." Colin sniffled as he headed for the bar.

They found themselves surrounded by Nate, Skye, Drew, Lucy, Sly, Zack and Daniel and Lizzie who was strangely alone. Dane was gonna speak to Lucy about that later.

"So, who told you?" Dane asked them all, looking at Zack.

"Not me," Zack said, holding up his hands in surrender.

"You knew!" Lucy said in mock outrage.

"Only because he found me after a particularly vicious bout of morning sickness," defended Lauren.

"Oh, I hear ya sister," said Lizzie, and Skye nodded her agreement.

"Your dad mentioned something that got me thinking," Nate said, "so we paid attention and when we noticed you downloading 'what to expect when you're expecting' onto your iPad we guessed."

"So, you've been spying on me and gossiping like old women."

"Well, Lucy did that bit," Drew said.

Lucy looked at Drew then with her hands on her hips "Thanks, buddy."

Dane looked at Lucy and was about to lecture her when Zack interrupted.

"We'll talk about the gross misuse of company property on Monday." But everyone knew he didn't mean it.

"Seriously though congratulations. We couldn't be happier for you," said Lizzie, hugging them both. "If I can do anything to help or if you need to ask anything just call," she said this to Lauren but turned to include Dane. "You too. I know you and you'll drive her crazy so if you're worried, call me."

"Thanks sis," he said hugging her. "So where is Marco tonight?" Lizzie looked around but luckily people had started to wander off.

"Oh, um he had to work. He sends his apologies."

"Um okay," he said not believing a word of it, but he knew better than to push too hard right now. Lizzie was very different from Lucy. She was intensely private and hated to show any sort of weakness in front of people. He'd talk to Lucy later and see if she knew.

Dane watched Lizzie walk back over to Lucy and relaxed a little as she smiled at something Nate said.

"So how long before we can leave?" Dane asked as he nuzzled Lauren's neck. She looked at him lovingly.

"Not long. It's eleven thirty and we pregnant women get very tired very quickly."

Dane looked up at her, suddenly serious. "Really? If you're tired, why didn't you say so. Let's sit down," he said feeling like an inconsiderate jerk.

"Relax, Dane. I'm joking. I just meant if we leave early nobody will wonder why."

"Oh, I see!" Understanding dawned on him. "Oh, I see."

"Let's do the rounds and say goodbye to everyone and then we can go."

~~~

Sly sipped his whisky and watched Lucy as she danced and laughed with Smithy. He'd realised when Nate walked in with Skye that Lucy and Nate were not together and felt foolish. But she was still not his and he had no right to ask her to wait until he came back from the second half of his tour. Sly had been ridiculously pleased when they had granted his request for his two weeks of R&R to fall in line with the engagement party for his friend, and even happier that it had been Lucy that had asked.

When he did come back, he was going to claim his woman. He'd taken enough time to try and get her out of his system, but it just wasn't happening. So, friend or not, Dane would have to get used to it. He loved him like a brother, but his feelings for Lucy had never been brotherly. She'd held his heart for so long now he didn't even know how it felt not to love her.

He was going to have to take his time with this, though. Lucy deserved to be wooed and that was what he was going to do. Sly wasn't sure how yet but he had some time to think about it while he was away.

She loved to collect shoes—anything to do with shoes—rare shoes, baby shoes, famous shoes. She even had a 'shoe' lamp. One bedroom at her place was filled with just shoes that she looked at but never wore. He didn't understand it himself, but it was one of her little quirks and he loved it. Maybe he would try to find out what rare shoe she was after and try to get it for her.

He watched her now, gliding around the dance floor and laughing at something Dane said as he and Lauren danced by. She was sunshine and light; he loved how she was so friendly with everyone around her, from the postman to the chief of police—all received the same warmth and kindness from Lucy.

She looked beautiful tonight. That dress clung to her like a second skin and her toned legs seemed to go on for miles. The look on her face as she laughed at something Smithy said made him want to be the one holding her in his arms. Crossing the dance floor, he politely cut in.

"May I?" he asked turning to his friend.

"Yeah, of course, man." Smithy said, stepping aside. Pulling her into his arms, the voice of Adele filled the air. He fitted her against him, tucking her head under his chin. He just held her there as they swayed slightly to the song, each quiet in their own thoughts. He inhaled her sweet scent and rubbed his face in the softness of her silky hair.

~~~

Lucy's heart was in her mouth. Something felt different this time. She had danced with Jace before and had never felt the raw need that she did now and it wasn't only her. With him pressed so tightly against her it was impossible to ignore the reaction he was having to her and it thrilled her.

The song ended and they slowly pulled apart. He looked at her with such need; never before had she seen that look on his face aimed at her. He cupped her cheek in his large palm.

"I'm gonna miss you when I do this last tour, but I have a way to make sure you won't forget me." He kissed her then, as if she was the only person in the room. It was brief but packed a serious wallop. When he pulled back, they were both breathless.

Lucy went to say something to him but, before she could decide what to say, he left leaving her standing in the middle of the dance floor. Lucy was stunned. She stood there for second before anger took control.

He did not just leave her standing there after kissing her senseless! Racing after him, she caught up with him as he was slipping out through the French doors. Grabbing his arm, she swung him around to face her and promptly found herself pressed up against the cold rough stone of the stately home by the solid hard muscle of a very aroused man.

Oh man, he was so hot like this—all dominant and commanding. Lowering his head, he feathered light kisses along her neck as he held her wrists tight to her sides. He was so tender and yet so commanding it made her heart ache and her body sing. Lifting his head, he looked at her with so much raw passion in his eyes she thought she would go up in flames on the spot.

He lowered his head and took her mouth like a starving man at an oasis. He licked and nipped at her mouth until, on a sigh, she opened to him and then their tongues were duelling for dominance. She could feel the hard ridge of him pressed against her core and it was more than she had ever dreamt. She always knew it would be good between them, but this was so much more. He was so powerful, and she could feel the leashed power making his body tremble. Pulling his mouth from hers, he pressed his forehead to hers while they got control of themselves.

"I can't do this now but when I get back from this last tour, this ends. All this trying to get you out of my system is over. You are mine, Lucy, and I intend to make sure everyone understands it." He then turned and walked away.

"Jace!" She chased him down in her new Jimmy Choo's. "Jace, stop."

She saw him slow and turn to her. "Go back inside, Lucy. It's freezing out here."

She walked up to him then. Lucy reached out and put her palm along his rough jaw. He'd let a beard grow in while he was away, and it tickled her hand.

"What did you mean by all that?"

"For years I've watched you—your humour, your caring nature, your compassion—and I've wanted you and that's not even touching on your beautiful face and heavenly body. I just can't fight it anymore. I want you to be mine. You deserve so much better than me. But I'm selfish enough not to care."

"But I don't want anyone else. I never have." Lucy said.

She saw him suck in a breath and he closed his eyes. "When I come home, will you give us a chance? I don't mind going slow."

"Jace, this is like a dream come true for me," she said, stroking his jaw.

He pressed his lips to her palm.

"Will you email me while I'm away? Nothing saucy mind, I can't be sharing a bunk with Smithy with an erection." He scrubbed his eyes and pulled a silly face of revulsion which made her laugh.

"Okay, I promise, no naked pictures."

"Argh no. No talk of nakedness either."

"You're crazy," she said patting him on the chest playfully. That was one of the things she loved about Jace; he was never serious for too long.

"I have to go or I'm going to forget all my good intentions of wooing you and drag you to bed." He kissed her gently on the cheek and left.

Lucy watched him go and had never been so happy. She touched her lips that still tingled from their explosive kiss. If that was what a kiss felt like, then how would it feel to have him in her bed? This was gonna be a long couple of months.

"Dream of me." She heard him shout as he disappeared from sight. Ha, as if there had ever been a time when she hadn't.

~~~

Nate had been bowled over when he'd picked Skye up tonight. He'd been trying so hard to keep his distance and take his time with her. She was so strong and perfect and he was so scared of scaring her off that he'd held back which had nearly killed him.

They'd talked for hours but hadn't even kissed properly. He was scared that if he did, he wouldn't be able to hold back. He enjoyed spending time with them and getting to know Noah. He was an amazing boy and so resilient and upbeat. He'd come to love the boy so much and couldn't wait to donate the bone marrow so that he could be a normal little boy again.

The call that they had received to say he was a match was one of the best of his life. The procedure was scheduled for next week. He'd paid to go private for them all as the NHS wanted to hold off on things after Nate's recent shooting and trauma, but Nate hadn't wanted to and had insisted they go private to get things moving.

He'd wanted to hold back from making things serious between him and Skye until after the procedure as he didn't want her to feel like she had to sleep with him to get the bone marrow. He wanted no confusion about what this was. She was his in his mind. They'd become his the moment he'd walked in that hospital room.

He just had to do things properly and convince Skye of that. He'd been surprised when she asked him to stay over tonight but pleased. She looked stunning tonight, her face giving off the most radiant glow and that dress... wow, he'd nearly swallowed his tongue when she opened the door.

He was torn between wanting to rip the dress off with his teeth or cover her up so nobody else could see all that creamy flesh. It was some sort of halter neck that cinched at her tiny waist and then flared out to her knee, which seemed fine until she turned around and it was backless. He had never considered himself a back man but hers made him a believer.

He kept touching his hand to her all night in some sort of silent possessiveness and every time he did, he could feel a tiny shiver run through her, which pleased him greatly.

Maybe he was going to have to re-think his no sleeping together policy—he wasn't sure he had that much willpower. He also wanted to talk to her about the test results he'd received earlier in the summer. It wasn't fair to make things serious between them until she knew everything. But that could wait until after the bone marrow transplant though.

~~~

Nursing a large snifter of the finest brandy, the man lifted the phone and dialled the number from memory. Seconds later it was answered.

"Yes," came the hard voice.

"We have a problem. Fortis is still digging, and they have far too many contacts for us to control." The line went silent for a minute.

"Fine. We'll give them something to divert their attention. Have Kanan take the boy tonight and I will have some of my contacts in the Middle East sort out a diversion there."

"Um ah." The man blustered.

"What? What is the problem now?" The voice barked out.

"Kanan is getting increasingly harder to control. I don't think he'll do it."

"He will do it. He is utilising his position in SIS to track down the woman and he wouldn't want to lose that, but if that's not enough use the sister."

"Okay, I'll arrange that now. What about Preedy?"

"Don't worry about him. I'll deal with him." The line disconnected and, as was usual with these encounters, the man was left feeling unnerved.

He'd risen to the highest echelons with his job and commanded respect from everyone he dealt with, but that woman scared him. It was like she was dead inside. He had only met her once and to look at—she was beautiful and glamorous—but if you truly looked you could see in her eyes that she was dead. He took a swig of the Brandy to calm his nerves and called Kanan.

~~~

Kanan Phillips threw the phone across the room. How did this happen? How did he get into this position? He'd done some pretty heinous things in his time working for the government but taking kids from their homes, and sick kids at that, was not his thing.

He couldn't really blame the government though; this was all on him. He just couldn't give up on her and this was the best way for him to track her. He wished he could just forget about her and move on. It had only been one week they had spent together before she had betrayed him. Then she'd disappeared, but what a week it had been, and try as he might he couldn't forget about her.

She had gone off the radar for three years, but he had caught bits of information that suggested that she might be back in the US now. As if that wasn't enough, they'd now threatened his baby sister, the baby sister who knew nothing about him.

He'd only discovered her by accident when he had been home on leave and run into one of his useless father's old girlfriends. She had been very smug and introduced him to his sister who had only been three at the time.

He sent money home for her and kept track of her too. So, when her druggie mother had overdosed, he'd quickly stepped in and had her fostered by a retired army medic and his wife that he had served under. The man had been a good friend to him—more of a father really—and had never told Celeste about him.

He hadn't wanted to put her in danger and by then he had been working for SIS. Somehow, they'd found her, and he wasn't sure what to do now. He couldn't just walk away. When he joined the army at sixteen, he had been so idealistic.

Two tours of Iraq had sorted that out

He'd decided to quit and then he had been approached by SIS. He had naively thought that being a spook would give him more powers to correct the wrongs. He had been both right and wrong.

He had done a lot of good. Some of the terror plots he and his fellow spooks had foiled had saved thousands of lives, but it was usually at the cost of someone's life or soul. He shook his head to clear the depressing thoughts. What would he do if he left anyway, he didn't know anything else. Resigned that he was going to hell for this, he put the wheels in motion for the job he had to do. First, he was calling in a favour.

~~~

Zack stood at the back of the room by the bar studying the group of people assembled. He was pleased with the way the people that worked for him got on. They were a tight-knit group of loyal skilled and now gifted individuals, but as a team they were something special.

Now with Sly and Drew, not to mention Lauren, coming on board, the team was expanding. He looked over at Daniel. He seemed to be coping but he knew appearances could be deceptive and that Daniel faced a long road before he came to terms with losing Claire.

When they'd talked and he'd agreed to stay on with Fortis he had made Zack promise not to send him into the field and take him away from Paige. He hoped the new training facility would give him the challenge he needed to help him with his grief.

The timing with Sly couldn't be better and he had been pleased he'd decided to sign on with them. Zack looked at Drew who was horsing around with Lucy again. Those two were like kids but Zack knew it was because Drew was finally relaxing with his new family. The boy had amazing skills on a computer and was already as talented as Will, which was good because he had a feeling that he wasn't coming back anytime soon if ever.

His phone buzzed in his pocket and he took it out. He stepped outside before answering as he was unsure of who was calling.

"Cunningham," he said curtly.

"Zack, I need a favour."

"K, is that you?" Zack couldn't believe it; they hadn't spoken in years.

"Yeah it's me. I'm calling in my favour." Zack straightened. He'd known this day would come. He'd followed K's career and was proud of how well he had done. He had wondered though when he heard that SIS was causing problems with GCHQ, if it was him. K had always been slightly on the wild side, but he'd also been Zack's best friend for the first eighteen years of his life until that afternoon when they were both eighteen, but Zack couldn't think about that now.

"What do you need?"

"Well if you could leave the Divine Watchers alone that would be good, but I guess that isn't going to happen is it?"

"No," Zack replied calmly "it's not. They're dangerous and need stopping."

"Yes, well I happen to agree with you there but not everyone has the luxury of doing what they want to," K said angrily.

"We all have our choices to make K, you know that," Zack replied.

"Yeah well, I need you to protect my sister. She's just lost her job at the tattoo parlour and some very bad people have threatened her if I don't do certain things. Please don't start about choices again either because I don't have any. I just need to know she is safe first and, despite our differences, you're the most honourable man I know."

Zack thought for a minute. "Fine I'll do it. I'll protect her, but make no mistake, if you hurt any of my people with this, I will come after you, history or not."

"I wouldn't expect anything less. Oh, and Zack she knows nothing about my existence so please keep that little nugget to yourself."

Zack was about to reply when the phone went dead. Lucky, he knew how to get in touch with Celeste. He would call her and offer her the receptionist job—that way he could keep an eye on her. He would tell her the extra security in her flat was a perk of the job.

Zack felt unsettled by the call; it had been so long since he and K had spoken. Something bad was in the wind he just knew it, and he had a very bad feeling that things were about to get worse for his team.

Zack walked back inside to see Lauren and Dane and join the others. He was happy Dane had found his soul mate. He did believe in love and soul mates, just not for him. He had forfeited his right to those years ago. He wandered over and settled in at the back of the group his ear only half on the conversation.

~~~

Dane and Lauren walked over to his friends, who had commandeered a large table.

"Ah here he is, the man of the hour," Lucy said with an evil grin.

"So, who wants to hear a really funny story?" He knew what she was up to and gave her his best 'don't do this' angry stare but he'd never been able to intimidate her, and she just laughed.

"So earlier today, I'm at home minding my own business getting myself beautified for tonight and I get a call from big brother here to go pick them up from the swanky private hospital on the old Hereford Road. Now, my interest was piqued," she said really getting into her story and building it up. "So, like a dutiful sister I went to pick them up and do you know what. Dane had been hurt!"

Lauren snickered then as everyone looked at Dane for signs of injury. She felt him squirm and squeezed his hand.

"It will soon be over, baby," she whispered in his ear.

"Well," Lucy continued "poor big bro here had gone and fainted at the news of his impending double joy and on the way down hit his thick head."

Dane knew it was coming and was not surprised when the whole table burst into loud laughter. Oh, there were a few 'are you okay' questions from Skye and Lizzie but his teammates and even Zack were nearly doubled over with mirth.

"Ha, laugh it up boys. It might be you one day and then we will see who has the last laugh." They sobered a bit at that. "And you," he said, pointing a finger at Lucy, "you will pay for this." Lucy just laughed and poked out her tongue.

"Well now you have all laughed at my expense, we will say goodnight. Lauren's tired."

~~~

After they had said goodbye to all their guests and had finally made it home, Dane locked all the doors and checked all the windows as was his routine now. Lauren had gone upstairs ahead of him as she usually did. He took a moment to walk around his home and tried to imagine what it would look like a year from now.

When the doctor had said they were having twins, he had just gone into shock and he was embarrassed as hell that he had fainted. What sort of father would he be if he couldn't even get through the ultra-sound?

Dane wasn't one for doubts normally, but this had him freaked out. She was his world and the thought of anything happening to her or his children killed him. He was trying not to show it because he didn't want to spoil her joy or make her think he wasn't happy because he was. He was so happy it scared him.

Maybe he would talk to Lizzie, although he had a feeling there was something going on with her. He walked upstairs and saw Lauren standing in the room next to theirs.

"Hey honey, what are you doing in here?"

"Just trying to imagine it with two cots. It's funny, I always wanted twins. Do you think it will be one of each or two the same?" Dane came up behind her and wrapped his arms around her.

"I don't know, honey, but I do know they will be the luckiest kids in the world to have you as a mum."

She turned in his arms then. "Do you think so?"

"I know so. Now, come on let's go to bed and I will show you how wonderful I think you are."

"I love you, Dane."

"I love you too, honey. So much."

Lauren followed him to their room where some of her self-doubts were assuaged.

THE END

Read on for a sneak peek at Nate and Skye's story.

Stolen Dreams
Fortis Security Book Two

Prologue

Nate Jones walked past the football stadium on his way to see his fiancée. It was early autumn and he could smell the sweet scent of apples from the cider factory across town. Every year, that smell of apple pie signified the start of autumn.

He loved this time of year; it was cooler, and everything seemed calmer. The hot summer nights had cooled, the kids were all back to school, and life was quieter as if everyone was taking a breath before the madness of Christmas began.

He wasn't thinking about any of that right then, though. Nate was wondering how he was going to break the life-altering news of his diagnosis to his fiancée, Nikki.

He hadn't worn a jacket as the air had been relatively warm earlier but now the wind was picking up. He tucked his hands in his pockets as he crossed the busy road by the football ground.

It couldn't really be called a stadium. He was more of a rugby man himself, but he had admired the way the fans had stepped up to keep the football club going after the last owners had run it into the ground. He and Nikki had even gone to a few games. She was a big fan.

He knew what he had to say to Nikki would upset her. She wanted everything in life to be perfect… and now he wasn't. He had been pretty upset too but he was sure they could get through this together. They just had to figure out a way to move forward. Maybe they could look at some different treatments? That was what commitment was about, he thought. Figuring out the tough stuff together.

So why was he feeling so unsure of the future? Why was his heart pounding so hard? It was just shock, he reassured himself, it would be fine. His parents had gone through some tough times and they were like newlyweds half the time.

His mum was a force of nature. She was the kindest and strongest person he knew. Always there with a wise word or a tongue-lashing if you needed it. Even now at thirty-two, he wouldn't dream of swearing in her presence and neither did anyone else.

She was from a province in Castile-La Mancha in Spain called Cuenca. She was a practising Catholic and had raised her children that way, although Nate was very much lapsed. His parents had met when his father had gone out there for work. From all accounts, it was a whirlwind romance. They had married and moved back to his father's native Wales soon after.

Nate had been brought up speaking English and Spanish in equal measure, so he was fluent in both. His mother had felt it was important for her children to know and embrace their Spanish roots and had often spoken only Spanish to them.

His parents were the best and always had his back. He wasn't sure if he was going to tell them this latest news yet. He didn't want to worry them.

As Nate crossed behind the Courtyard Theatre and walked around the back of the garages, he thought about Nikki. She had seemed off lately and he couldn't put his finger on why. He wondered not for the first time if maybe he was making a mistake by ignoring his mum's cautious words about her commitment to him.

Mimi Jones possessed an innate sense for spotting a person's true nature and he had followed in her footsteps. It was very rare for him to be wrong about someone. Nobody was infallible though.

No, he was being paranoid. Nikki would support him, and they would be fine, he knew it.

~~~

Nate used the key Nikki had given him to quietly let himself in the front door so he didn't wake her. She'd worked a night shift at the hospital and he knew she would be tired. She had one more night shift, then they had a few days off together.

He would wait until she woke up to talk to her; maybe surprise her with breakfast in bed. Although it would be dinner for him by then.

He wasn't supposed to see her today. He was working a VIP close protection job, but Daniel had agreed to swap with him, and he didn't mind owing him a favour. He could have waited until the weekend, but he hadn't wanted to let this news fester.

Easing closed the new front door that he'd fitted in the summer Nate entered the two-bedroom mid-terrace house Nikki called home. It was a quaint little house on a street filled with 1920s terraced houses. It backed onto the new theatre and the noise from the football stadium across the road was deafening on match days. She liked it though, and had decorated it herself.

He found the large amount of black and purple she painted on the walls a bit harsh. It wasn't to his taste at all, but she liked it and that was all that mattered. She'd agreed that, once she finished her nursing degree, she would move in with him. She was waiting to move in together since they were going to be married and he hadn't pushed it.

Cocking his ear towards the stairs, Nate thought he heard a noise. It sounded like a giggle. Maybe she was awake? He quickly bounded up the short flight of stairs and froze when he heard the unmistakable sound of people having sex. His stomach flipped as he listened to Nikki moaning and mewling.

His mind went blank, his fists clenched tightly as he listened. Anger made his hand tighten on the bannister and he realised he was pulling it off the wall.

Nate pushed open the door of her bedroom and stopped short. In the middle of the bed was his fiancée. She was so intent on riding whoever was underneath her she didn't see him. His vision turned red; all he could hear was the roaring in his ears. The room reeked of sex and perfume and almost made him gag.

He stepped forward, intent on seeing the motherfucker that Nikki was going all cowgirl on. She turned, sensing his movement and gasped. Jumping up from the man, she tried to cover her nakedness to deny what she had been doing.

Nate wasn't looking at her though he was looking at the arrogant self-satisfied smile of his childhood nemesis.

"Nate, it's not what you think," Nikki whimpered as big tears fell from her lying eyes.

"Oh, of course it is, sweet Nikki. You and I have been fucking like rabbits for months behind poor old Nate's back," said the arrogant twat who'd ruined his teenage life. He looked so pleased with himself, Nate wanted to smash the smile right off the bastard's face. Nate knew that was what he wanted. Using every ounce of restraint that he could manage, he turned his gaze to Nikki.

"It's you I love ,Nate! Please!" She had mascara streaking down her face, her nails gripping the sheet trying to hide her fake breasts and he realised his mum had been right. Nikki was a scheming bitch. *How had he been so blind?*

Love. Ha! What a joke; she had never loved him. She simply liked the idea of a tough-guy boyfriend. She'd always bragged to her friends about him being an ex-para. He thought it cute that she was proud of him, but she wasn't. He was just a trophy boyfriend.

Nate started to smile at the irony. How many times had he warned his sister about dating men who only saw her for her looks? And here he was, a victim of his own lecture.

He turned back to look at the man that had plagued his teenage years. The snide comments and sexual innuendos had crippled Nate's shy teenage self. He'd spent years trying to ignore the teasing and jibes, the casual touches and overall intimidation from this man and his friends.

Nate thought it would end after he'd come back from the Army, but it had gotten worse. This asshole always wanted any and everything Nate had, and he'd made it his mission to take things from him, including girlfriends and friends. He didn't understand it. This guy could literally have anything he wanted. Women fell for his charm and looks and still it wasn't enough. He had to torture Nate.

He couldn't put it into words why he behaved that way, but he had a feeling it was a power thing. During his school years, Nate was always the quiet scrawny kid. It wasn't until college that he started to develop into the man everyone saw today.

He hadn't seen the asshole for years, not since he'd joined the Army and then the Parachute Regiment. *Bloody typical.* Now a shit day had turned into an even shittier day. And he was back on this prick's radar.

Well, no more. He was sick and tired of this sick evil bastard taking from him.

"You can have her," Nate sneered at the man, causing Nikki to cry harder. "I'm done with her, she's all yours. You and your games? Won't work. Get this through your thick head, asshole. You cannot bully or manipulate me for your own sick reasons anymore. You're a sociopathic motherfucker who relishes people's pain. You make me want to vomit. Just looking at you makes my skin crawl. Stay the fuck away from me and my family or you won't like what happens next." Nate glowered at the man with so much disgust and fury it was almost tangible.

He turned then and walked away. His news didn't matter now.

~~~

Calmly picking his clothes up off the floor, the man contemplated what had transpired. He'd wanted Nate to catch them. It had taken months of fucking the pathetic bitch until Nate caught them. He had pictured what the expression on his face would be and it had not disappointed.

He'd wanted him for years and had done everything he could to manipulate him into bed, but Nate wouldn't take the bait. He didn't know what it was about Nate Jones that made him want to consume him physically and mentally. Perhaps it was because Nate had always evaded his charms?

He shook his head as he looked at Nikki crying in the corner of the bed. She hadn't been a bad fuck, but she chose to betray her boyfriend, so it was her own fault she was now left alone. Walking over to her, he leaned down and roughly grabbed her hair, twisted her face up to his and kissed her viciously, biting her lip hard as he did. She liked a bit of rough and he knew her whimper wasn't one of pain.

"Come on, Nikki. You knew it was going to end badly. Stop your crying and pull yourself together."

She looked at him with hate then and it made him smile. "I fucking hate you," she spat, which made him laugh.

"You might hate me, Nikki, but you sure did love my cock when it was pounding into you, making you scream." He pushed her roughly onto the bed and turned to gather his things as she curled into herself and cried.

When would people learn not to do stupid things if they didn't want to get caught? He whistled as he turned and walked out of her tiny townhouse. Time to up his game with Nate. It would take time and careful planning. Luckily, he had lots of time and loved to make plans and strategise. It was time for Nate to see that he always got his way. People didn't say no to him—ever!

Read More: <u>Stolen Dreams Fortis Book 2</u>

Books by Maddie Wade

Fortis Security

Healing Danger
Stolen Dreams
Love Divided
Secret Redemption
Broken Butterfly
Arctic Fire
Phoenix Rising
Nate & Skye Wedding Novella (Available 27 November 2018)
Digital Desire (Releasing January 2019)

Alliance Agency Series (co-written with India Kells)

Deadly Alliance

Tightrope Duet

Tightrope One
Tightrope Two

Contact Me

Email: info.maddiewade@gmail.com

If stalking an author is your thing and I sure hope it is then here are the links to my social media pages.

If you prefer your stalking to be more intimate then my group Maddie's Minxes will welcome you with open arms.

Email: maddie@maddiewadeauthor.co.uk

Website: http://www.maddiewadeauthor.co.uk

Facebook page: https://www.facebook.com/maddieuk/

Facebook group: https://www.facebook.com/groups/546325035557882/

Amazon Author page: amazon.com/author/maddiewade

Goodreads: https://www.goodreads.com/author/show/14854265.Maddie_Wade

Bookbub: https://partners.bookbub.com/authors/3711690/edit

Twitter:@mwadeauthor

Pinterest:@maddie_wade

Instagram:Maddie Author

Printed in Great Britain
by Amazon

13214819R00163